# THE DIVINE

Mary Grundberg

THE DIVINE



978-1-7398687-0-3 (paperback)
978-1-7398687-1-0 (hardback)
978-1-7398687-2-7 (ebook)

First published 2021 by Corrennie Press Ltd.

This novel is a work of fiction. The names, characters and incidents portrayed in it are the work of the author's imagination. Any resemblance to actual persons, living or dead, is entirely coincidental.

For my family – past and present

# PART ONE

# SILVER CITY

# CHAPTER 1

# ELPHINSTONE KIRK

***A divine n. a priest, one learned in theology, associated with religion or worship, a man of God, possessing gifts of supreme excellence or worth***

Aberdeen, Scotland – Friday 21st September 1860

Later, Frederick Black would remember the date as the day when his life changed for ever. Yet there had been no clues that that might be the case. Up until that point his existence had seemed calm and ordered, leading irrevocably to the moment when he would finally stand, fully ordained, in the pulpit and prove the naysayers wrong. The memory of their jeering response when he had first admitted to his ambition still inflamed him.

'*You, a minister? A wee bastard who nivvir kent his faither.*'

He would show them. The elders at Elphinstone Kirk had invited him to speak at their Friday evening service, a rare honour, and he wanted to make a good impression. He had asked the Reverend Richard Kelman, his friend and mentor, for guidance but had been told to be his own man and say what was in his heart. So he was. Dressed in his customary black garments, long legs pulled under his chair, Fred wrote hurriedly, muttering to himself under his breath. What would it sound like to them, he wondered?

So intent was he on his task, he had barely noticed the drop in temperature in the cold north facing room nor the passing of time. It was only when the clock struck five that he looked up in surprise. How had the afternoon passed so quickly? The sermon was nearly done but some new thoughts had come to him and he was anxious to commit them to paper as soon as possible. Narrowing his eyes, he gripped his pen and scratched away on the yellowing paper. There wasn't much time left and Fred could feel his nerves get the better of him.

Finally he ceased, replacing the pen by the ink well and straightening up. He thrust long fingers through his scrubby red hair, then covered his face for a few seconds. Much depended on this. He had spent seven years studying in this chilly, grey town, often homesick, hungry and ill. He had heard it said that men endured greater hardships up here to get an education than a traveller suffered in Central Africa. Maybe it was said in jest but at times it had felt like his very own banishment into the wilderness. He had come close to giving up last year, wracked with toothache and fever and his precious bursary funds running low. Why not return home to Strathmuir to be the dominie there? He would have a position and influence in the town, he could look after his mother and maybe in due course settle down himself. But Fred knew full well in his heart there could be no going back. That was not God's plan for him.

Richard Kelman had come to his rescue. Seeing how low Fred had seemed, he offered him lodgings at the manse in Bon Accord Crescent. Fred had accepted with joyful relief. This would now afford him a degree of comfort and privacy in which to complete his studies. And then, completely unexpectedly, he had heard from his father. The man he had never met who had left while he was an infant. He had tried to quiz his mother on the circumstances but she had refused to elaborate, saying merely that he had gone to America to make his fortune. He had his reasons, she said, but he always knew about his son and acknowledged him. And there he had remained, a shadowy figure about whom Fred sometimes day-dreamed but never imagined he would ever get to know or meet.

He had never had an address for his father but clearly someone in the town did as he was told later that a friend, seeing Fred's struggle and predicament, had written appealing for any help the older man could give to his son 'who will be a credit to you and make you proud.' Pulling open the drawer at his right hand side, Fred picked up the envelope which had arrived a couple of months earlier, a smudged New York postmark obscuring the small brown stamp. In slanting black hand-writing, it was addressed to him care of his mother's house in Strathmuir. Even now the shock and thrill of hearing from his father caused his hand to tremble.

> *'My dear son,'* he read. *'I was so pleased to have direct news of you after all this time and humbly ask your forgiveness for being absent in your life. I behaved badly towards your mother and let her down. She is to be praised for having brought up such a fine young man. It is a sadness to me that I cannot say this to you in person. I hope you will forgive me, unfortunate and ungodly creature that I am. I do hope and trust that all your prayers will be heard and answered. In a more practical vein I am aware and very proud of the great application you have shown in your studies. I understand that financial support would greatly assist your progress. I therefore wish to inform you that I intend sending you a cheque in the sum of £20 for this purpose. Please arrange to open a bank account so that this may be lodged safely for your sole benefit. I look forward to hearing news of your continuing progress and success and, if my life is spared, pray that one day we may meet.'*
>
> *Your loving Father'*

Fred would have given much to have had his father and mother present this evening, to see their son finally stand in the pulpit and address a congregation as a fully qualified minister of the Kirk. But this was not to be. His father's situation was completely understandable and Fred anticipated writing of the event to him with enthusiasm. He would paint as vivid a portrait of the occasion as he could. His dear mother had declined his invitation. Proud as she was of her only child, already the distance Fred had travelled in his life was beginning to show, and she admitted to feeling uncomfortable with 'city types and their fancy ways.' Fred protested that they were no different from their kith and kin in Strathmuir and would be pleased to see her, but she was not to be persuaded. She would wait to see him in the pulpit back home when he next visited, she announced firmly. And that was the end of the matter.

The door to his room opened and Fred was brought abruptly back to the present.

'Come and have some food, Fred,' Richard invited him. 'You'll need your strength for this evening. Have you finished your sermon?'

'Aye, I think so, Richard. I hope it lives up to your expectations.'

Fred's face creased into an anxious frown as he looked at his colleague for reassurance.

'I have no doubt it will, Fred. It is natural to have reservations. But once you start to speak it will come alive. You can do no more now.'

'Thank you, Richard. I will join you shortly.'

The service was due to start at half past six. It was now after five. While Fred knew he should have something to sustain him, his stomach churned with anxiety and he felt he would be unable to eat very much at all. In the fading light of the study, the young man bowed his head and prayed for strength and conviction in the coming hours. Then, returning his father's letter to the drawer, he tidied the sheaf of papers in front of him and stood up.

Richard and Fred walked out into the body of the kirk. On

either side of them the pews were so tightly packed that latecomers were left to stand in the aisle. No doubt the congregation was curious to see and hear this young preacher for themselves of whom so much had been said. Fred knew there were those who wondered what Richard saw in this tall, red-haired lad from the countryside, who it was rumoured had barely been to school. As Richard opened the service, Fred, sat dry-mouthed and tense beneath the pulpit. Then it was time.

Clad in a simple black Geneva gown, his head held high, Fred felt more like a young senator entering the Forum than an unknown country boy. Climbing the pulpit, he grasped the lectern with both hands and scanned the congregation intently as if seeking out a particular face. He waited until everyone was still. Then he knew he had their attention.

'Today is my birthday,' he announced. 'Not the day I was physically born into this world, of course, but the day on which I start the new life that God intends for me. You, my brethren, are witnesses to my rebirth. As I stand before you, I commit my body and soul to serving God and my fellow man.'

What followed would serve to change any doubters' minds. It was as though he were addressing each man and woman individually. How could he see into their souls so clearly and compassionately? He had been there, he said.

'It is within us all', he declaimed, 'good and evil. The choice is ours. We have the power within ourselves. It is not preordained. We cannot turn away for even one minute lest the Devil take the advantage. Think on what you have thought and done today. Would you, brothers and sisters, do it differently tomorrow? Be true to yourselves and to those you love and who love you. Thanks be to God, Amen.'

As Fred's final words faded into the high nave of the kirk, there was a hushed silence. Many bowed their heads in prayer, lips moving as they mouthed their innermost thoughts to their Maker. Fred sat down slowly within the pulpit and started to give silent thanks to God when he was aware of movement immediately beneath him. Suddenly he was startled to hear a man's indignant voice calling out.

'Who are you to tell me you know my thoughts? Only the Lord God Almighty has that privilege. You have much to learn, Reverend Black!'

Fred caught the sound of a woman's softer voice appealing to the man to calm down and cautiously lent forward to identify the individual. Then the speaker stood up. It was Donald Ferguson, owner of Ferguson and MacKintosh, the largest department store in the city, a senior elder of the kirk and one of its most important benefactors.

'I'll nae calm down! I've heard enough!' He barked out, shaking off his companion's restraining arm.

A tall, white-haired man, whose florid complexion was rendered even redder by his anger, was now making his way out of the pew and down the aisle towards the exit. Fred was aware that the congregation had started to whisper amongst themselves not quite sure what to make of such an interruption. Ferguson now flung open one of the heavy double doors with a crash that echoed round the church. Without a backward glance, he jammed his black felt hat on to his head and strode out into the darkness.

For a moment Fred froze with confusion and embarrassment, then he felt the heat of pure anger rise in his veins at this man's arrogance and sense of entitlement. Clearly no-one had challenged his soul or opinions recently. Forcing his face into a sad smile, Fred rose once again to face his congregation.

'Aye, indeed the Lord's words seem to have shocked our brother, but understand that these are not my words as a mere mortal man but the thoughts of the Almighty Himself!'

As he spoke the last few words, Fred let his voice rise up in strength and tone and once again, to his relief, saw that he had regained the attention of his congregation. He would not let a wealthy, self-satisfied bigot get the upper hand. He regretted any upset caused to Richard or the other parishioners but not the saying of those words. With whispered exchanges, a shuffling of feet and the adjusting of winter garments, the men and women now started to file out slowly from the church. Beyond the doors, on the wide granite thresh-hold, Fred was glad of Richard's company as they stood side by side to meet the congregation. Perhaps they too shared Donald Ferguson's views of him? Richard placed an encouraging hand on Fred's back as the first of the parishioners came up to greet them.

'Dinnae dwell on it, Fred,' he said softly. 'It was a splendid sermon, rest assured.'

And so it proved to be. Without exception each person approached Fred to shake his hand and utter words of support and appreciation.

'Truly inspirational. You must return to us again soon.'

'That was so heartfelt, it certainly made me think.'

'For such a young laddie, you have an auld heid on your shoulders!'

'There's no hiding from you, Reverend Black. You told it straight.'

And it continued thus for quite some time, the handshakes and smiles, nodding heads and pats on the shoulder. Finally, when the last of the worshippers had departed, Richard turned to Fred.

'Well, Fred lad, I think you made your mark there. They are hard to please this congregation. You can be proud of yourself.'

Putting his hand into his pocket, Richard withdrew a gold pocket watch and glanced at it.

'Eight thirty. Will you be coming back to the house now?'

After such exertion and drama, Fred felt suddenly drained. For a moment he hesitated. Then out of the corner of his eye he caught sight of two young fellows, about his age, making their way into the town. They were talking animatedly, seemingly without a care in the world.

'Thank you, Richard, but I think I'll get myself changed and take a wee walk. The air will do me good. I have my latch-key so please don't either of you wait up for me. I'll let myself in.'

"Of course, lad, I quite understand. You take your time. We'll see you in the morning.'

# CHAPTER 2

# DOUGLAS QUAY

STEPPING OUT FROM ELPHINSTONE KIRK ON TO THE STREET beyond, Fred was hit by a sudden surge of relief and exhilaration. No doubt there would be many hurdles and challenges ahead of him in his career but for now he delighted in having lived up to Richard's expectations and met with the approval of this most discerning of congregations - Mr Ferguson apart. His calling was beyond doubt but the endless self-discipline bore down on him sometimes. This evening Fred felt he had earned a couple of hours of relaxation.

Although the autumn day had been fine, now, as the evening drew in, a sea haar had fallen on the city leaving a fine sheen of moisture on everything it touched. Fat herring gulls called mournfully above his head and the pungent smell of fish which hung in the air following the safe return of the fleet, reminded Fred that the sea was not far off. He would head down towards the harbour.

Turning right along Union Terrace, he passed, on one side, stately, granite buildings housing the offices of local solicitors and accountants, then the imposing presence of the Douglas

Hotel, pink granite steps leading up to heavy swing glass doors with gleaming brass handles. Within, Fred could make out the genteel outlines of the city's bourgeoisie as they celebrated the end of another week of commerce and achievement.

He could have walked inside to join them but this was not for him he felt, at least not yet. While he no doubt looked the part with his tall, slim figure and handsome, earnest face, within himself he knew he was still the "*teuchter frae Strathmuir*". That would never leave him, nor did he want to forget his roots, they made him what he was, but at this moment Fred Black was not quite ready for the new life that one day would be his.

No, he would continue his walk to clear his head and calm his thoughts. Over Union Street now, down the hard, grey cobbles of Market Street and on towards the harbour. As he had guessed, the fishing fleet had made it safely back to port. In contrast to the evening tranquillity of the main street up the hill, here on Douglas Quay, there was a wave of human activity with heavy canvas sails being taken down by the skippers and the precious catch being poured in silver cascades into creels on the quayside, bound for the fish-market.

'Oot the road, man!'

Startled, Fred looked down to see a short, sturdy young woman looking up at him. She was about his age with strands of light brown hair escaping from the faded red cotton scarf she had tied about her head. On her back was a large basket full of shining grey fish – the herring, the "silver darlings".

'This load's fuckin' heavy, man, or are ye gang tae help me wi' it?' This time Fred could see she was also grinning up at him, her small blue eyes nearly disappearing into her round, rosy face.

'I'm sorry, lassie, I was miles away,' Fred started to explain, holding his hands in front of him apologetically.

'Nae bother, jist move yersel unless ye fancy a load of these criturs on yer boots.'

Fred smiled wryly and shook his head.

'No' really,' he admitted as he stepped out of the girl's path.

Fred watched her as she passed and took in her solid, comely frame, so purposeful and unaffected. Despite the strong odour of fish and sweat that followed her, he felt an unexpected wave of affection. Then he realised that he was still hungry. Despite Mary-Ann's encouragement, Fred had only managed a few mouthfuls of a very good steak and kidney pudding and had declined any dessert. Now that his debut was past, he regretted not having eaten more. He was reluctant to retrace his steps to the hotel where he would no doubt have to pay over the odds for some fancy food. No, he would seek out a bap or a pie in one of the public houses which lined the quayside and then make his way back to the manse before nightfall.

Fred surveyed his options. The Ship Inn, The Royal Bar, The Blue Lamp or Ma' Donaldson's, all lined up in front of him for the choosing. The brown glass windows and drab facades of the drinking houses gave little away. The sailors and fishermen were starting to gravitate towards the various hostelries, their week's wages already burning a hole in their pockets. The quayside would remain busy for quite some time to come.

In front of the Ship some men were spoiling for a fight with raised voices and flailing arms. The Royal was packed as Fred approached with small, work-weary men standing three deep at the bar. There would be no food on offer there. It was the same story at the Blue Lamp, a smoky fug hung over the crowd within and the strong, sweet, hoppy smell of Younger's ale hit the young man's nostrils. His guts rumbled unhappily. It reminded him of the annual Harvest Fair back home in Strathmuir where he had had his first illicit taste of beer and much else besides.

Unwelcome though it was at that moment, Fred knew all too well what his mother's thoughts on the matter would be. A "den of iniquity", provider of the "demon drink" and not a threshold any respectable, God-fearing person should pass over. She was right of course. There was still time, part of him reasoned, to cut his losses and return back to the quiet, safe seclusion of the manse in Bon Accord Crescent. Bread, oatcakes, cheese and pickle would be his for the asking and he would be sure to go to sleep satisfied. But something held him back. A small perverse voice in his head chided him for being a coward

'Can ye nae take the temptation, son?' it seemed to be saying mockingly. 'Stand up tae it, dinnae run awa' like a feart bairn!'

Fred felt emboldened, almost as though he were to be put to the test. He had to manage his own demons. He was a grown man after all. He hesitated for just a moment then, making his decision, he opened the door to Ma' Donaldson's and pushed his way to the bar. Folk barely turned their heads, so intent were they in getting served themselves, that if they noticed the tall, red-haired stranger in their midst, they did not show it. Fred was relieved by this new found anonymity. Out of his clerical gown he felt lighter, freer. Just another young loon out to shed his cares on a Friday night.

While there had been a damp chill in the air outside, now in the smoky interior of Ma' Donaldson's, the atmosphere seemed suddenly close and stuffy. Fred undid his overcoat and tugged at the top button of his plain, white shirt, looking around him as he did so. He stood a full head above most of the clientele, his red hair falling over the collar of his coat and a modest showing of whiskers on his cheeks.

'Yessir!' The short, dark-eyed barman addressed him. 'What'll ye hae?'

'I fancy a pie or a bap, if ye hae such a thing. I'm famished.' Came Fred's urgent response.

'Well, mebbe, mebbe. Let's see. But fit's yer poison, sir?' Answered the publican, doubtfully, his hand hovering over the beer taps.

'I'll have a pint o' porter then.'

'Right ye are, sir. Comin' up. That'll be tuppence.' The barman filled the glass with the dark liquid topped with a creamy foam and held out his hand for payment.

'And ma pie?' Fred reminded him as he handed over a couple of coins.

'Ye'd better speak tae Ma' hersel' – she's oot the back there...' instructed the publican, jabbing his thumb behind the counter as he scooped up the payment and turned away to serve another drinker.

There seemed to be no sign of the landlady so, ignoring his hunger, Fred lifted his glass to his lips and drank deeply. The rich, iron-flavoured liquid filled his mouth for a moment as he savoured the long-forgotten taste. Then another. The hunger was starting to abate. He looked down at his glass and saw to his surprise that it was already half empty. He would finish it off and make his way back home. It might not be too late to beg some late night sustenance before he turned in.

'We've nae seen ye here afore.'

The statement in Fred's right ear startled him. On turning he found he was looking at the quizzical, cunning face of one of the fishermen, who was still wearing his heavy oiled wool jumper, his weather-beaten cheeks aflame with the beer and the warmth in the tavern.

'Cat got yer tongue? We dinnae bite!'

A gale of derisive, drunken laughter followed this comment. Fred tried to step back so he could focus. Already he was feeling distanced and uncoordinated.

'Aye, I'm nae frae Aberdeen. I stay doon Brechin way. Just visiting ma sister. She'll be wondering where I am.'

'Aw, sweet, her wee pet then? She's yer big sister I suppose? Better run awa' hame then!'

The speaker, pleased with his wit, turned round to grin at his companions. There was more laughter and nodding of heads, as the fishermen swayed in agreement. Fred felt a wave of anger and irritation hit him.

'*Wee shites*!' he thought.

Out loud he heard himself say, more calmly than he felt, 'Oh aye I'm a good boy I am! And it's ma birthday so am awa' oot tae celebrate!'

'Well ye'd better get us a drink then, man!' came the response and half a dozen flushed, expectant faces leered towards him.

He looked around the group which now encircled him. His earlier plan to melt away into the night no longer looked like it was going to work. There was nothing for it, he would have to buy a round and try to extricate himself later. Feeling down into his trouser pocket he caught hold of a couple of silver shilling pieces. That was supposed to last him all weekend. Pushing his way to the counter, Fred, raised his hand.

'Another round please.' He addressed the barman, who wiped his hands on a stained white apron and nodded.

'All round,' added the young man, indicating his new drinking companions.

'Right ye are, porter again is it?'

Fred nodded and started to distribute overflowing pint glasses to outstretched hands. The first of his shillings was handed to the barman and he turned back to the dishevelled band who were already quaffing the dark brown liquid thirstily.

'Slainte!' exclaimed Fred, lifting his glass.

The bitter, fruity drink went down even more easily this time and standing in the midst of all this noisy humanity Fred felt a not unpleasant sense of well-being and confidence growing within him. He was vaguely aware that he still had not found anything to eat but this seemed now less urgent than it had an hour earlier. The beer was now flowing round his body raising his pulse and making his cheeks glow.

'A wee dram for yer birthday…' Fred turned to his right and found he was looking at the same young seaman who had quizzed him earlier. A small tumbler filled with an inch of pungent golden liquid was pushed into his free hand.

'Quick, afore I change ma mind!' chuckled the fisherman, as Fred hesitated in surprise at the gesture.

'Thanks, man, Slainte!'

The fumes hit his nostrils making his eyes water. Then the burning kick of the liquid at the back of his throat as he swallowed a large mouthful. Suppressing a cough, Fred nodded in appreciation and waved his glass at the group.

After a couple of minutes, through the din and the chatter, Fred became aware of an annoying tug in his bladder. He shifted his position to ease the pressure and tried to ignore the persistent reminder that he had not had a piss for hours. Hell! He'd have to go outside. Even in his present relaxed state, he would not risk the privies out the back of the tavern. Tipping the last of the whisky down his gullet, he placed the glass on the counter and unsteadily turned to make his way out through the Friday night throng to the street outside.

What happened next Fred could not exactly recall except for realising that he had misread the height of the kerb and found himself sprawled face down on the wet pavement. His mouth felt cold and numb. Tentatively licking his lips, Fred could taste blood in his mouth and felt a sharp jagged edge where his front tooth should have been.

'What have I done?' he groaned. "Idiot, idiot, idiot!"

Slowly he tried to raise his supine body on to one arm. For the moment the effect of shock and alcohol served to deaden the pain. That would no doubt come but for now he wondered how he would get back home, preferably unseen?

'My, my and aren't you a sight for sore eyes!'

With effort, Fred turned his head slowly towards the speaker. Taking in the black boots and heavy black skirts by his head, he realised it was a woman.

'Hae we nae met afore?' she continued. Fred groaned again and tried to turn his head away.

'Aye, I thought it was you – d'ye nae mind when I had my wee fishies on me?' And she chuckled in recollection. 'So fit ye daein' doon there?'

When Fred said nothing, the girl exclaimed 'Well, ye cannae stay there a' night, ken. Dinnae be sae high an' mighty!'

And she dropped to her haunches to take a closer look.

'For fuck's sake, yer bleedin'. Ye bin fightin'? Yer a real sight!'

At this Fred turned as best he could to face her. Yes, she was right, they had met before. It was the fish lassie he had nearly bumped into a few hours ago. Now he felt a need to explain himself.

'Nae fightin', lassie, just fell an' hit ma face. Smashed ma tooth,' he slurred, pointing to his mouth.

'Fit's yer name? I'm Jessie, Jessie Duthie.'

'Fred, just Fred.'

'Ah, a man o' mystery? Where d' ye stay then, Fred? Can I help ye hame?'

'Too far,' Fred mumbled through his swollen lips. He was starting to feel sick and just wanted to be left alone. But Jessie was having none of it.

'Ye cannae stay here. Ye'd better come back wi' me. Dinnae worry, I willnae try onythin' on!' And she let out a chirrup of amusement. She was just a wee thing but strong with it. Slowly she helped Fred to his feet where he swayed uncertainly for a moment.

'Aw right? I'm nae far,' and she indicated a tall, dark tenement building at the end of the street.

He made it as far as the front door when the nausea he had tried so hard to quell finally overcame him. Flinging himself towards the gutter, Fred vomited with relief, bitter bile mixing with blood-soaked saliva. Oblivious to his surroundings, his head spinning, Fred was vaguely aware that his mouth had started to throb painfully. Jessie's voice once again broke into his consciousness.

'Fred, Fred…Can ye make it up the stairs. We'll clean you up a bittie. God, you're gang tae reek the morn!'

For a second time, the young woman helped him to his feet, turning her face away from the splattered frontage of his coat. She pushed at the peeling front door with her left foot and together they tottered into the dark, stone lobby. The stench of stale urine and refuse nearly made Fred retch again. He swallowed hard to control it then, holding the dirty brown banister on one side and Jessie on the other, he started to climb the worn stone staircase. All he wanted now was to sleep, to lose consciousness. He would worry about tomorrow in a few hours' time.

# CHAPTER 3

# GOOD SAMARITAN

THE FIRST THING FRED NOTICED ON WAKING WAS THE smell. A mixture of stale sweat, dry vomit and the sweeter background aroma of smoke and putrid fish hit his nostrils causing him to gasp in disgust. Then, as he tried to raise his head, the pain in his mouth and the throbbing behind his eyes, brought a fresh wave of nausea. Once again his aching stomach turned and he clenched his teeth. Every part of his body seemed to be resisting his return to consciousness.

'Dear Christ, where am I?'

Beneath his head was a lumpy pillow and his half-dressed body was covered with a rough, grey blanket now tangled between his naked legs. Fred peered into the semi-darkness of the room. A cough from a figure slumped on a chair in the corner startled him before patchy recollections of the previous evening started to filter through.

'The lassie – who was she again?' Fred ran a dry tongue over his lips and then his teeth. 'Sweet Jesus, my tooth…'

He started to remember and groaned again. There were no curtains at the east facing attic window and the sun rose illuminating the dingy room without mercy. Outside, early morning sounds - a bairn crying, a mewing gull on a chimney pot and the trundle of cart wheels on the quayside - made Fred realise he had to get home.

'Jess, Jessie. That was her name. Should I wake her? She looks exhausted, poor lassie. Let her sleep. But I need tae thank her. I cannae steal off without thanking her.'

The young woman gave another cough and shuddered awake. She turned her head and saw him staring at her.

'Oh yer still here. That's nice tae see. Ma visitors dinnae usually wait around.' And she stretched lazily and unselfconsciously.

'I'm sorry to have put you to so much trouble, Jessie. I cannae mind exactly what happened but you were a wee Samaritan to me. I couldnae leave without thanking you.'

Then Fred caught sight of his bare legs and stopped in embarrassment. Where were his clothes? As if reading his thoughts, Jessie pointed to a hook on the back of the door.

'They've dried out a bittie but I think yer mither'll hae somethin' tae say.' And she gave a low chuckle.

Ignoring the pounding in his head as best he could, Fred stood up unsteadily and reached for his trousers and jacket. Slowly and reluctantly he put on the rank garments and looked for his boots. There was a clatter as the second of his shilling pieces fell on to the wooden floor and started to roll under the bed. He stamped his foot on it and picked it up.

'Can I give you this for yer trouble, Jess?'

The amused expression on the girl's face changed.

'I'm nae a whore, ken! I was happy tae help ye. I dinnae want yer siller.'

'I didnae mean that at a'. I want to thank ye. I was a mess and ye helped me. Many folk widdnae. Please, dinnae be angry.'

With a sigh the young woman hesitated, looked at Fred's outstretched hand then around the sparsely furnished room. Slowly she extended her fingers and took the small coin.

'Thank ye, Fred. Yer a good man, ye are. Mebbe I'll see ye again at Ma's? If ye've learnt yer lesson?' And a small smile returned once again to her face.

There was a silence in the attic room as they observed each other. The tall, bedraggled red-headed man with the broken tooth and the short, brown-haired fish lassie, standing bare foot on the floorboards, her blue eyes staring intently at her overnight visitor.

'Aye I have. That's the truth. Take care of yersel', Jessie.'

And Fred held out his hand once again to the young woman. Then, with the realisation that the day had started, he turned to the door and with as much dignity as he could summon up, walked out on to the landing and down the dark stairway. When he opened the main door of the tenement on to the street the morning sun hit him full in the face. Shutting his eyes tightly for a moment, he did not see the stocky fisherman who was standing just outside and nearly tripped over him. By the time he had started to apologise, the man had cursed under his breath and pushed past Fred into the building behind him.

It took Fred a moment or two to gather himself. Down here by the harbour his dishevelled appearance was unlikely to draw attention. However up on Union Street it would be a different matter. And the reception he might get from Richard and Mary-Ann caused him to hesitate with shame.

'Well, Freddie lad, you got yourself into this pickle, you'll have to get yourself out o' it.'

Then he smoothed his hair and attempted to brush down his garments as best he could. If he could have washed properly ....

His thoughts were suddenly interrupted by the loud insistent rapping of a knuckle on a window pane far above his head. Any more of that and the glass would break. As it continued he also became aware of a woman's voice raised in alarm. Looking skywards, Fred, to his shock and surprise, saw that the woman was Jessie. Behind her was a male figure who rapidly pulled her back from the window.

'*What the hell?*

Any thought of returning timidly to the manse had now

departed and Fred turned back into the tenement building. Nearly tripping in his haste, he rushed up the stairs until he reached the shabby front door of Jessie's attic apartment. It was open and inside Fred could see the back of the muscular seaman he had just encountered on the street.

'Billy, leave me alone! I've nae done onythin'. Yer oot yer mind!'

'Fuckin' whore! I told ye tae wait for me. But ye've better fish tae fry I see.'

'It wisnae…'

The man was about to bring his hand down on the girl's head when Fred pushed past. He stood a good head higher than the assailant and grabbed the man's shoulders to face him. Looking directly at the angry, red face spitting venom in front of him Fred tried to control an irresistible urge to punch the intruder.

'Leave her be, you coward! What are ye thinking of? Get yerself out o' here before I lose my temper!'

For a brief moment the two men glared at each other, their breath heavy and laboured in the cool morning air. Then suddenly the fisherman wrenched himself out of Fred's grasp and retreated out of the door.

'Ye'll regret this, ye cow. I'm nae jokin',' he hissed over his shoulder, then ran down the stone stairway his metal capped boots ringing harshly in the darkness.

Fred turned back to Jessie who was standing shaking and weeping, her hands covering her face. All the fight was gone from him now and his head suddenly felt clear. Hesitantly, he reached out to touch the girl lightly on her shoulder.

'Who was that, Jess? Has he hurt ye?'

Her body continued to heave but a slight movement of her head indicated that he had not.

'Who is he, Jess?' Fred repeated. 'I've caused you so much trouble. I'm truly sorry.'

'Billy, ma man,' came a whisper finally. 'He gets sae jealous.'

'Ye dinnae have tae stay with him, lassie.'

'Oh aye I do. He kens too much aboot me.'

'What do ye mean?'

'I cannae tell ye, Fred,' Jess sighed deeply, raising a small, reddened hand to her face.

'Tell me if it will help ye. I willnae tell a soul, I swear. I'm nae gang tae walk out on ye. Ye cannae rest here.'

Jessie let out a short snort of exasperation.

'Oh, really. And where would I go, Fred? I've ma work. Money disnae grow on trees, as you ken well.'

Fred paused and looked again at Jess now facing him with anger and defiance in her eyes. She was right, why should she trust him? What did he know of her life? Perhaps he should not have interfered? But it was because of him she now faced this threat.

'We all have secrets, Jessie.' Fred placed both hands on her shoulders and willed her to look up at him. 'I could help you. But you'll have to trust me.'

'Oh and why should I do that, Mr Fred? A drunken loon frae Brechin? Ye'll be awa' shootin' yer mouth next time yer pissed!'

Fred dropped his hands from her shoulders, stung by her angry accusations. Was that how he appeared to her?

'Alright, I'll go first. Sit yourself down and hear me out.' And before she could object, Fred gently pushed her back towards the tangled bed he had just left.

'I ken a' about poverty, Jessie,' he said half to himself. 'I come frae Strathmuir. I nivvir kent ma faither. He left afore I wis born. So it was jist me and ma mither. She was a weaver and when she wisnae dain' that, she wis helpin' oot in the fields. There wisnae much money. But the Kirk wis aye important and ma mither took me wi' her tae a' the services. They are my earliest memories. That's when I decided I wanted to be a minister mysel'. That one day I would be in the pulpit holding a'body's attention.'

There was a slight intake of breath from Jessie.

'Am I boring you, Jessie?' Fred tried not to sound offended.

'No, Fred, not at a'. I'm jist that tired. Remember there wis someone in ma bed last night so I didnae get much sleep.' Jessie raised her eyebrows and Fred dropped his gaze in embarrassment.

'Go on, Fred, please.'

'At first we couldnae afford for me tae go tae the university, so I became a shoe-mender. And a really bad one. It was clearly not my calling.'

Fred smiled at the memory.

'We saved everything we could. It wis really hard but ma mither wis determined. At last I got a bursary to the university here in Aberdeen. That was seven long years ago but jist last week, I learned I had passed my final examinations and will now graduate as a minister.'

Just saying the words out loud caused such relief to flood through Fred's body. Outside, the bells of St Nicholas' Kirk rang the hour with eight tolls.

'So tell me, Jessie, how can I just walk out and leave ye? I dinnae ken why our paths crossed but they did. That man attacked ye because of me and he could be back. I would never forgive mysel' if anything happened.'

Glancing down, Fred realised he had gathered both Jessie's hands in his. She remained silent, her face turned away from him. He gave her hands a little shake as if to remind her of his presence. When she finally looked up there was a different expression on her face. Still wary but softer and more hopeful.

'Ye hid it well, Fred. I nivvir guessed ye was an educated gentleman. I wish I could hae had an education but I cannae even read or write, well a wee bit mebbe…ma name. Perhaps you could teach me?' And she leant into him with a low laugh.

'Mebbe, Jess, but just now ye need to get awa' from here. It's nae safe. We'll go back tae the manse. I've got some explaining tae dae. The Kelmans will be sending out a search party if I'm nae back soon.'

'And fit aboot me? Fit'll they dae wi' me, Fred? Look at me! They'll nae want me in their fine hoose.'

'No, Jess. Why would ye think that? They are good folk. They will be upset wi' me that is true but I deserve it. But ye've done nothing wrong. Mebbe they can help ye. Come awa' now, Jessie.'

By the time Fred and Jessie finally emerged on to the Shiprow it was well after eight o' clock. They turned up Market Street, Fred retracing his steps from the night before. He cut a very different figure now. With his broken tooth and soiled clothes he looked ready for shelter in the nearest doss house rather than a West-End manse. They should take a hansom cab but who would stop for such a pair?

Approaching Union Street, Fred hoped he was unrecognisable. There were still few people about at this hour but before long Saturday shoppers would start to throng the broad pavements of the city's main thoroughfare. If he were spotted in this state his illustrious career in the pulpit would be over before it started. The station might be a better bet.

'Ye'll need some siller I dare say,' observed Jessie, quietly offering her open palm to Fred. On it lay the small coin he had recently given her. His humiliation felt complete but she was right. If they could find a cab to take them, the driver would need to be paid.

'Wait here,' instructed Fred, 'When I find a cab to take us I'll raise my hand.'

Standing as straight and tall as he could, Fred approached the first of three hansom cabs lined up in front of the railway station. In his best-spoken manner Fred addressed the driver.

'I have an urgent appointment at Bon Accord Manse, Sir. I would be much obliged if you would take me as soon as possible.' And holding out the silver shilling he added 'I have the fare, Sir.'

The cabbie, a stocky man with a round, red face, turned to look at him. He cast his eyes over the figure in front of him, while Fred hoped the anxiety he was feeling did not show. He just needed to be away from this place. The driver paused for a moment then, to Fred's greatest relief, nodded.

'Aye, I'll take ye tae the manse. Jist yersel?'

'No. I have a parishioner with me who needs his advice. Thank you, Sir, I am much indebted.'

Fred raised his arm and waved to Jessie. Lowering her head

and wrapping her shawl around her, she walked resolutely towards him. However, as she approached the hansom, the driver had a change of heart.

'Is she the parishioner then?' The driver demanded of Fred. His earlier bonhomie seemed to have departed. Fred nodded.

'I cannae hae her in ma cab! It'll stink tae high heaven.'

'For pity's sake, man!' Fred remonstrated with him angrily. 'She needs help. I'm nae leaving her here.'

'Weel that's your decision, sir, but I've a livin' tae make and I'm nae takin' her.'

At the sound of the men's raised voices, Jessie, stopped and stood where she was. Now she came up to Fred and took hold of his sleeve.

'Leave it, Fred! I dinnae want this.'

'No, Jess. This isnae right. He agreed. We hae the fare.'

'Weel, Fred, I'm nae stayin' here tae be embarrassed.' And she turned and starting walking away.

Torn between standing his ground and his fear of losing sight of Jessie, Fred finally let go of the cab door. 'Nae a very Christian thing to do,' he pronounced acidly. 'If anything happens to her it'll be on your conscience, man.'

'I'll tak ma chances.' And the driver turned away.

By this time Jessie was standing with her back to Fred and appeared to be surveying the street beyond. She was a feisty little thing, he gave her that. You had to be to survive in her world. Then she turned back to look at him and to his surprise and amusement she put her fingers to her mouth and whistled, while her free hand beckoned to him urgently. Fred hastened his pace and caught up with her.

'He'll tak us,' explained Jessie, pointing up the street to where another solitary hansom was standing.

The driver, a young man about their age, his cap pulled down over his forehead, was holding a grey Highland pony by its bridle. Catching sight of them he held up his hand in acknowledgement.

'It's Alan Massie, I ken his sister,' said Jessie by way of

explanation. He's going up town wi' some parcels.'

Fred opened the door to the hansom cab and Jessie climbed in. With a final glance around him, Fred ducked his head and followed her, slamming the door behind him.

# CHAPTER 4

# BON ACCORD CRESCENT

JESSIE DUTHIE HAD NEVER BEEN IN A HANSOM BEFORE. SHE had taken the coach a couple of years back when she left Dundee, but she had been in such tumult she could recall very little of that particular journey. Now as the driver flicked his whip and clicked at his horse, 'Come on now, Bobby' and the cab started to roll forward, she felt suddenly self-conscious and vulnerable.

She looked sideways at the gangly red-haired youth sitting bolt upright at her side, slightly too much of him to sit at ease in the confined space. Bony wrists extended from the sleeves of his dark overcoat and rested on his knees. At the moment he seemed lost in his own thoughts, his tongue poking out absent-mindedly and running over the gap left by his broken tooth. So he was a minister, or so he said? A 'holy Wully'. So earnest, so solemn, but still a lad for all that.

Did she feel differently towards him now? Perhaps she should have declined his offer of help. She could not just walk out on her life like that, or could she? If Billy came back and found her gone, what would he do? Well he would be away with the fleet come Monday and that would give her time to think. She looked down at her chapped, red hands, the bitten nails and, in the confined space, was all too aware of the strong smell of fish that came off them. She pulled the shawl around herself more tightly and tried to conceal her hands in the folds.

Outside, the horse and cab strained as they climbed the steep incline of Windmill Brae and approached Union Street. The wheels rattled and clattered under them, as the gelding's hooves clipped the hard, granite cobbles. Turning westwards on to the main thoroughfare the coachman cracked his whip above their heads and with another call to his horse, it broke into a trot. As the light cab moved rapidly along the road, Jessie's attention was caught by the street beyond.

Looking through the small square window in the side of the cab she stared at the majestic buildings, built from solid slabs of pink and grey granite, sparkling in the morning sunshine. Only a quarter of a mile from the harbour but it could be another world. Decorated with columns and turrets and flag poles reaching skywards, they looked like castles to her. Grand shops, their names picked out in prominent gold lettering, displayed their wares behind huge polished glass windows. What would it be like to wear those beautiful gowns and dresses? Some even boasted a Royal Appointment emblem. The city had become a favourite of the Queen ever since they had built the big castle up the Dee. Jessie heard she came by train all the way from London. She could barely imagine such a thing.

'A penny for your thoughts, Jessie?'

With a start Jessie turned away from the window to look at the young man sitting beside her. For just a moment she had forgotten about why she was here and what had just happened.

'Fit am I daeing, Fred?' she sighed shaking her head. 'I cannae jist up and awa'.

'Ye couldnae stay there for now, Jess. It wisnae safe. And what did ye mean that Billy kent too much aboot ye?'

Jess looked away and dropped her chin, her lips pressed

tightly together as though words of explanation might jump out of their own accord.

'Weel, Jessie? Ye ken a' aboot me. Your turn now.' And Fred turned towards her, his blue eyes willing her to confide. Should she tell him the truth? Could she trust him? Perhaps in telling Fred it would give her some protection from Billy Smith.

'If I tell you, Fred, you must swear you will *nivvir* tell anither soul. Swear it!'

'I swear, Jessie, on ma mither's soul.'

Then in a low, quiet voice, Jessie started to give her account.

'I used tae stay in Dundee wi' ma mither and sister. Ma faither died. He worked at the jute mill. His lungs gave up. Ma mither stayed at hame wi' ma wee sister and I went tae work at the mill instead. There wis a foreman there, a real bastard, a drunken bully. He'd aye pick on ye and try to get ye tae say somethin' so he could report ye. Make up reasons for ye tae dae mair work. We wisnae friends!'

And she laughed mirthlessly.

'Onyways, one day he told me and ma friend, Annie we had tae stay late tae tidy up, while he went aff tae the boozer. When he came back tae check, he wis pissed an' fell over a bobbin. He wis sae angry he wis gang tae hit ma friend. I couldnae stand by, I jist went to stop him but he fell and hit his heid. We thought he wis deid! I could hae hung. Naebody wud believe a pair, common, wee lassie.'

At the recollection, Jessie, paused and put her hands over her face. Fred said nothing, his face solemn.

'Ma mither wis beside herself. She'd jist lost ma faither. But she's a strong woman and she heard there were jobs going in the fish up here in Aberdeen. She put me on the coach one mornin'. Told the works I wis in the family way and wis awa' tae relatives in the country. She took over ma job.'

'And the foreman, wis he deid?' Fred frowned at Jessie. She leaned back and surveyed him for a moment.

'No, he wisnae. The mill owner found him lying on the flair.

Unconscious but nae deid. The boss thought he wis deid drunk and fired him. If Charlie McNab wisnae ma friend afore he certainly isnae now!'

'And how does Billy ken a' this, Jessie?'

'Ma fault. I met him up here soon after I'd arrived. I quite fancied him tae start wi'. We had a nice wee time at the beginning and I'd had a bittie tae drink and….' Her voice tailed off and she shook her head. 'But he's a jealous critter and keeps coming back wi' it, says he kens Charlie and will tell him where I am.'

There was a sudden shudder as the hansom came to a halt. The driver coughed, cleared his throat and spat into the gutter. Jessie ceased her story and saw to her surprise that they had turned off Union Street and were now stopped in an elegant crescent of tall granite houses separated from the pavement by uniform black railings.

'Bon Accord Crescent, Sir,' announced the cabbie. 'Which number?'

'This will do very well, thank you,' replied Fred, feeling in his pocket for the fare. Jessie observed her destination with trepidation. Holy folk or no, Fred had some explaining to do. He had been out all night and she… well what did she look like? They wouldn't have had the likes of her through their doors very often, would they? Fred had jumped down from the cab and passed his coin up to the driver. He then came round to Jessie's side of the hansom and held out his hand to help her alight.

'This is the manse, Jessie. Best you wait here till I speak tae Reverend Kelman. Dinnae worry, I won't be long.' Fred smiled encouragingly.

Dinnae worry? That was easy to say, she thought but before she could respond Fred had turned away from her and was walking up to the house.

For what seemed like an eternity, Jessie stood on the pavement looking up at the house, waiting for Fred to reappear. She was all too aware of her impoverished appearance and wished she were not so exposed. Fortunately, it was still early enough in the morning and there were few passers-by. Whenever Jessie heard foot-steps approaching, she made sure she had her back turned and bent down as if to secure her boot-lace. In the background she could hear a bell striking the hour. Nine o'clock. Her stomach grumbled and she realised that she had had no breakfast. Oh, she could so do with a bannock and a cup of hot sweet tea right now. Feeling light-headed, Jessie sank down on to one of the broad granite steps.

She could only guess at what Fred was saying to explain his absence and the surprise visitor. It was likely they would be very vexed and send her back immediately. She went through in her head what she might say to them. But look at herself! A dirty, wee tink. Who was she fooling? Maybe they would send Fred away? Because of her? She could not have that on her conscience. She forced herself to stand up again and looked nervously at the unforgiving grey façade in front of her. No, this could not be. She had been a fool to think she could just run away again, disappear from her life, her job. Better to get herself back before more harm was done.

Her mind made up, Jessie turned her head eastwards to where the North Sea lay sparkling in the distance. Then, with a quick backward glance at the house which might have been her salvation, she hurried away as quickly as she could.

*

Standing in the familiar hallway, Fred wondered if he should call out to announce his arrival. Taking a deep breath, he inhaled the comforting smell of furniture polish and Richard's pipe tobacco and sighed with relief to be back at last at the manse. However, catching his unkempt and dirty reflection in the hall mirror caused him to stop in shock. He was filthy. Was he really come to this, what had he been thinking of last night? The broken tooth continued to throb but with so much on his mind Fred had become almost accustomed to its presence. He moved closer to the glass to scrutinise the damage. Almost immediately he heard a door open and turning round Fred saw Mary-Ann emerge holding a tray of used breakfast dishes. Her eyes widened and for a moment neither spoke.

'Fred! There you are!' Mrs Kelman placed the tray on the hall table and approached him, an anxious frown on her kindly face. 'What in God's name has happened to you? Are you alright?'

'Yes, yes, I am. Forgive me, please. I….'

'When you did not come down to breakfast we checked your room and saw your bed had not been slept in. We did not know what to think. Thank the Lord you are alright!'

And she paused a couple of paces from the young man.

'Where is Richard? Is he very angry?'

'Richard? Angry? No, we have just been so worried. He felt he should have looked after you more carefully yesterday but I told him you needed some time on your own. But when you weren't here this morning, well….you start to fear the worst.'

'Fred! For God's sake man! Where have you been?'

A raised voice from the top of the staircase caused both Mary-Ann and Fred to look up. Richard stood with his hand on the newel post.

'Come upstairs, we'll talk in my study,' he instructed.

'I will, Richard, but I'm not alone.'

'Not alone? What do you mean?'

'I will explain everything, I promise, but, Mary-Ann, will you go and speak to the girl please? She's just outside. I had to persuade her to come. She needs some shelter for now. Please? She'll need some food and some fresh clothes if we have some to spare?'

'Fred, what on earth have you been up to?'

'Just check on her please. I'll tell you everything.'

'Very well. You go upstairs with Richard and I will try to tend to the lassie. What's her name?'

'Jess, Jessie.'

# CHAPTER 5

# LOST AND FOUND

FRED STOOD IN RICHARD'S STUDY FEELING SHAME AND embarrassment in equal measure. The fact that his friend had not castigated him made him feel worse as did the anxious look of disappointment on the older man's face. In the confines of this quiet, academic room, with its rows of leather bound books and solemn portraits of earlier incumbents, Fred felt more out of place than ever. It should not have been so. Had he not in many ways grown up in this room spending long days and evenings studying his calling? Richard, always so patient and understanding, would talk him out of his moods and doubts and get him to think beyond these four walls, about what the texts really meant and how he could apply them in the present day.

'Sit down, Fred,' he was instructed.

Self-consciously he lowered himself on to the upright chair being pointed out to him. Now that the artificial glow and false confidence gained from the alcohol had long worn off, Fred could not understand his actions. How could he have jeopardised all he had worked for in one evening? If he could not explain things to himself, how was he going to explain it to Richard? As he sat in silence, staring at his hands, he heard his friend address him.

'Fred, I am not angry. What you did was foolish but understandable. You are a very young man yet and have achieved a great deal. This is both a blessing and a curse. The opportunity is there for you and you have the makings of a great preacher, precisely because you can see both sides of man's predicament. But with so many expecting greatness from you I can see that the burden must sometimes seem intolerable. From an elevated position it is too easy to fall.'

Fred raised his head at last and looked directly at his teacher. He had never known his father and while his mother's family had provided companionship and friendship during his childhood, Richard Kelman was the person who had filled the paternal void for him.

'Thank you, Richard. I am truly sorry. I ask your forgiveness. You have always treated me with respect, consideration and friendship and I have let you down. What I did was weak and thoughtless.'

'Your apology is accepted, Fred, but what is even more important to me is your assurance that you understand your road through life. So many people have made sacrifices, and I am not talking of myself here, to enable you to embark on your calling. There will always be temptation. You have free will whether or not to follow it. I am confident you have the strength of character to make the right decisions. But perhaps you need to experience the consequences of actions to fully comprehend the power that choice has. You will not stay here forever. This is just your starting point. Wherever you go I will be watching out for you, so make me proud, Fred.'

A knock at the study door interrupted their conversation and Mary-Ann's muffled voice called through the wooden panels.

'Richard, Fred, may I come in?

'Yes, come in, Mary-Ann. We are done here.'

The minister's wife opened the door and entered, a concerned expression on her face.

'I went outside to speak to Jessie as you requested, Fred, but she wasn't there. Maybe she has thought better of it. I hurried down to the end of the road to see if I could catch sight of her, but to no avail. I am sorry.'

Fred felt his stomach tighten and stood up in alarm.

'We need to find her. It is not safe for her to return to the harbour. This is my doing.'

As he made to leave the room, Mary-Ann caught hold of his sleeve.

'Fred, we'll go and look for her but just now you need to change your clothes, wash and get some rest. You are over-tired and over-wrought.'

'How can I rest? I really fear she will be hurt again. In return for her kindness I have compromised her safety. I must find her!'

'Douglas Quay you say, Fred?' asked Richard. 'I'll send word to James MacDonald at St Nicholas Kirk. He knows everybody down there. If she has returned there he will find her and we can see how matters lie. Trust me, Fred. You now need to return to your real life.'

'Let me come with you then when you visit the Reverend MacDonald? Please.'

And Fred looked at Richard with such an urgent expression on his face, that the older man felt compelled to agree.

'Very well, but not until you have cleaned yourself up, Fred. It is fortunate my sermon for tomorrow is already prepared otherwise I might not be so amenable. I will go and prepare the pony and trap. Make yourself respectable and be ready in half an hour.'

THE BRIGHT WEATHER of the early morning was now wearing off and a chilly east wind had started to blow as the open pony cart bearing the two men set off along the cobbles of Bon Accord Crescent. Fred pulled up his collar and was thankful that he had thought to grasp his hat as he left the manse. He scanned the streets anxiously for signs of Jessie, but without success.

There were so many back lanes and streets she could have taken, perhaps it was not surprising, but nonetheless he felt a sense of disappointment and worry that they might not find her. Sensing his friend's disquiet, Richard turned to Fred to reassure him.

'She will be found, have no fear, Fred. If not today very soon afterwards I am sure. Reverend MacDonald will not fail us. But you must be prepared for the lassie to have had a change of mind.'

'But why would she want to stay somewhere where she was at risk?'

'People act strangely, Fred. From what you have told me, she sounds like an independent young woman who may not want to be beholden to us.'

'Do you think I am wrong to feel responsible for her, Richard?'

'Well it seems she has made quite an impression on you one way or another, Fred, so my opinion is unlikely to make you change your mind. Am I not right?'

'I do feel responsible for the situation she now finds herself in. I could have ignored her cries and turned my back but I would not have slept easy if I had done so.'

'It is her life, Fred, and she has to fight her own battles. Maybe she realised this and that is why she took flight?'

This might be true, Fred realised, and he was surprised how down-hearted this possibility made him feel.

The reek of smoke hit them as soon as they turned into the Shiprow. At first the two men put the smell down to an over-productive chimney but, as they raised their eyes to the rooftops, Fred saw immediately that the top floor of the tenement building where he had spent the previous night was on fire, the rooms behind the windows full of smoke. A crowd of people stood on the pavement passing leather buckets of water inside the building, while another group held on to a scruffy little man who was struggling furiously and shouting obscenities.

'She's a fuckin' whore! She had it comin'. I'm nae sorry. A pity she wisnae in there hersel'.'

'Far's the fire brigade?' A voice shouted 'We have'nae ony mair water.'

'I dinnae ken, man. Bob ran awa' up the street tae ring the bell jist as soon as he saw the smoke. It wis that mad-man Billy Smith wha's done it. He's lucky a'bodys oot the building.'

'Mind oot, here they come, thank goodness!'

'Richard! That's Jessie's place!'

Fred jumped out of the trap, twisting his head around, but there was no sign of her. Two snorting horses pulling the fire-cart clattered to a halt, ears flattened and eyes bulging. The air was thick with the ominous, acrid smell of burning. With much pointing and waving of hands the four firefighters were shown the upper floor where the blaze, thanks to the efforts of the neighbours, had yet to take hold. Encumbered with their bulky oilskin coats, metal helmets and heavy black boots, the men tramped towards the tenement block.

'Man the pumps,' shouted out the chief fireman, enlisting some of the onlookers. 'We cannae dae it a' ourselves. Hurry up there!'

There was a low cheer when a jet of water first appeared over their heads to be directed at the upper windows. It was not a minute too soon. The wind had come up and the dust and rotten wood inside the tenement would act like tinder. They had seen it all before. Number ten, just down the way had been gutted only six months previously, with a young mother and two bairns dying.

'Everyone oot you say?' Fred addressed an elderly woman standing close by, one hand over her mouth in alarm.

'Aye, I think so.'

'D'ye ken Jessie Duthie?' Fred continued.

'Jessie? Aye I do. It's her place that's on fire. Her man's a lunatic. He didnae even deny fit he's done. The police had better get here afore the crowd set on him. He's always been an angry man but he's gone too far this time.'

'Have you seen Jessie at all?'

'No I hav'nae. It's Saturday so she's probably awa' somewhere. Lucky for her.'

Behind him, over and above the muttering of onlookers, Fred could hear raised voices and the unmistakeable harsh tones of Billy Smith, who continued to shout profanities and defend his actions aggressively. Then a higher pitched note of alarm entered the man's voice which caused Fred to turn. He could see now that two men had grabbed Billy by each arm and were attempting to drag him towards the oily waters of the harbour.

'I cannae swim!' Billy squealed in panic.

'You should hae thocht o' that afore. Time to cool that temper o' yours.'

The metal toes of his boots scraped along the cobbles as Billy desperately tried to resist his captors. No-one came to his assistance. He had few friends in these parts it seemed. For a moment Fred felt frozen to the spot then suddenly he called out to the two vigilantes.

'Stop there! Stop it now! If he drowns, you will be his murderers. And then what will happen to your wives and your bairns? This is nae your business. Let him answer to the court.'

The two men slowed their pace but did not reply nor release their quarry who continued to wrestle frantically in their grasp.

'Do you hear me?' Fred repeated with even greater urgency. 'This is nae your affair. There's enough harm been done already this morning - dinnae add tae it.'

For a moment there was no reaction and it crossed Fred's mind that his words might have no effect. Then, to his relief, the men paused. Their prisoner, seizing his chance, wriggled free and ran off along the harbour side towards the beach. Fred approached the two seamen who were looking down the quayside at the small dark figure disappearing into the distance.

'Thank you,' he said simply. 'This is'nae your fight.'

'Excuse me, sir, did you say you were looking for Jessie Duthie?'

Fred turned to the voice behind him.

'I heard ye speaking tae Belle Wishart over there.' The speaker was pointing to the woman Fred has questioned just minutes earlier.

'Aye, have ye seen her? I'm a friend o' hers and I heard she'd been having trouble wi' Billy.' Fred allowed himself this mild fabrication.

'I think she's o'er in the Ship. I saw her arguing wi' Billy jist efter he'd come oot the building. Pair lassie she wisnae able to save onythin'.'

Fred could feel his heart pounding. Whether this was due to his intervention with the sailors or in anticipation of finding Jessie he was not sure. He looked across at the Ship Inn which did not look open for business; the tatty brown door was closed to passers-by and there were no lights within. However, Jessie's neighbour seemed to be of the opinion that she had sought sanctuary there so he would investigate. Walking a few paces back to the pony cart, Fred updated his companion.

'Richard, she's been seen in the Ship Inn. I will check there. Will you wait until I return?'

'Yes, go and see how she is.'

'And if I can persuade her to come with us, will you speak with her please?'

'Yes, of course. Go.'

Realising he was procrastinating, maybe fearful of the outcome of the next few minutes, Fred turned back abruptly to the harbour-side and strode up to the entrance of the public house. Raising his right hand he pushed at the door with his palm. It remained closed. Undeterred, he rapped a couple of times and waited. After a short period, the door was opened cautiously by the publican.

'We're closed. Nae open 'til eleven.'

'I dinnae want a drink, sir. I'm looking for Jessie Duthie? I'm a friend o' hers.'

Fred tried to see past the man who was blocking his path.

'Oh aye, that's fit they a' say. I dinnae think she wants tae spik tae onyone jist noo. Did you see fit happened tae her room?'

'Aye I did. That's why I'm here. She needs somewhere tae stay nae doot?'

'Weel she's safe enough here.'

'Can I speak to her then?'

'Did ye nae hear me? She disnae want tae speak tae onyone. Jist leave her alone!'

'Can I no' hear that from her?' Fred appealed once again. But the door had already closed in his face.

Fred stood for some seconds, head bowed and arms at his sides. He should leave. He had his answer. But not from Jessie. He did not want to intrude on her difficulty but it was important to him to know this was what she wanted.

'Jessie! Are you there?'

Fred had pressed his face up against the weather-beaten entrance and called through it.

'Jess, it's Fred! Come back with us – if you want to. I've spoken tae the Kelmans. They understand. We're in the Shiprow. We'll wait for you by the water trough. If we dinnae see you by eleven we'll leave you be.'

He could do no more. Turning away he suddenly felt abashed. Half a dozen passers-by were watching him with curiosity as he made his way back to Richard and the pony cart.

'I think she's in there. I don't know if she heard me. Can we wait until eleven, please?'

Richard, despite his charitable nature, sighed with some impatience. It had been an unexpectedly long morning. He checked his pocket watch.

'That's fifteen minutes. Very well, but then I think if the young lady does not appear we must away. We can still call by St Nicholas Kirk and let Reverend MacDonald know of our quest.'

All was now calm. The onlookers of the earlier drama had dispersed and normal activity had returned to the quayside. The firemen had succeeded in putting out the top floor blaze and all that remained were soot darkened windows, pools of water in the gutter and the smell of smoke. The bells of St Nicholas started to chime the hour.

'Sorry, lad, but it's time to go.' Richard Kelman placed a

consoling hand on his young friend's shoulder.

Taking up the reins and laying his whip across the pony's back, the pony cart started to move off.

'Wait! Wait for me, Fred!'

A woman's voice rang out. It was Jessie.

# CHAPTER 6

# ALPHABET

FRED BARELY RECOGNISED THE DISTRAUGHT FIGURE STANDING in front of him. Jessie's face was smudged with soot and, around her eyes, where she had being crying, there was a greasy dark residue. Her hair was streaked with black deposits and her hands and finger nails were cut and bleeding.

'What's he done to you, Jessie?'

Fred had leapt down from the pony trap as soon as he had heard Jessie's distressed voice. Oblivious to the groups of curious bystanders and to Richard sitting, reins in hand, above him, Fred held out his arms and pulled the young woman close to him. Jessie, unable to speak, leant against him trembling. He could smell the smoke in her matted hair and heard her shallow breathing.

'Thank the Lord you weren't in there, Jess. You're alive.'

'There's naethin' left,' she muttered eventually. 'I tried to get back in but there was too much smoke. He's done fer me, the bastard!' And her body started to shake.

'Hush, dinnae greet, lassie.' Fred tried to comfort her. 'We'll take care o' ye.'

Jessie raised her head and stared up at him. She had made no attempt to wipe her nose and her eyes were red, whether from smoke or crying, Fred was uncertain. Very gently, he pulled away from the young woman and started to guide her towards Richard and the pony cart. Then he was aware that she had stopped, her body tensing.

'So this is my life from now on!' Jessie spat out to no-one in particular. 'Charity frae others! I should be grateful I suppose but I'm muckle tired o' bein' grateful. I work hard, God knows, but it's nivvir enough! Nivvir! There's always some bastard waiting tae spoil it fer me!'

Then she dropped to her haunches and howled, her hands beating an angry tirade on her head.

'Jess, Jess, come awa'. We'll see ye are a' right.'

Fred knelt down beside the small distressed figure and, placing his hands around her shoulders, tried to get her to stand up again. After a couple of minutes Jessie finally raised her head, got to her feet and allowed herself to be led to the pony cart.

MARY-ANN WAS WAITING at the front door when they arrived at the manse some ten minutes later. Fred found it difficult to read her expression as they walked up the steps towards her. Whether it was a frown of anxiety or disapproval he was not sure and for a fraction of a second his confidence that they were doing the right thing by Jessie faded. But then, feeling Jessie cautiously take hold of his arm as if to steady herself, he felt all doubts recede.

'Well, she is found,' Fred declared, putting his arm around Jessie's shoulders. 'But it has been a sad story, I am afraid. She has lost everything, Mary-Ann. And it's my fault. While she was out, her man came back and set fire to her rooms. She could have been killed. We have to help her.'

Fred was aware that he had raised his voice and stopped speaking. A horrified look had crossed Mary-Ann's normally calm face.

'Good Lord, Fred! This is terrible. This means she is destitute? I will ask Mrs Milne to come and help. I will see if she can bring something for her to wear. But first Jessie needs to wash and rest and then we will see what can be done. She can have Betty's room for now. We have had nobody there since she left to get married last spring.'

Mary-Ann took a step towards and held out her hand to Jessie.

'Miss Duthie. Please come in. I am truly sorry to hear of your troubles.'

Briefly her anxious glance took in the dishevelled figure in front of her, then she turned and led the way inside.

'Well, it is decided!'

Mary-Ann entered the drawing room where Fred and Richard now sat.

'It is indeed fortunate timing as since Betty left us last spring we have had no live-in help. Jessie is willing to learn a house-maid's skills in return for her board and lodgings. When she is fully trained we will review the situation. Jessie, please come in and introduce yourself properly.'

Fred had to stop himself staring as Jessie presented herself hesitantly to her new employer. Bathed and now clad in fresh, plain clothes, she presented a total contrast from a few hours previously. Some colour had returned to her cheeks and the soft brown hair had been washed and was now plaited and pinned up demurely on the top of her head. The small blue eyes were still wary but a polite smile played on her lips. She turned to Richard.

'Good afternoon, sir. I'm Jessie.'

Richard got to his feet and approached the young woman who hovered shyly in the door-way.

'Good afternoon to you, Jessie. Well you look much improved now, I must say. How do you feel after your ordeal?'

'Better, Sir, thank you. But I can'nae quite believe it. I feel as though I am in a dream and I will wake up in a wee bit.' Jessie laughed briefly.

'Oh this is real enough, Jessie. Mrs Kelman has explained everything to you, I hope. We live plainly here but you will be safe.'

'Yes, sir, thank you.'

Faced with Jessie's unfamiliar appearance amid the sober surroundings of the manse, Fred suddenly felt shy and awkward. Unmoving, he observed the young woman in silence. It was only when she made to leave the room that he found his tongue.

'Forgive me, Jessie. I am standing here like a glaikit loon, jist admiring ye.'

Then he stepped forward and held his hand out to shake hers. Tentatively, Jessie also extended hers. Fred took it and enclosed it in his. Holding on slightly longer than he should have, he was once again drawn to look at her face. The blue eyes held his for a fraction before Jessie bent her head down again and sought to release her hand from Fred's grasp.

'I'd better awa'. Mrs Kelman has some lunch for me and then she is gang tae show me fit needs daeing.'

While the drama of the morning had sustained Fred thus far, by early afternoon he was suddenly overcome by exhaustion and wanted nothing more than to lie down and close his eyes for an hour or so. Excusing himself after lunch, he returned to his room and sat down on his bed. Looking about him he took in the peaceful and comfortable surroundings he had enjoyed for the past few years. By comparison to the cramped cottage he had shared with his mother and then the cold austere room he had lived in as a student, this was a palace. But for the first time he began to think of when he might have his own home, his own books and furniture, a companion, a wife even. Now he was qualified he could start to think ahead to such a time.

He stood up and walked over to the window to close the curtains. Gazing over the roofs of Aberdeen all the way to the sea, Fred reflected on how much he loved this view. He felt liberated. Suddenly, a movement on the ground caught his eye. A small figure clad in a simple grey and white dress was hanging the day's washing on the clothes line. It was Jessie, now so calm and purposeful. Bending down to the wicker washing basket, a wooden peg clamped in her teeth, she picked up a garment, giving it a gentle shake before reaching up to secure it to the line. Fred paused half concealed by the curtain and continued to observe her. Her work done, Jessie straightened up. Just in time Fred withdrew from her eye line as she turned towards the house and glanced briefly upwards. After a couple of paces, she disappeared from view and Fred was left alone with his thoughts.

'Jessie tells me you are going to teach her to read and write? Is that so?'

It was Monday morning. Despite all that had occurred in the preceding couple of days, normality had returned to life at the manse. Now Mary-Anne addressed Fred across the breakfast table. He raised his head from the morning edition of the Press and Journal and looked at her directly.

'Aye, we discussed it. She can'nae read nor write just now. That's nae' right. Would you mind?'

'Not at all, provided it does not interfere with your work and your own studies. She seems intelligent enough. She should learn quickly I dare say.'

Mary-Ann seemed about to add a further comment but hesitated.

'You are sure?' Fred pressed her.

'Yes, but be careful, Fred. She is vulnerable and no doubt impressionable.'

'But of course, Mary-Ann. I would never…'

Mary-Ann held her hand up to silence him.

'We understand each other, Fred, you need not say anything else. I will look out some of the boys' old books and an alphabet. There will be paper and pencils in the study. Perhaps between eleven and twelve in the morning? I will have a word with her as soon as we are done with breakfast.'

Jessie started to laugh when she saw the colourful children's book laid out on the table in front of her.

'I'm nae a bairn!' she exclaimed in mock indignation. 'I ken ma ABC.'

'You're feeling better,' remarked Fred with amusement. 'These belonged to the Kelmans' sons. It's just to start you off.'

Fred and Jessie were now seated in the window of the study with paper, pencils and an assortment of books ready for their attention. The morning sunlight lay in a dappled pattern across the sturdy table and, apart from the steady ticking of the carriage clock on the mantelpiece, there was silence in the room. Fred was only too aware of Jessie's physical proximity. Close enough for the warmth of her body to reach him. The strong little hand resting lightly on the book in front of them. She smelt of soap and lavender water and cleared her throat once or twice unselfconsciously. Then she turned her face expectantly towards Fred and he forced his thoughts back to the lesson.

'ABC - those are their names if you like but when you read them they make different sounds,' he explained, pointing to the first illustration. 'Also when you read and write it is usually the small letters you use rather than the big ones. We call them capital letters. You see them at the start of a sentence.'

'Sentence?' queried Jessie. 'I ken a prison sentence but I suppose this is different?'

'Ah yes, indeed. Look here.' And Fred opened one of the books, The Sleeping Beauty by Charles Perrault, and turned to the first page.

'*Once upon a time.*' He read out pointing to each word. 'That is the first sentence. A group of words that tell you something. The first letter is always a capital and you finish it with a dot called a full stop. Now you show me the sentences.'

With a brief glance at her instructor, Jessie pulled the book in front of her and with her forefinger lightly traced each of the subsequent sentences. Then she stopped and looked at Fred.

'Correct first time, Jessie. You are going to be good student, I know it.'

Now they returned to the alphabet book. Each letter was

accompanied by a short rhyme which was now read out by Fred to be repeated by Jessie.

*'A is for Apples that Auntie will bring. B is for Bells that loudly ring, C is for Crackers that Kate pulls with Fred.'*

Now Jessie stopped and retraced the rhyme replacing Kate's name with her own.

*'..that Jess pulls with Fred!'*

Fred started to correct her but as he glanced up, Jess caught his eye and smiled. His stomach shifted slightly and he turned away. When he looked again Jess had assumed her earlier solemn stance poring over the illustrations, one finger resting lightly on the page.

'Well said, Jess. I'm proud of you,' exclaimed Fred. 'We'll have you reading in no time.'

'And one day mebbe I'll write letters like fancy folk. Mebbe I'll write you a letter, Fred. Would you like that?'

She was watching him again. Fred had no doubt she was completely earnest.

'Aye, I would, Jess,' he admitted softly. 'But we need to carry on now otherwise Mrs Kelman will think I'm nae doing ma job.'

Jessie nodded her head without speaking and lightly brushed his hand with her fingers before turning her attention once again to her books.

# CHAPTER 7

# THE CEILIDH

MORE THAN TWO MONTHS HAD PASSED SINCE JESSIE FIRST entered the Kelman household at Bon Accord Crescent. There had been no sign of Billy Smith – perhaps he had left town or maybe even cadged a passage on a ship bound for America. Jessie had begun to relax. Sometimes she mourned the loss of her few possessions, her name embroidered on a scrap of material by her granny or the hairbrush her mother had given her, but there was nothing to gain by looking back she decided. What was done was done.

Life had taken on a peaceful routine of laying fires, serving wholesome food on solid blue and white china, clearing tables and doing the laundry, interspersed with her lessons with Fred. Jessie enjoyed the diversion and was pleased with her progress. She took pride in practising her handwriting, signing her name with a flourish over and over again. Fred was a patient and encouraging teacher but remained an enigma to her. They enjoyed each other's company and she found herself listening out for his voice and being aware which room he was in. Sometimes she would catch him observing her but if she reacted to this Fred seemed awkward and shy.

As autumn turned into winter, the days grew shorter. Curtains were drawn and fires lit by four o'clock in the afternoon. Christmas was fast approaching and Mary-Ann had let Jessie know that they would be visiting relatives in Inverness for a few days between Christmas and New Year. Fred would be going to see his mother in Strathmuir but Jessie was welcome to stay on at the manse or visit her own family perhaps. Her heart sank at the thought of being left on her own but she doubted if she could afford to travel to Dundee and indeed if there would be room now that her sister was grown.

Jessie saw the advertisement for the ceilidh on the way to the post-office with a bundle of Christmas cards for Mrs Kelman. Standing beside the pillar box her attention was caught by the colourful announcement. Peering at it carefully Jessie read that the event was to be held in the church hall on Saturday 15$^{th}$ December at 7 p.m. Charlie MacCrae's band would be playing and there would be a singer and a fiddler for their entertainment as well. Tea and cakes would be served at 9 p.m. All for 6 pence each. Unaccustomed excitement flared within her for a moment. Could she persuade Fred to come? Would that be permitted? Or would the Kelmans consider it inappropriate – the minister and the maid?

'Fred?' Jessie addressed him cautiously when they were next together in the study. She had now advanced to a plentiful library of fairy stories and cautionary tales from the Kelman nursery. She was about to start on The Little Mermaid by Hans Christian Andersen when she decided to ask Fred about the dance.

'Fred?' She repeated. 'Can I ask you something, please? Nae to do wi' ma books.'

Fred had turned to her in surprise. 'Yes, of course, Jessie.'

'There's tae be a ceilidh in the church hall next Saturday. I'd like tae go. Would you be allowed to come wi' me, Fred?'

The last sentence had come out very fast as if Jessie feared what the answer might be.

'Ah, a ceilidh. I mind those from when I was a boy,' Fred mused. 'I'm nae much of a dancer, Jessie. Would you really want someone wi' two left feet? Plenty other nice dancers for ye I dare say!'

Jessie fell silent. All animation gone from her face.

'I dinnae want ither nice dancers. I want you to be there,' she whispered, looking down. 'I think it would be nice. I've nae bin oot since I came here and a girl needs a wee bit of fun.'

There was silence in the room as the question was left unanswered. Fred ran his hands through his hair. Jessie noticed he did this when he was considering something.

'D'ye nae want to go wi' me then?' Jessie made a final appeal.

Fred put his hands on the table and turned to her.

'Aye I do, that's the difficulty. D'ye nae see how much I care for ye, Jessie? But I don't think we can be together. People hae expectations of me. I cannae stay in Aberdeen.'

'Fred, I've jist asked ye to a ceilidh, nae tae marry me!' Jessie retorted indignantly, the gaze from her blue eyes now directed at her teacher. 'There'll be plenty folk there and ye can ask the Kelmans first if ye care to.'

'I dinnae want tae mislead ye, Jess. So long as we understand each other?'

'Aye, Fred, I promise. We're friends are we not? So you'll speak to Mrs Kelman?'

Mary-Ann addressed Jessie the next morning as she was busy stuffing the used bed linen into the copper. Hot, sticky and absorbed in her task, at first she did not hear her employer speak.

'Jessie, I hear you would like to go to the parish ceilidh with Fred?'

Jessie immediately straightened up, initially apprehensive that it might be a negative response.

'Cheer up, young lady,' teased Mary-Ann. 'You shall go to the ball! I'll see if I have something for you to wear. A wee bit more fancy and festive.'

'Oh Mrs Kelman! Thank ye, thank ye. This means so much.'

Impulsively, Jessie grasped the older woman's hand in gratitude.

'Hush now, Jessie. You are more than welcome. You have worked very well for us since you arrived and with Christmas coming up I think you have earned a little treat. Fred will be your chaperone. I cannot vouch for the other guests but everybody will have a good time if last year is anything to go by.'

The usually dour and unadorned church hall now had a semblance of merriment about it as Jessie and Fred approached the entrance. Red and green bunting was strung out across the room and ropes of ivy were draped around the door and windows. Fat candles flickered in the deep window sills, safely shielded from passing clothing with glass covers.

Jessie stood self-consciously at Fred's side as Mr Burns, one of the kirk elders, held out his hand for their entrance fee.

'Good evening, Fred. Glad to see ye're taking a break from your studies.' He remarked jovially. 'I didnae ken ye were a dancing man, though?'

Fred's serious demeanour broke into an embarrassed smile.

'I have to blame it on this young lady,' he apologised indicating his companion.

Jessie's hands nervously smoothed the heavy dark green cotton material of the dress she had been loaned by Mary-Ann. It fitted her perfectly. There was a jolly band of tartan fixed around the base of the crinoline and small green buttons up the front. It was a little long perhaps but she was wearing her boots and would have to remember to hold up her skirts during the dancing.

'I hae ma ticket money, Fred,' Jessie started to undo a small money pouch.

'Dinnae be silly, this is my treat. I insist.' And Fred gently pushed Jessie's hand away and reached into his pocket. Two silver sixpenny pieces were placed on the counter and Mr Burns handed over two pink tickets.

'Thank you kindly. Enjoy yersels!'

Although it was not yet 7 pm the hall was already full of bustling and excited people. Children skipped and ran among the adults absorbed in their own games and young couples shyly stood as close to each other as they dared. On the small stage the ceilidh band was warming up. Charlie MacCrae sat centre stage, his fingers tinkering with the keys of his accordion as he warmed up for the evening's entertainment. To his right a thin, young man in a black coat was tuning his violin and on the other side a red-haired young woman, about the same age as Jessie, was leafing through sheet music of popular Scottish ballads.

'Thank you, Fred. This is the best day of my life!'

Jessie's eyes sparkled as she surveyed the scene in front of her. Spontaneously she grasped Fred's arm. She just wanted to hold the moment for ever. The sense of belonging, of friendship, of having a good man by her side. Above her Fred smiled and very briefly passed his hand over hers. Suddenly there was a short toot from the accordion and Mr MacCrae got to his feet and cleared his throat.

'Good evening everybody and a very warm welcome tae oor Christmas ceilidh. It may be cold outside but in here once we get ye dancin' we'll be nice and cosy I can assure you! On my right here is my son Robert who's a fine fiddler as you'll discover and on my left is my daughter Lizzie who has some bonnie songs lined up for you. So without further ado let's get to know each other wi' the Dashing White Sergeant.'

There was a general rumble of approval as the festive crowd stood up and approached the dance floor. One man, two women or one woman, two men. What was it to be? Jessie looked up expectantly at her companion.

'Fred, d'ye ken this one? Surely ye do.'

'A wee bittie, Jess, but I promise you ah'm nae much o' a dancer.'

'We'll find anither lassie and ye can go in the middle o' us.'

And excitedly she searched the room and pulled Fred impatiently by the sleeve.

'Look Fred, there's Betty Milne over there. Mebbe she'll make up a three wi' us?'

And before Fred could comment further, Jessie had rushed over to the other side of the crowded hall returning triumphantly a few seconds later with a short, plump young woman already apparently feeling the heat in her buttoned up gown and sensible black boots.

'Good evening to you, Betty.' Fred addressed. 'Is William nae here?'

'No, he disnae like the dancing,' Betty pulled a disdainful face then laughed. 'But he disnae mind me coming so I'm here wi' ma sister.'

'Well, he had a lucky escape,' riposted Fred under his breath.

'Come on you two, they're about tae start.' Jessie grabbed both of her companions by the arm and drew them towards the body of dancers now standing expectantly in rows of three facing each other.

The little band started up with the jaunty refrain of The Bonnie Lass of Fyvie.

'Oh I love this one. Fred, you've tae hold oor hands. There, now we're ready.

And the dance started up with the crowd advancing and retreating and circling amid whoops and claps and laughter when one of the party forgot a step or went the wrong way. It was all part of the fun. When the last chord was played a cheer went up from the assembled company, eager for the next tune. But not everybody shared their enthusiasm.

'Ah'm awa' tae sit doon, Jessie. I'll catch my breath,' Fred explained, dabbing his forehead with a handkerchief, as he nodded to Betty and made to sit down on one the chairs vacated around the dance-floor.

'Already, Fred?' The disappointment was clear in Jessie's voice. 'We've jist started. Ye're nae an auld man yet!'

But Fred was adamant. Reluctantly, realising she was in the

way of the others, Jessie also retreated to the side of the hall. The pair sat down in silence. Jessie could feel the sense of anti-climax settle within her like a physical weight. This special evening was spoilt before it had barely begun. Furious tears of disappointment began to form in her eyes but just as she was about to wipe them away, a voice above her caught her attention.

'Why's a bonnie lassie like you nae dancin'? Davie Brown at your service.'

Looking up she saw she was being addressed by a stocky young man about her age with short fair hair and a happy expression. Judging by his confident manner it was likely he had already consumed a bit to set him up for the evening. Jess looked from him to Fred sitting bolt upright beside her.

'Oh, apologies, you're wi' him?' The young man looked crest-fallen.

'Jessie, you can dance if you wish. You've my blessing.' Fred announced flatly. 'I'm nae much o' a dancer.' He added by way of an explanation to the newcomer.

'Really, Fred?' Jessie appealed to her friend.

'Yes, Jessie. This is your evening and I dinnae want tae spoil it. Go on, it's starting.'

The band leader had now announced the Gay Gordons and couples were pairing up and threading their arms around each other's shoulders. Jessie stood up and followed her dance partner to the floor to take up their positions. Once the music started and she was held firmly in Davie Brown's strong arms she began to forget her earlier upset. She would just enjoy herself as had been her plan and if Fred chose to be a killjoy, well, that was his affair. There was the smell of beer and sweat and the slightly cloying aroma of hair oil. It has been a while since Jessie's senses had been awoken like this. Calm and secure and peaceful though her life was at the manse, she was only half alive she realised. The whirling and circling and polkaing was making her feel slightly dizzy and light headed and on one turn she nearly lost her balance. Davie caught her and pulled her close to his chest.

'Careful there, lassie. I dinnae want tae return ye wi' injuries!'

Jessie laughed and briefly lent her head on her partner's shoulder to steady herself. As the music ended the couple's arms dropped to their sides and they smiled at each other.

'Thank ye, Davie. That wis grand. I think I need a cup of tea now. I'm parched.'

Jessie turned back to where she had left Fred but saw only an empty chair where he had been seated. Scanning the room she was still unable to see him. The exhilaration she had experienced after the last dance was fast draining away to be replaced with a feeling of unease. Surely he would not have departed without her? Was he feeling ill perhaps? She spotted Betty Milne approaching her.

'Betty, have ye seen Fred at all? He wis here a few minutes ago.'

'Mebbe outside, Jessie? It's gey hot in here.'

There were a few souls standing about outside the entrance to the church hall. At first Jessie was unable to spot Fred but then she caught sight of him leaning up against the notice board. The pale light of the gas street lamp illuminated his sombre face. He looked deep in thought. She wondered why he had agreed to come with her when it seemed clear this was not to his taste at all.

'Fred, there you are. I thought you had abandoned me.'

'You seemed quite happy wi' things from where I was sitting,' came Fred's terse response.

'You said I could dance, Fred. What's got into you? I've been looking forward to this so much. You ken that fine. Now you're being a soor Wully. It's nae fair, Fred!'

Jessie stood immediately in front of Fred, her face tilted indignantly before his.

'I've.....'

Before she could continue she felt Fred's hands take hold of her head and he pressed his lips to hers, stopping any further conversation. In shock, Jessie held her breath, barely aware of her surroundings, only able to absorb the immediacy of Fred's presence, a clash of teeth, the grazing of his beard and the faintest whiff of their last meal on his breath.

# CHAPTER 8

# A VISITOR

FRED AND JESSIE STARTED TO WALK HOME IN SILENCE. AFTER what had passed between them, neither had the heart to return to the dance. The temperature had dropped and the pavements were now covered with a frosting of ice. Jessie took tiny cautious steps to prevent herself from slipping while gripping her shawl tightly across her chest. Fred slowed his pace and offered Jessie his arm. Without looking at him she took it and continued walking.

'Jessie, I apologise,' Fred spoke suddenly. 'What I did was wrong. I should'nae hae spoken to you like that and kissing ye after what I said earlier. I don't know what ye will think o' me. Forgive me, Jessie. I am conflicted.'

Now Jessie stopped and turned to him.

'I think ye were jealous. There wis nae need, Fred. I wanted tae dance wi' ye. I'm nae interested in a'body else. Do ye nae trust me?'

'Aye I trust ye, Jessie. I dinnae trust mesself. That's the trouble.'

'But ye told me we could'nae be together, Fred. I ken this.'

'I care a lot for ye, Jessie, and I dinnae want tae hurt ye. I wish it were all simpler.'

'The Kelmans hae been very guid tae me. I dinnae want tae let them doon. We should forget this happened, Fred. Mebbe we can be friends again like before?'

Fred laughed softly under his breath.

'Mebbe, Jess, I'll try,' he murmured.

A strand of Jessie's hair had fallen across her face and Fred had to restrain himself from stretching out a hand to tidy it behind one of her ears.

The sounds of merriment and music behind them were starting to fade as they turned into Bon Accord Crescent. Their footsteps crunched on the icy ground and their breath blew white in the cold dark air. The outer doors to the manse were still open and the St Columba's bell was just striking the half hour as the couple entered the house. The sound of the door opening brought Mary-Ann out of her parlour to see who was there.

Looking from Fred to Jessie, she exclaimed in surprise. 'You are back! So soon?'

'Aye, it's my fault,' volunteered Fred. 'I did'nae want tae dance and I made Jessie feel bad. I am sorry. It wis'nae very Christian behaviour.'

Jessie stood in embarrassed silence before her employer.

'Oh Fred, that's such a shame. You could have made more of an effort. Jessie, I'm sorry. We must make it up to you somehow.'

'Excuse me, Mrs Kelman,' Jessie addressed Mary-Ann directly. 'Thank ye for your kindness and the loan of the dress. If I may I will retire now and give it ye back the morrow?'

'Of course. There is no rush, Jessie. Good night to you.'

In her rush to escape the awkward encounter, Jessie nearly tripped over the hem of her borrowed gown. With a start Fred extended his arm to catch her. Jessie, however, recovered her balance and, steadying herself with a hand on the banister, grasped the full skirt in her free hand and proceeded to climb the staircase. Fred remained standing in the hall, watching her until she disappeared from view.

'Come and sit with me for a while, Fred,' Mary-Ann invited

him. 'Richard's finishing off his sermon for tomorrow so it will be good to have some company.'

As Fred hesitated in the hallway, Mary-Ann placed a light hand on his arm and ushered him through to the smaller reception room to the back of the house. A fire burned brightly in the grate and at that moment the warm room seemed a haven of peace and security. Tempted as he was to confide all to Mary-Ann, despite her obvious affection for both him and Jessie, he felt he could not take the risk. He would not compromise Jessie in this way. She had had to change her old way of life completely because of him and now that she was clearly more settled he could not disturb that.

Mary-Ann picked up the copy of *Cranford* she had been reading from the small upright sofa, to make space for them both to sit comfortably side by side.

'I was going to have a cup of tea. There is enough for two. Will you join me, Fred?'

'Thank you, Mary-Ann. That would be most welcome.'

Mary-Ann lifted the little silver teapot and filled a cup for him. Fred stretched out one of his large hands, quite dwarfing it between his thumb and forefinger.

'You may need a refill, Fred,' smiled Mary-Ann noting her friend down his drink in two gulps.

'No, no, thank you. That was perfect. I was thirstier than I thought.'

'So, Fred,' Mary-Ann observed him intently, her head on one side like a curious blackbird. 'I'm sorry Jessie's special evening was cut short. This is not like you I would say.'

Fred took a deep breath, hoping his expression gave nothing away.

'I'm nae a dancer. I told her that when she first asked me. But she was insistent so I did'nae want to disappoint her. We had a couple o' dances wi' other folk but the White Sergeant had me confused and I felt a fool, frankly. I know I should'nae care but I still hae my pride.'

Fred looked down at his hands spread out on his lap and paused.

'Did she not get to dance with anyone else then?' Mary-Ann persisted.

'Aye, she did, with my blessing, but she said she did'nae want to dance wi' anyone else so she left the dance floor in a bit of a mood. Then we decided we should come home. Maybe I should have tried harder, Mary-Ann, I'm sorry. I have apologised to her.'

'Well, what's done is done but it's a shame nonetheless. She was looking forward to it all so much.'

Mary-Ann leant forward and lifted her tea-cup to her lips. Then returning it to the saucer, she turned anew to Fred.

'I am glad to have this opportunity to speak to you, Fred, unplanned though it was. Richard will no doubt see you himself as well but seeing as you are here, I wanted to ask what your plans are for the future? Now that you have graduated and showing such promise, it is an exciting time for you, is it not?'

Fred felt caught unawares by Mary-Ann's directness. Trying to deal with his feelings for Jessie as he was, this question placed yet another weight on his shoulders.

'Aye it is indeed,' he replied slowly. 'But I feel there is no rush. I am still young and I think I would like to stay awhile here in Aberdeen. Of course maybe you feel it is time for me to find my own lodgings now that I have a stipend?'

'Certainly not, Fred!' retorted Mary-Ann. 'That was not the purpose of my question. You are like a son to us and always welcome under our roof. No, it is just that an old friend and former colleague of Richard's, William Russell, has let it be known that he is in need of an assistant. He is the minister at St Ninian's in Edinburgh, so it would be a very good opportunity to advance yourself if you were to be offered the post.'

'Ah, Edinburgh,' repeated Fred, almost to himself. 'When does Reverend Russell want his assistant to start?'

'Some time next year, I believe. But I am getting ahead of myself. It is best you speak to Richard for more details.'

'I appreciate the thought but I am still very attached to this city, Mary-Ann. I would need to think about it.'

'Of course, Fred. It would be a big step but chances such as this do not come about very often. It is lucky timing for you. Sleep on it and Richard will speak with you further tomorrow after the service.'

Suddenly the clear, urgent tone of the front door bell sounded throughout the manse. Looking up at the clock on the mantelpiece, Mary-Ann saw that it was already nine o' clock. Fred stood up and moved towards the door.

'Shall I see who that is, Mary-Ann? Quite late for callers is it not?'

'It is but it's probably Willie Burns with tonight's takings. He was on the door and expected a good turn-out. Let us hope that is the case.'

Although his hand was already on the door-handle, Fred could hear voices in the hallway as Richard Kelman welcomed his colleague in from the cold.

'Mary-Ann, thank you for the tea but I think I'll away to my bed now. Mr Burns will no doubt want to see you himself.'

Unwilling to come face to face with the visitor, Fred started to excuse himself. However, before he had time to leave the snug parlour, the door opened to reveal Richard and Willie Burns. The latter still had his overcoat on and was rubbing his hands vigorously.

'My, it's turned chilly the night but it's fine and warm in here, Mrs Kelman. I winnae take up too much o' your time. Ah Fred!'

The church elder turned to Fred and nodded up at him.

'Enjoy yerself this evening then?'

Fred thought he detected a slight note of sarcasm, but maybe it was just his guilty conscience. His embrace with Jessie had been outside. With the ceilidh in full swing, he was sure they had been unnoticed.

'It seemed a good evening, Mr Burns. Did you sell plenty tickets?'

'Aye, we did thank you. I thought I would bring the money up tae ye afore I went hame. I dinnae want the responsibility!'

And he chuckled wryly, rubbing his moustache with his free hand.

'Thank you, Willie, it is appreciated. Will you take a wee dram while you're here?'

Richard Kelman took the black metal cash-box from the visitor and invited him to sit down.

'Weel, mebbe I could be persuaded.' Mr Burns winked and glanced round the room.

'Fred, will you join us?'

'Thank you, Richard, but I have some things to prepare for tomorrow. If you will excuse me, I'll bid you all good night.'

Fred nodded to the three figures standing around the fire and, closing the door behind him, retreated thankfully to the sanctuary of the empty hall. As he climbed the staircase, the sound of sociable chat and laughter could be heard from behind the parlour door. On the landing he paused and found himself straining to catch part of the conversation, without success. What was he trying to learn, he wondered? The man had brought the proceeds from the ceilidh and was enjoying a quick dram with Richard and Mary-Ann. He would be on his way soon enough.

The sound of the parlour door opening again caused Fred to draw back rapidly. He took a couple of paces towards his bedroom and entered as unobtrusively as he could. His books and papers were strewn across his desk where he had left them. The theme of his sermon was to be temptation. On a piece of paper were written the words "*Keep watching and praying that you may not enter into temptation; the spirit is willing, but the flesh is weak.*" Ah, and now he had failed the test. How weak was he? He was a hypocrite! Angrily, Fred gathered the sheets together and flung them down. He could write no more this evening. He had to sleep, if he could, and try to seek some temporary peace.

Divesting himself of his day clothes, Fred changed into his night-shirt and splashed some cold water over his face and neck.

Lying down he was only too aware of Jessie's presence upstairs. Was she safely asleep he wondered or dwelling on events as was he? He may have dozed off, he was not sure, but he was vaguely aware of a firm single rap on his door followed by Richard's voice.

'Fred, are you awake? I would like a brief word if I may.'

Fred lay completely still as the door opened slowly and Richard's head peered into the darkness of Fred's bedroom.

'Fred? Are you awake?'

Fred forced himself to breath slowly, as if comatose. In and out, in and out. He could not speak with Richard now. The man continued to stand there in the darkness. Finally, to Fred's greatest relief, Richard accepted that he was indeed asleep and turned very quietly and departed the room. Fred let out a long breath and opened his eyes. For now there was a reprieve. He would face the consequences tomorrow.

# CHAPTER 9

# CONFESSION

It was not until after morning service that Fred found himself alone with Richard. Breakfast had been a strained affair with Richard barely uttering a word and Mary-Ann chatting brightly to compensate. Fred, never a man of many words in the morning, out of courtesy to his hostess, felt obliged to respond. Unusually, Jessie was nowhere to be seen.

'I've given her the morning off,' clarified Mary-Ann as she brought the breakfast dishes to the table. 'She has been working so hard doing everything more or less by herself. We don't want her falling ill over Christmas.'

There had been a full congregation at the kirk as was often the case in the approach to Christmas and Fred's sermon on resisting temptation had been well received. Despite his inner turmoil, his voice was clear and resonant and his gaze unflinching on his audience.

'Just as Jesus was led into the wilderness to be tempted by the Devil, so we all have our own wildernesses. They will not be barren, rocky wastes as He faced, but wildernesses nonetheless. You will recognise them and must resist the temptations therein.

What is hardest for us all is that while our spirits are strong, our weak flesh finds it hard to turn away from short term pleasures. With a time of celebration coming upon us when we remember the dear Lord's birth, we must also be mindful of our human responsibilities and remain in control at all times. We are all vulnerable and it takes only a tiny slip to fall down a precipice.'

Fred was only too aware of how hypocritical he sounded and he deliberately avoided Richard's eye, fixed solemn and unsmiling as it was on him from the front pew. As he climbed down from the pulpit, he could see Willie Burns out of the corner of his eye, standing ready to pass the offering plate amongst the congregation. The man's face gave nothing away and Fred began to wonder if he was imagining things.

Now, however, with the church empty once more, Richard and Fred faced each other as they changed from their religious gowns into their regular attire.

'Fred,' started Richard, gently closing the vestry door. 'I think it is appropriate that we are on our own for what I am about to say. Some things are better stated away from home.'

Fred opened his mouth to respond but Richard held up his right hand firmly.

'Please hear me out. You will have plenty time to respond, never fear. You know how much I respect you and, indeed love you, Fred. You are as a son to me and Mary-Ann. But as a father figure I also have a responsibility to guide you even if that means facing unpleasant truths. Promise me you will always tell the truth. If we in our profession are to be held in regard we have to be above reproach so that our parishioners can believe in us completely. Without that our calling is built on sand and will come to nothing.'

Fred was standing by a high window through which the morning sun now shone. He followed its beam as it lit up the solid oak furniture in the small ante-room and the flecks of dust caught in its rays. The truth of Richard's words pierced him and caused him to swallow suddenly. Linking his fingers in front of him, he twisted them nervously as his colleague continued.

'I will not beat about the bush, Fred. As you know Willie Burns called by yesterday evening. To start with I understood it was to bring the takings of the ceilidh but it became apparent something else was on his mind. Do you have any idea what this might have been, Fred?'

Aware that Richard had stopped speaking, Fred reluctantly raised his head to look at his mentor.

'What did he say, Richard?'

Even at this late stage, Fred held out one last hope that this was not to do with Jessie. But in his heart he knew this was unlikely. He was being a coward as well as a hypocrite.

'Forgive me, Richard, I shall tell you the truth.' Fred lowered his head and paused before continuing. 'I cannot tell what Mr Burns reported to you but I will give you my side. I believe what he had to say to you was that he saw me kiss Jessie Duthie outside the church hall. It was not her fault. She was quite shocked. The blame is entirely mine.'

Now that the words were out, Fred felt a wave of relief followed rapidly by one of extreme anxiety.

'Please understand that Jessie did nothing to encourage me and I do not want her to suffer for my inexcusable behaviour.'

Fred faced his friend, an expression of urgent appeal on his handsome features.

'You are correct,' confirmed Richard. 'Willie did say the young lady seemed taken aback, as indeed was he. He had believed you were her chaperone not her beau. But he thinks it unlikely anyone else saw the encounter as the ceilidh was in full swing by then and he has sworn to keep silent on the subject. I have no doubt it will not happen again, but a line has been crossed, Fred, which makes it difficult for Jessie to stay on with us for as long as you are also living in the house.'

'Ah no!' Fred let out a deep sigh. 'But she is innocent. The fault is entirely mine.'

'Hush, Fred, Mary-Ann and I have spoken about the situation

and we feel confident that we can find Jessie a similar position elsewhere among the clergy.'

'But what reason will you give her and a future employer?'

'Mrs Milne has always been interested in working full time for us, now that her daughter is away and married. We will merely say that we are honouring a promise made to her quite a while back.'

'Does Jessie know?' Fred queried softly.

'Not yet but I think she knows changes are afoot. Mary-Ann was going to speak with her this morning.'

Fred stood, head bowed, in heavy-hearted silence.

'One day perhaps I can make amends. I fear I have let everybody down.'

'Well, Fred, that day may come sooner than you think. There is another matter I wanted to discuss with you before this issue presented itself. I will give you the outline now but we can talk at greater length back at the manse this afternoon.'

Suddenly Fred recalled his conversation with Mary-Ann the evening before. In his concern for Jessie it had completely gone from his mind. St Ninian's in Edinburgh – that was it.

'Mary-Ann mentioned you wished to speak to me about a post in Edinburgh.'

'That is correct, Fred. And it may be more opportune than I had first imagined. My old friend William Russell - we were scholars together at Edinburgh back in the '30s - wrote to me recently. He is in need of an assistant at that big church of his, St Ninian's. He has heard me sing your praises more than once and had you in mind for the position. It would be a fine start for your career, Fred, and taking everything into consideration this could be the opportunity you need.'

'Sir, I am truly grateful but do you think I am ready for such a responsibility?'

Fred wondered why he did not feel more excitement and enthusiasm on hearing Richard's words. A man could wait half a lifetime for such an offer and here he was at the tender age of just twenty five being given the opportunity of working in the capital city, something he could have only dreamed of just a few years ago. He knew he should grasp this with both hands.

'Come now, Fred, why the long face? Do not doubt your own abilities. Yes, you still have much to learn but I have every confidence you have the necessary intellect and determination to make a success of this. But you do not need to decide now. Come, let us return to the house or Mary-Ann will be sending out a search party for us.'

Richard chuckled at his little joke and patted the younger man affectionately on the back. The morning sun was higher in the sky now as two clerics left the church by a side door. A skittish wind was whipping up the brown, fallen leaves that lay on the adjacent pavement, causing Fred and Richard simultaneously to raise a protective hand to their hats. Heads bent they set off at a brisk pace for the half mile or so to the manse.

The warm, fatty aroma of roasting meat greeted the men some ten minutes later as they entered the house.

'That smells delicious, my dear. Apologies for our late arrival,' Richard called out to announce their arrival. 'We have had a good conversation, Fred and I, but I think we are now ready for lunch.'

Unusually, Mary-Ann was neither in the dining room nor her little parlour. On turning back into the hallway Fred noticed her approaching them, an intent expression on her face, bearing a large china ashet on which lay a generous leg of lamb.

'Let me assist you, Mary-Ann.' He stepped forward, arms held out, to take the hefty dish.

'I can manage, thank you, Fred, but perhaps you could bring through the vegetables from the kitchen?'

It was only as he entered the kitchen that Jessie's absence suddenly struck him. Where was she? Surely she would be assisting at the family Sunday lunch? He cast his eye around the high ceilinged room, noting the paraphernalia from the preparation of the meal covering all available surfaces from the plain wooden table in the centre of the room to the deep china sink by the window. No attempt had yet been made to render any kind of order here.

'I expected to see Jessie back to help you, Mary-Ann?' queried Fred as he returned to the dining room. 'Have you not had any help this morning?'

'Mrs Milne came in earlier and she will be back later. Jessie is gone, Fred.'

'Gone? Gone where? So soon? I would have liked to say good-bye.'

Despite himself, Fred could hear the tone of his voice rising.

'Fred, do not take on so. She has gone to the Reverend MacDonald. He has a young family and was happy to take her at short notice. It is for the best. Things could not continue as they were after yesterday's events. We will talk later but for now let us eat before the food is spoiled.'

From feeling hungry with a keen anticipation of his Sunday lunch, Fred now felt a physical sinking within him. It was as if his stomach had closed tight and shrunk within his abdomen. He doubted he would be able to swallow a thing. Richard was sharpening the carving knife with gusto as Fred sat down silently at the dining table. He had brought this upon himself with his stupid jealousy and pride – a fine example of a holy man to be sure. He felt a fraud. He knew Richard and Mary-Ann expected him to go to Edinburgh. It was part of the plan. He could not let people down now. But what about his heart?

'There, Fred. That will make you feel better!'

A large plate brimming over with thin pinkish slices of lamb, golden potatoes and orange and yellow carrots and parsnips was placed in front of him by Richard. A tiny drip of gravy spilt on to the white table cloth and started to seep into the starched cloth. Mary-Ann pushed a small glass bowl of mint sauce towards him which he declined. Lifting up his knife and fork Fred started to cut up the food, raising it to his mouth, chewing and swallowing. He could taste nothing. His appetite had completely deserted him. But it would be rude to leave such a meal so persist he must.

When luncheon was finally over, Fred made to clear the table, but was dissuaded by Mary-Ann.

'Thank you for offering, Fred, but Mrs Milne will be here shortly.'

'Well, if I may, I will retire to my room for an hour or so? Richard, I believe you wish to speak further with me?'

'I do, that is correct, but it can wait. By all means take some time to collect your thoughts on what we discussed. You have an exciting future, Fred.'

With a brief nod to his hosts, Fred stood up and left the room. Climbing the stairs to the first landing, he suddenly felt the urge to investigate the upper floor where Jessie's room had been. Was she really gone so quickly? Treading softly on the slightly steeper stairs, Fred looked up at the skylight which illuminated the stairwell and hall. The blue sky of the morning was now deepening as it approached the early winter dusk of this northern city. Stopping in front of Jessie's door, Fred knocked softly on one of the dark wooden panels. Leaning his ear against it, as he already expected, there was no sound within. His hand rested on the doorknob and with a brief turn the door opened and he stepped inside, closing the door quietly behind him.

It was true. She was really gone. No sign that she had been here at all. The high single bed with a patterned eiderdown on it sat abandoned in the middle of the worn carpet. A marble topped washstand with a pink and white pitcher and ewer was set at the window and a large brown wardrobe with a thin mirror inset was pressed up against the near wall. The room was not completely empty however. On the back of the door hung the borrowed dress Jessie had worn only the night before. Without thinking, Fred unhooked it and clasped it to him. He closed his eyes and held the fabric close to his face, breathing in the faintest scent of soap and lavender water. Yes, finally something of Jessie was here. Overcome with fatigue and remorse, Fred placed the dress on top of the eiderdown and lay down beside it, his hands clasping the smooth fabric until, before too long, he fell asleep.

# CHAPTER 10

# THE LETTER

IT TOOK JESSIE A FEW DAYS TO ADJUST TO HER NEW POSITION. The initial flare of tearful indignation she had felt when Mrs Kelman had explained the situation had been replaced with a weary resignation and the hope that the MacDonald household would prove longer lasting than her stay at Bon Accord Crescent. Mrs MacDonald was not as friendly as Mrs Kelman but then she appeared permanently distracted by her four young children who seemed to rule the roost on the nursery floor.

Jessie was surprised and a little hurt that she had heard nothing from Fred. No word of farewell, nothing. Despite her lowly position she saw quite clearly that it had been Fred who had been in the wrong and not her. He had apologised. She hoped he had the courage and decency to explain the situation fully to the Kelmans. Jessie thought it likely as Mary-Ann had been most solicitous of her feelings emphasising that that she had already promised a post to Mrs Milne and that Jessie's appointment at the manse could only have been temporary. No mention was made of Fred but Jessie could not believe the move was unrelated to his behaviour the previous Saturday evening.

Her day had started early as it always did. The kitchen range was to be stoked up, the household water fetched from the pump in the back yard and the breakfast table laid. Afterwards, the fetching and carrying, the cleaning and washing kept Jessie busy until mid-morning. She had just paused briefly in the kitchen to take a welcome cup of tea when she was aware of a couple of knocks on the back door. Not expecting any visitors or tradesmen, she was surprised to find Mrs Milne, cheeks reddened by the chill wind, standing on the doorstep. She had not seen her since her own sudden departure from the Kelmans and, with a nervous lurch of her stomach, she wondered what the reason for the visit might be.

'Hello, Jessie,' Mrs Milne smiled awkwardly and spoke softly. 'I'm sorry tae disturb ye. I'm on ma way to visit ma mither. She's a wee bit poorly. I thought I would jist see how ye were doin'?'

'I am keepin' well, thank you, Ishbel. I'm sorry tae hear aboot yer mither.'

'Aye, aye, lassie. Thank ye.' Mrs Milne looked about her for a moment then dipped her hand into the basket that hung from her left arm.

'I've brought you some bramble jelly, and … this.'

She held out an envelope on which Jessie could see her name was written in dense black ink. With a start she realised it was Fred's handwriting and for a moment she stood motionless, gazing at her visitor.

'Take it quickly, lassie. It's for you. From Reverend Black.'

With a shaking hand Jessie took the letter and pushed it deep into her apron pocket.

'Is he well? I've nae heard onythin' since I left.'

'Well enough I think. I am sure he will explain more in his letter.'

'Thank ye, Ishbel. Tell them, him, I'm keepin' fine. I wis sorry nae tae be able to say good-bye. Thank ye for coming and for the jelly. I hope your mither gets better soon.'

Jessie laid her hand lightly on Mrs Milne's arm. The older

woman nodded and, gathering up her basket, announced she must away. No sooner had the back door closed than the sound of footsteps crossing the tiled hall caused Jessie to turn her head.

'Was that the back-door, Jessie? We were not expecting anyone this morning were we?' Mrs MacDonald was looking at her with curiosity.

'Aye, it was Mrs Milne from the Kelmans. Her mither isnae well and she wis on her way tae visit her. She brought us a wee pot o' bramble jelly.'

'That was kind of her. You should have let me know, Jessie. I would like to have expressed my thanks in person.'

'I'm sorry, Madam, I didnae ken if ye wanted tae be disturbed?'

'Ah well, no harm done,' Mrs MacDonald mused, looking at the jar of purple conserve that now sat on the kitchen table. 'I wanted to speak to you about this evening's meal, Jessie. There are a few provisions I would like you to purchase this afternoon.'

Mrs MacDonald then proceeded to list the items that should be obtained for the family dinner, reminding Jessie which merchant she favoured.

'Thank you, Jessie,' Mrs MacDonald concluded. 'If you have finished your morning duties you may take an hour to yourself. We will have lunch at one o' clock, so please be back here at midday.'

Only when she heard the click of the drawing room door on the first floor above her as it closed, did Jessie feel confident she was alone. The kitchen clock above the mantel, ticked steadily as a heartbeat, and the cool, grey light of the December morning spread over the tiled floor. Sitting down at the kitchen table, Jessie took the letter out of her pocket and held it for a moment between her fingers. Then breaking open the sealing wax on the back, she pulled out a single sheet of paper and laid it in front of her. Bending her head, she started to read.

*25 Bon Accord Crescent*
*20$^{th}$ December 1860*

*My dear Jessie*

*Forgive me for not writing to you until now. I have no excuses save that I wanted to have time to think of the right words. I had not realised you were to leave so suddenly without giving me the opportunity of speaking to you. I have now had time to understand how I feel. First of all, my dear little Jess, you are not to blame for any of this. I behaved very badly. Too proud and yes, you were right, jealous. I was fooling myself that we were just friends. I so wanted that to be the case. It would be so much easier would it not? But when I realised you had gone and that I might never see your sweet, kind face again, I felt so sad and downcast. That is more than just friendship is it not? I cannot tell how you feel towards me. I will understand if you feel let down and wish to be left in peace but I pray this is not the case. I do not know what the future holds for me but I believe fate has brought us together. I can promise nothing but my heart at the moment. Please let me know your thoughts. Send me your reply care of Mrs Milne. She is a friend and can be trusted. Her address is 10 Rose Street. I send you all my love, Jessie, and will pray for us both.*

*Yours aye, Fred*

She had been here before, Jessie thought to herself. They swear undying love and then once you let your guard down and open your heart, they change their minds and it is you who is left counting the cost and feeling an angry, hurt fool. She retraced Fred's words carefully with her finger and, despite herself, her heart swelled and a slight smile crept across her face. She had never received a love letter before and might never again so that in itself was a special moment. Lifting the sheet of paper to her face she touched it lightly with her lips. Upstairs, Jessie heard Mrs MacDonald's voice addressing her husband. She might return to the kitchen at any moment. Jessie had but a short time to herself. She would go to her room to consider her reply.

Treading softly, Jessie took herself upstairs to her attic room. She still had pencils and a sheaf of rough paper taken from her previous school-room but no pen and ink. Would a pencilled note suffice? She could never hope to write as Fred had done and suddenly Jessie felt frustrated and angry that so much of life seemed closed to her. Yet it was important to her that she should impress this intense, educated man. But first of all, she needed to read Fred's letter again and decide what her response would be.

The writing was tiny but regularly formed. '*My dear little Jess*', '*sad and downcast*', '*fate*', '*promise nothing but my heart*'. It seemed heartfelt but only weeks before Fred had told her they had no future. What was she to make of it? Maybe, just maybe they might have a future after all? She could read and write now and was determined somehow to leave behind the rough and ready life she had endured down at the harbour. She would not go back to that. She would rather die. So what did she have to lose? Jessie pulled a sheet of yellowing paper towards her and carefully started to write.

*My dear Fred*

*Thank you for your letter. I was surprised but happy as well. You told me that we couldnae be together so until the dance I didnae expect anything from you. My life hasnae been easy and I dinnae want to lose what I have now. I dinnae want my heart broken either. But to think I might never see you again also makes me very sad. So, dear Fred, let us write to each other and I hope that we may meet again soon.*

*With my love, your Jessie xx*

When she had finished Jessie held up the sheet of paper in front of her and scrutinised each word, imagining Fred doing the same thing in a few days' time. Then spontaneously Jessie picked up her pencil again and started to draw two small figures at the bottom of the page. Her skills were undeveloped but it was unmistakeably a tiny minister and an even smaller female companion dressed in a crinoline. Jessie smiled gently, pleased with her after-thought. All she needed now was a stamp and an envelope.

Once luncheon had been consumed and cleared, Jessie checked through the shopping list Mrs MacDonald had written out for her. Apart from the skirt steak which she would have to obtain from MacNab the butcher, everything else would be available at Mr Strachan's, the grocer. After the final item, Jessie added *envelopes*. Satisfied she had omitted nothing, Jessie folded the list and, together with the florin Mrs MacDonald had given her to pay for the messages, put them in her purse and tucked it into her coat pocket. Wrapping a shawl around her shoulders against the December cold, Jessie picked up her basket and left the house.

Hurrying up Wilson Wynd towards the high street, she realised that she was not that far from Rose Street. This was fortunate as it meant she could deliver her letter directly to Mrs Milne. It would not take long and she calculated she could fit in a quick detour after completing her shopping. The grocer's shop was situated prominently on a corner site with windows over-looking two streets. A satisfying aroma of cheese, ham and coffee greeted Jessie as she opened the entrance with a warning tinkle from the bell above her.

'Good day tae you, young lady! And what can we get you today?'

Jessie placed her basket on the counter top and pushed the list towards the shopkeeper.

'And d'ye hae ony envelopes, Mr Strachan?'

'Aye over in the windae there.' The grocer pointed behind Jessie to a basket of stationery displayed in the shop window. 'They are tuppence the pack.'

Jessie added the stationery to the basket and pulled out an

extra couple of pennies from her own purse to pay for it. While Mr Strachan was busy seeking out the various provisions on the list, Jessie slipped her letter into one of the envelopes. There was a pen and inkwell at the far end of the counter so she carefully wrote Fred's name on the front, care of Mrs Ishbel Milne. The shopping completed, Jessie thanked the grocer and stepped out of the shop.

Number 10 Rose Street was a solid granite building built over three floors. A row of smoking chimney pots was now silhouetted against the darkening sky of the December afternoon. On which floor Mrs Milne lived, Jessie did not know, but she had to trust that her letter would find its way to Fred. Pushing her fingers with difficulty against the heavy cast-iron letter-box, Jessie forced the flimsy envelope through on to the hallway floor beyond. In the background she could hear the bells of St Nicholas Kirk striking three o' clock. It would be dark soon. Time to get back.

# CHAPTER 11

# CHRISTMAS

On waking, Fred was alerted by the muffled silence and the bright reflected light in his bedroom. It could only mean one thing. Looking out of the window, the garden below was now blanketed in drifts of fresh snow. Fluffy and pristine, it was piled up on walls and sills, hedges and ledges. On the garden path, a tiny robin hopped forlornly in the hope of uncovering something to eat, its tawny breast a vivid note of colour in the neutral palette of whites and greys, where the putty coloured sky was almost the same colour as the roofs.

The days since Jessie's departure weighed heavily on Fred. He had gained some relief in writing to her but had yet to know what her feelings on the matter were. Preparations for the festive season were in full swing but Fred found he could not share in the excitement. He tried to draw reassurance and inspiration from Christmas itself. Was this not the original story of hope and the promise of a better future despite the most modest and humble of origins? To doubt this would be to undermine all he had been working towards.

Downstairs, the long-case clock chimed the hour and

reminded Fred that he had agreed to accompany Richard to visit parishioners in need. Time to put his own woes to one side. There were those in much greater difficulty than he. With the drop in temperature he would need to wrap up warmly. He knew only too well how unforgiving an Aberdeen winter could be.

'Good morning, Fred.' Richard was already standing in the hall and greeted him as he descended. 'I missed you at breakfast. I made an early start with some writing. Are you ready to depart?'

'Indeed I am, Richard. Who are we visiting today?'

'Time permitting I hope to call in on five families. We'll start off with the Andersons. They are having a hard time of it since Bill Anderson had his accident. His arm's taking a long time to heal and Mrs Anderson is working all hours at the Station Hotel to help make ends meet. There are four bairns as well so they need our support, especially at this time of year.'

By one o' clock the two men had completed their rounds. In the cold, damp weather, parishioners struggled to keep warm and the cost of fuel and adequate food was a constant worry. Fred was always deeply affected by the courage and determination they showed and wished he could make more of an impact on their lives. Spiritual reassurance was easier to provide but faced with chronic illness and a sick child, even he found it difficult to accept God's will at times.

On their return to the manse, Fred saw that there was a letter waiting for him. For a moment a small flare of excitement sparked within him. Might it be a reply from Jessie? On lifting the envelope from the brass letter tray however, the careful script and the Strathmuir postmark immediately told him it was from his mother. She would no doubt be outlining plans for his forthcoming visit. He tried to quell the stab of disappointment he now felt. His dear mother who was so proud of him and to whom he owed everything. Indeed he was looking forward to seeing her and to returning, albeit briefly, to his home-town.

The next few days were busy ones. Both Richard and Fred

preached Christmas sermons and, along with Mary-Ann, brought baskets of provisions to house-bound members of their congregation. Fred was kept fully occupied and for a time almost managed to forget his anxiety about Jessie. Perhaps it was for the best. On Christmas Day it was agreed that dinner would be taken in the evening and Mrs Milne and Betty would help out.

As Fred entered the dining room he was taken by surprise when Mrs Milne approached him and, without a word, handed him a letter. She indicated he should conceal it and before he could reply, she had turned and left the room. There was no time to look at it as almost immediately Richard and Mary-Ann presented themselves and took their places at the dining table. The contents would have to wait. Standing by the sideboard, Fred picked up the heavy bone-handled carving knife and fork and started to slice into the golden-skinned festive turkey which sat majestically alongside bowls of dark green Brussels sprouts and steaming roasted potatoes. Betty appeared by his side to carry the plates to the waiting diners.

'Well, a toast is called for I think,' announced Richard, lifting his glass as Fred sat down to join them. 'Firstly, a very merry Christmas to you, my dear wife, to you, dear Fred, and to absent friends.'

Three crystal wine-glasses were raised and candlelight shone through the garnet coloured claret for a moment until an appreciative sip was taken and the glasses were lowered once again to the table.

'Secondly, Fred, here's to your future in Edinburgh and all success and good fortune in your career.'

It was nearing ten o' clock by the time Fred finally retired for the night. Pulling out Jessie's letter from his jacket pocket, he sat down on his bed and studied it. He felt a small flare of triumph as he realised that his declaration of love had not been rejected. Suddenly there were possibilities but he must tread carefully. If he disappointed her again, there might not be a second chance.

'God bless you, Jessie,' he whispered as he placed the letter in his bedside drawer.

In the grate the fire had died down. Walking over to the fireplace, Fred stoked up the embers and added a few pieces of coal before blowing out his candle and climbing into bed.

The following morning he could barely lift his head off the pillow. Should he put it down to an excess of claret? No, he thought not. Shivering, he attempted to pull the eiderdown, which had slipped off during the night, around his shoulders. He then realised his night-gown was damp with sweat and his eyes felt as if each had received a good punch. What bad timing! Fred cursed inwardly. Today, Mary-Ann and Richard were heading off to Inverness for a well-earned break and he was due to depart for Strathmuir.

With difficulty he rolled on to his back and tried to focus on the interior of his room. He had felt like this before. More than once in fact. It was the influenza come to taunt him again. He would have to let the Kelmans know. Gritting his teeth, Fred forced himself upright and sat swaying on the edge of his bed. He reached out to the low upholstered chair beside him and with effort pulled a maroon dressing gown towards him. With fumbling fingers and half closed eyes he put it on and stood up. Grasping hold of the bedstead, he made it unsteadily to the door.

'Mary-Ann!' He called out urgently. 'Mary-Ann! I am unwell.'

This was as much as he could manage and he turned back into the room and slumped once more on the bed as a paroxysm of coughing over-took him.

'Fred, you poor thing!' Mary-Ann had appeared at the door and was now approaching his bed-side.

She stretched out a small, cool hand and placed it on his forehead.

'Oh my goodness, you indeed have a fever. You poor man! Let me fetch the thermometer.'

She returned after a couple of minutes holding a small mercury thermometer which she proceeded to place under Fred's tongue.

'Try to hold it steady, Fred, while I count the seconds.'

Fred felt too ill to be embarrassed by his friend's solicitude and lay still as instructed.

'102, I'm afraid,' announced Mary-Ann finally after peering at the tiny scale. 'Shall we call Dr Taylor?'

'No need, Mary-Ann,' croaked Fred. 'It's the influenza. I've had it before. Nothing to be done but lie still and sweat it out.'

'But you cannot stay here on your own. We will have to cancel our visit to Inverness.'

'No, no, Mary-Ann. You must go. You've been looking forward to this so much. Maybe Mrs Milne could come in till I'm stronger?'

Fred was unable to continue speaking and started to cough again, covering his face with both hands.

'I will speak to Richard. We won't abandon you, never fear.'

Fred raised a hand and whispered,

'My mother is expecting me in two days' time. I will not be over this by then. We must let her know.'

'I will send a telegram this afternoon, Fred. Now you must rest. I will make up a foot-warmer for you and make sure the fire is stoked up.'

After that Fred fell asleep. Mary-Ann had given him a small dose of laudanum and he slept for several hours as a result. When he awoke, dry-mouthed and disorientated, he reached for the glass of water that stood by his bed. His fever seemed to have abated but his head and joints continued to throb relentlessly.

'Ah, you are awake at last, Fred.' Mary-Ann's voice came from out of the shadows.

Startled, Fred, turned towards her.

'What time is it? How long have I been asleep?'

'It is nearly five o' clock. You have slept for most of the day. We have delayed our visit by twenty four hours and sent a telegram to your mother. Mrs Milne will come and stay until we are back and we have asked Dr Taylor to visit you as well. How are you feeling now, Fred?'

'Very poorly.'

'Are you hungry? Do you want to eat anything?'

'I have no appetite, Mary-Ann, but perhaps a cup of tea would ease my throat and cough.'

Fred must have fallen asleep once more as when he awoke it was dark save for a small oil lamp left burning in the corner of the room. A now cold cup of tea sat on the top of the commode beside him. Oh, this was intolerable! He truly felt good for nothing. What time was it now he wondered? As if in reply the silver chimes of the hall clock struck ten. With difficulty Fred raised himself up, reached out for the cup beside him and swallowed the contents in one draught. Pulling the bedclothes around him once again he slumped back on to the pillows thankful for the heat of the fire that was still glowing in the grate. Pray to God he would feel stronger in the morning.

The small grey clad figure leaning over him startled Fred when he next woke up. Expecting Mary-Ann, in his sleep and fever befuddled state, Fred could only gaze uncertainly at the newcomer, aware only that it was not Mary-Ann. Nor Mrs Milne it seemed.

'Dinnae fash yersel' Fred. It's me, Jessie.'

The soft voice so close to him caused Fred to jump in surprise. Was he dreaming? This could not be possible. As if reading his thoughts, Jessie continued.

'Mrs Milne has had to go and see her mither. She's nae well. She asked me tae look in on ye, Fred. You're nae well an a' I can see. Pair thing.'

And she stretched out one of her hands and touched Fred's cheek.

'Shall I wash yer face a wee bit. Make ye feel fresher?'

Before Fred could reply, Jessie went over to the fire and picked up the copper pitcher that was standing on the hearth. Pouring out some warm water into a large earthenware bowl Jessie dipped a large sponge into it, wringing it out thoroughly and began very gently and rhythmically to wash Fred's face and then his hands, turning them over one by one. Then she sat down on the edge of the bed which shuddered slightly under the extra weight. Fred was overwhelmingly aware of Jessie's presence and despite his weak state his heart started to pulse uncomfortably. He closed his eyes and tried to resist the urge to grasp hold of her. Hold her and never let her go. Then he felt her fingers start to untie his night-shirt and his neck was laid bare. The sponge was applied again in small circular movements.

'Feeling better now, Fred?' She whispered.

Fred started to reply but was overtaken with another bout of coughing. Turning his head away from Jessie, he was aware, with a feeling of helplessness, that she had straightened up as if to remove herself. Catching hold of her wrist, Fred drew her to him.

'Stay wi' me, Jess, dinnae leave!'

The urgency in his voice caused Jessie to pause and lean into him. A few moments passed then Fred felt his hand being placed on the smoothest, warmest, softest place he could imagine. He knew then he was lost. Turning her round and placing her head gently on the pillow, Fred allowed himself finally to succumb to Jessie's embrace.

'You'll be the ruin of me, Jessie Duthie,' he sighed into her hair.

# CHAPTER 12

# STRATHMUIR

FRED COULD NOT REMEMBER WHEN HE HAD LAST SLEPT SO well. Falling asleep cupped around Jessie's body with his face against the nape of her neck, all the anxieties and troubles of the previous few days evaporated. He slept so deeply he did not awaken when Jessie, after a couple of hours, gently disengaged herself from his hold nor even when she kissed him on his forehead before letting herself out of the bedroom.

Consciousness crept upon Fred gradually. For a few fleeting moments he wondered what the reason for his relaxed state was. Then, with a rush of emotions, the recollection of the previous few hours came back to him. He could see from the tangled bedclothes that he had not dreamt the whole encounter. His head felt clear and, for the first time in several days, his body no longer ached. Pulling himself up against the pillows, Fred noticed a folded piece of paper propped up against a glass of milk on his bedside table. Opening it slowly Fred cast his eyes over the short message.

*Dearest, I did not want to wake you. Sleep well. I hope you are better very soon. Jessie xx*

Only a very few words but such precious ones. Fred gazed at them for several minutes then reached out for his Bible. Turning to the back he inserted the note carefully between the end papers and then replaced the holy book by his bed.

MRS MILNE HAD arranged for her son-in-law to take Fred to the station for which he was truly grateful. He could not delay his visit to his mother any longer. The daily train to Strathmuir departed at ten o' clock and he wanted to get to the station with plenty of time to spare. His illness had left him feeling weak and distracted but the solid presence of Charlie Cuthbertson, as he lifted Fred's valise into the back of the pony cart and tucked a rug around his passenger's legs, was reassuring. There had been no further snow since he had fallen ill and the streets were now covered with a dirty grey slush which splashed against the sides of the vehicle as the cart-wheels spun round. Charlie was a skilful driver and they made good progress arriving in front of the station by twenty to ten.

'Wait there, Sir.' Fred was instructed, as Charlie jumped down from the cart and came round to help Fred down from the vehicle.

Looking about him, Fred recalled the last time he was here, several months ago, when he had first met Jessie. He winced inwardly when he remembered the circumstances of their meeting and how he must have appeared to the cabbie who rescued them on that inauspicious occasion. His front tooth, though broken, had been saved fortunately. Subconsciously, Fred ran his tongue over the rough surface remembering the pain and shock when he first fell.

'Here you are, Sir.' Charlie looked up at him and held out a hand to take Fred's bag.

Cautiously, Fred stepped down from the pony cart on to the slippery wet cobbles and, despite a protestation from Charlie, insisted he take a sixpence for his trouble.

'Have a good journey, Sir.'

Settled in a quiet compartment with only one other occupant,

Fred began to relax. Sitting by the window, he pulled out his copy of *Paradise Lost* and then pushed his case under the seat. Mrs Milne had given him a good breakfast which, despite his lack of appetite, he had attempted to eat. His mother would no doubt have prepared a hearty lunch to welcome him on arrival. With a gloved hand Fred smeared away the condensation on the inside of the window and looked out. To his left stretched an iron-grey sea topped with white breakers, seagulls wheeling and whirling in the sky, but Fred found that all he could see in front of him was Jessie's face, her eyes closed, her lips slightly parted, her breath light but steady and the tiniest of whimpers as he pulled her to him.

'Awa' for Hogmanay?' A voice cut into Fred's thoughts.

'Aye, a family visit,' was Fred's hurried response as he forced himself back to the present.

Lifting his head to look at his fellow passenger, his clerical collar was revealed.

'Ah, yer a minister, I see. I've been speaking tae one recently. I'm tae be married in the spring.'

Fred, unwilling to seem rude, wished the speaker well.

'Are you a married man, sir?' continued the traveller.

'No, I'm not, not yet, but God willing one day,' responded Fred.

'I'm awa' tae visit ma lassie's family in Stonehaven. They want us tae wait anither year but I'm a' fer getting married this year. I'm nae getting ony younger!' And the man laughed merrily.

Suddenly Fred wished he were in the man's uncomplicated shoes, about to spend some days with his lassie and her family in Stonehaven. It seemed so simple and appealing. Then it came to him. He would tell his mother about Jessie. What he felt about her. If he could have her blessing then maybe they might have a future.

'Weel, this is me,' announced the traveller, wrestling his bag down from the luggage rack, as the train slowed in its approach to Stonehaven. 'A pleasure to have met you, sir, and a Guid New Year to you.'

'Thank you. The same to you and all blessings for your marriage.' Fred smiled as the man slid the compartment door open and exited into the corridor awaiting his stop.

He must have dozed off after that, as the next thing Fred knew was the locomotive shuddering to a steaming halt at its final destination – Strathmuir. A fine drizzle was coursing down the compartment window, obscuring the view of the red sandstone town. Fred felt a wave of emotion as he regained consciousness and stood up to gather his possessions. This was home, the neighbourhood that had nurtured him as a child and now welcomed him back as a man. The pull of the place was strong. Perhaps this was where he was meant to be after all?

Despite the drizzle, Fred decided to walk the short distance between the station and his mother's cottage in South Row. The air would do him good he considered after so long spent indoors. And then there he was approaching the familiar low front door to his mother's house, knocking once and then turning the handle and calling out her name.

'Hello, Mother, I'm here!'

'Fred, Fred, there you are! I thought mebbe ye wisnae coming?'

Janet Thomson threw her arms around her son, pressing her face against his damp, dark coat. Fred in turn bent his head to kiss his mother's hair. This dear familiar person who was his rock.

'I sent ye a telegram, mother. I hope ye received it?'

'Aye, son, but I thought mebbe ye were still sick.'

She drew back and looked up anxiously at Fred.

'It's so cold and damp but I've built us up a good fire. I want ye tae be comfortable.'

To their right was the heavy frame of his mother's handloom. Along with many other women in the town, Janet made her living weaving jute into cloth. Fred worried that she worked too hard and that her cough was caused by breathing in the fibres she handled. One day, he determined, he would be able to support her without her having to work herself into an early grave. Today, however, was a holiday and Janet shooed her son into the cosy kitchen on the left. Taking his coat and bag, she pushed him gently down into the only armchair and set about offering refreshments to her cherished visitor.

'It's been so long, Fred,' sighed his mother. 'I want to hear a' your news. Dinnae miss a thing.'

For the first time, Fred felt a flicker of foreboding and his earlier resolve that he would tell Janet about Jessie began to waiver. No, give her time, he reasoned. He would tell her all about his graduation, the sermons he had preached and how pleased Richard was with his progress. Soon he could have a parish of his own, with a manse to call home. It would be natural for a man to want companionship, to marry. Why should his wife not be Jessie?

'Aye, I will, mother, all in good time. But how are you doing? I hope you have some help with your work now?' Fred indicated the workshop across the hall.

'Aye, May MacPhie, comes in most days. I manage but when my arthritis is playing up she'll lend a hand. The winter months are the worst. It takes me a gey long time tae get started wi' ma creaky joints!'

Janet Thomson held out her hands and waggled the fingers theatrically.

'But I dinnae want tae spik aboot mesel'. You must be famished and chilled tae the bone, Fred. Come and take some soup. Cockaleekie, your favourite. May brought me one of her mother's fowls jist yesterday. It's a meal in itself.'

Fred did not need asking twice. Having eaten so little over the past few days, he now realised how hungry he was and in no time the bowl of broth was finished and being replenished by his mother. Finally, pushing the bowl away from him and straightening up, Fred started to give his mother his news. As he expected she smiled warmly and nodded approvingly as he related his successes and achievements.

'I knew ye would dae me proud, Fred. And yer faither… his faith in ye has paid off. So this position in Edinburgh..? Do you think you will take it?'

'It is too early to say, Mother. I have not even met Reverend Russell yet. I believe Richard wishes to invite him up to Aberdeen to hear me preach and speak with me.'

There was a pause as Fred collected his thoughts. His mother was looking lovingly at him, her eyes alight with happiness. He was loath to break the mood but he knew he had to tell her what was on his mind.

'Mother, I also wanted to tell you that I have met a lassie who means a lot to me. She is not well-educated but she has a good heart. Now that I have graduated I thought I might start to think about such things. I have spoken about it with no-one else and your blessing is very important to me. '

At Fred's words, his mother sat up and assumed a serious expression.

'A lassie?' she whispered almost to herself. 'Perhaps it would be better to wait a wee bit before becoming involved in such things? You don't want to have your head turned by the first girl who sets her cap at you?'

'No, she's not like that. I care for her. She wants to better herself and she's become a good friend to me. I have waited years, mother, studying and preaching and doing everything that people have asked of me. I am twenty five. How much longer am I expected to wait for my own life to start?'

At his impassioned words, Janet, pulled her chair closer to her son and took both his hands in hers.

'Listen very carefully tae me, Fred. Of course I want you tae be happy – you are my son - but it is not as simple as you think. Now that you are qualified you have tae make yer mark. So much has gone into you becoming a minister. You are not just another preacher. You have a divine gift, Fred, and you will go further than Strathmuir and Aberdeen. You will move in different circles and meet people you can only dream of now. Do not commit yersel tae onyone now, Fred, please! You need tae be free. I have had a hard life but I have borne it gladly knowing that things would be different for you. Please dinnae throw away this opportunity otherwise my sacrifice will have been in vain. Do you understand me, Fred?'

Looking into his mother's face, he knew he could not refuse her.

'I understand, mother, forgive me for upsetting you so.'

'Thank you, son. We will not speak of this again.'

# CHAPTER 13

## THOU SHALT NOT

The memory of her night with Fred helped Jessie overcome the loneliness of a Christmas on her own. The warmth and security of his body against hers had made her feel, for the first time in her life, at one with the world and with this person. She felt no guilt in their encounter. It had been done with love and tenderness. It had been gentle and trusting and, in her mind, Jessie now felt committed to the deep, enigmatic man who had finally opened up his feelings to her. She wanted to think ahead to when they could be together again but she knew this might only lead to anguish and disappointment. No, she would hold on to this moment and prayed that God would be merciful and grant her wish.

Slipping back into St Nicholas' manse early in the morning, she hoped her absence had not been noticed. Mrs MacDonald and the children had departed, with much noise and excitement, for their grandparents' home in Peterculter. While they were away there was less for her to do. Only the Reverend MacDonald remained to attend to parish matters and his congregation. To the poor and needy, Christmas was just another difficult day, made more difficult when contrasted with those fortunate enough to have good food on the table and a warm fire to sit in front of.

Unlike his wife, who, though not unwelcoming, seemed in a state of perpetual harassment and simmering resentment with four children under ten, the Reverend MacDonald was friendly and took an interest in Jessie's welfare. When time allowed, he would drop into the kitchen to chat and ask about her day. He was an old friend of Reverend and Mrs Kelman, he said, and was happy to help them out by employing her. Jessie, on her part, though still frustrated and hurt by the injustice of her sudden departure from Bon Accord Crescent manse, appreciated that she had been quickly given a new position rather than being turned out on to the street.

Jessie was unused to such solicitude but, after initial reticence, allowed herself to be drawn on subjects such as her family, where she came from and what she hoped for in life. But one topic was out of bounds. Reverend Black was banished from her thoughts. That was her secret and her secret only. Maybe, probably, nothing more would come of it and though this thought filled Jessie with sadness, she would not share her memories with anyone else. They were hers alone.

A couple of days after seeing Fred, Jessie awoke from a deep sleep. Opening her eyes, she realised she had been disturbed by the sound of her bedroom door opening and was aware, with sleepy surprise, that the Reverend MacDonald was standing by her bed.

'Am I late, Sir?' Jessie queried, believing she had slept in. 'I beg yer pardon, I'll be up immediately.'

She then paused waiting for the minister to leave the room. However what she heard was the sound of the door closing followed by him sitting down heavily on the narrow bed. Jessie felt a jolt of shock through her body and lay stiffly with her back to the man.

'I'll be up immediately, Sir.' Jessie repeated herself half-heartedly, forcing herself to sound calm.

She was then aware that, far from taking his leave, the

Reverend MacDonald, still without saying a word, had placed his hands under the bedclothes. Taking hold of her taut body, he started to slide his fingers up and down, closing in on her curves. Bending down and putting his mouth close to her ear, he finally spoke.

'Dinnae be feared, young Jess. It's Christmas and I need a wee bit o' comfort. My wife has the bairns and disnae understand. Will ye no turn round?'

Jessie lay motionless, still with her back to the minister, fists and buttocks clenched. She knew this tone of voice and what it meant. The weasley softness and the accelerated breathing of the man made her feel nauseous.

'There's only the two of us here, Jess,' he murmured, 'so dinnae make a fuss. It can be our secret. I've admired yer bonnie wee figure for quite some time.'

'Please go, Sir!' appealed Jessie with growing desperation. 'I winnae say onythin'.'

Suddenly the Reverend MacDonald's demeanour changed. Grabbing Jessie's hair and pulling it back so violently that she cried out in pain and fright, he forced her face round to his.

'There is nothin' tae tell, Jessie. Who would believe ye? A wee whore frae the harbour, wi' a bit o' a reputation from what I hear. Now turn around if you don't want me to hurt you.'

Jessie had never heard the minister speak in this tone before. She had no doubt he meant what he said so with the greatest reluctance and her eyes tightly shut, Jessie turned over as he had instructed.

Now his hand gripped her face. She would not let him kiss her and twisted her head from side to side to avoid him. In such close proximity, she was very aware of his smell – a trace of alcohol on his early morning breath, cold tar soap on his hands after his ablutions and a whiff of sweat as he bore down on her. With his free hand he reached once again under the bedclothes and started to pull up her heavy cotton night-dress. Now he was tugging at his own garments, breathing heavily in a combination of exertion and desire. In one last attempt to bring her attacker to his senses, Jessie appealed to him.

'Let me be! I beseech you!'

She tried to keep the panic from her voice but from the high pitched shriek coming from her, she realised had not succeeded.

It made no difference. Reverend MacDonald's hand now came down firmly over her mouth as he hoisted himself upon her. A few thrusts and it was all over. For a few seconds the minister lay spent on top of her, then he rolled off to lie at her side. Abruptly he stood up, throwing a towel at Jessie with the instructions,

'Clean yersel' up and mind, if you speak o' this tae anyone you'll find yersel' wi'out a roof over yer head.'

Shocked and shivering, Jessie lay without moving until the minister had left. Clutching the blankets under her chin she tried to supress the nausea which once again bubbled up inside her. Then, finally unable to contain it, she turned her head and vomited into the chamber pot by her bed. Eyes watering and head pounding, she rolled into a ball hugging her knees around her bruised body.

'Bastard! Bastard! Evil hypocrite!' Jessie screamed silently to herself. At that moment she was too stunned to shed tears. Then a rush of disgust ran through her. She must wash all trace of that bastard from her body. It was icy cold in the room but despite that Jessie tore off her clothing and soaked a sponge with the nearly frozen water in the basin on her side table. Scrubbing, scrubbing at her skin while a still warm trickle ran down the inside of her thigh. Once again she spewed into the chamber pot, then wrapped in one of her blankets, fell exhausted on to her bed.

When she awoke, for a blissful moment of amnesia she wondered what had happened. Then the recollection of the assault hit her and she covered her face with her hands.

'What now? What now?'

She could not stay here in the same house as that…man. But where should she go? Not back to the harbour. Not to Bon Accord

Crescent. How would she explain matters to the Kelmans? She could never speak of this. Not to protect MacDonald – never that, he could burn in Hell for all she cared. No, to protect herself. She had done nothing to deserve this. Everything seemed to be stacked against her however hard she tried. Now, warm tears started to fill her eyes and she gave into the release of this emotion. With gulps and shudders, Jessie wept into her pillow.

Gradually she quietened and lay still. Beneath her something rustled and she remembered Fred's letter slipped under her mattress for safe keeping and away from prying eyes.

'Oh Fred, fit'll I dae? Will ye nae come and save me?'

Probing with her fingers, Jessie took hold of the envelope and pulled it out. Wiping her eyes with the back of her hand, she opened the sheet of paper and re-read Fred's words of love. She would try to see him at morning service when he returned from seeing his mother. He would help her, she was certain. But that was several days off. Where she would she go meantime? As her eyes scanned Fred's words, Jessie was reminded of Mrs Milne's help in the past. Perhaps she would take her in and help her? 10 Rose Street. She already knew her way there. She must go there today before the MacDonald family returned. She would not spend another night under this blighted roof.

Raising herself shakily from her bed, Jessie cast her eyes round the room. Her day clothes were lain over the back of a chair, where she had cast them off the evening before. New undergarments were all she needed. Trying hard not to make a sound she crossed the small attic room to her chest and cautiously opened one of the drawers. The garments she sought were inside and she pulled them on. Then with one ear alert for any sounds outside, Jessie picked up her black work dress and pulled it over her head. She had little enough by way of possessions so that would not take long. Her black valise was stowed on top of the single pine-wood wardrobe to the left of the window. But before she pulled it down, Jessie crept to the bedroom door and opened it a fraction to check that she was alone. For a few seconds there was silence apart from the ticking of the grandmother clock in the hall. Then, with a terrified jolt, Jessie could make out the sound of footsteps on the staircase. Was he coming back?

Closing the door, Jessie cursed the absence of a key. She had not thought she would need to barricade herself into her room. In a panic she threw herself back on to her bed pulling the blankets over herself and feigned sleep. The pounding of her heart was so loud she thought it must give her away. Eyes tight shut, Jessie lay still as a gravestone. Sure enough the door opened slowly and the minister took a step inside the room. She could hear his breathing and the slight clearing of his throat as if he were about to say something.

'Please God,' she prayed. 'Let him depart, don't let him hurt me again.'

What seemed like an age passed, before MacDonald sighed and clicked his tongue, as though he had thought better of something. To Jessie's greatest relief she then heard the man leave the room, pulling the door sharply behind him. A little later she heard the sound of the front door slamming and the minister's footsteps receding down the path. Only then did she dare open her eyes and raise her head. She might not have long to make her escape. Was he gone for the morning or just a few minutes, she wondered. There was no time to lose. Spurred on with a new found energy born of anger and fear, Jessie stood up, grasped the little wooden chair, and climbed up to retrieve her bag. Scooping her few possessions she crammed them into the case then pulled on her stockings and fastened her boots.

Without a backward glance, her heart still thumping in fear, Jessie made her way downstairs towards the kitchen as the clock struck ten. Realising how dry her mouth was she quickly poured herself a glass of water from a jug by the sink and then let herself out of the backdoor. She would get out through the back gate which would take her round to the street without having to cross the garden. After that it would not take her long to reach Rose Street. And if Mrs Milne was not there? Well she would worry about that later.

Lifting the latch to open the back gate, Jessie had just stepped outside on to the street when she heard the rumble of a carriage drawing up to the house. To her horror and despair, Mrs MacDonald's voice could be heard supervising the children as they clambered down to the pavement. If she left now she would be seen. And how would she explain her luggage. With a sinking heart, Jessie realised she had no choice but to retreat indoors, back where she had come from.

# CHAPTER 14

# NEW YEAR

THE NEW YEAR OF 1861 CREPT IN QUIETLY AND ALMOST apologetically. While Aberdeenshire often saw ferocious snow storms early in the year with the landscape swathed in deep white drifts, this January, so far at least, seemed different. Instead, a grey chill had settled on the rich, bare soil, the timeless hills and the solid, un-showy towns of the North East. This cold stillness seemed to echo Fred's mood since his visit to his mother. Where not so long ago he had allowed himself to be warmed by thoughts of a life with Jessie, of companionship and a purpose and direction to his endeavours, now he felt that once again this was to be closed to him – for the present at any rate. More than this he was tormented by a sense of having let the young woman down, not that any promises had been made – only implied. As he approached the city on his return journey, Fred's mood felt as grey and heavy as the imposing granite buildings which closed in on him as the countryside receded.

Although he had wired the details of his return journey to Richard and Mary-Ann, Fred had declined the services of Charlie Cuthbertson, preferring to take one of the hansom cabs that were lined up in the station forecourt. He did not want Charlie waiting in the cold for him should the train be delayed. Twenty minutes later, well-worn leather case in hand, Fred stood on the pavement outside the manse in Bon Accord Crescent. What would this year hold in store, he wondered? Then, with a sigh, he turned the handle of the front door and entered the hallway. Almost immediately he was greeted by Mrs Milne, who wished him a "Guid New Year" and hoped that his mother was keeping well.

'Aye, well enough, thank you. And how is your's? I hear she's nae been well hersel'?'

'Well, she's holding her own, thank you Sir, but she's auld, ken, and jist wants tae get awa'.'

There was a pause as though Mrs Milne wanted to add something, but at that moment Mary-Ann appeared on the staircase and greeted Fred.

'Well, here he is!' she exclaimed. 'You look so much better, Fred. Thank goodness. Your visit has done you good clearly. Happy New Year!'

'Thank you, Mary-Ann, and the same to you,' Fred approached the older woman and embraced her affectionately. 'Yes, I do feel so much better, thank the good Lord. And you and Richard… your visit to Inverness went well? You were both in need of a break, I am sure.'

'Yes, it was marvellous. We were so well looked after. I feel a new woman.' Mary-Ann chuckled briefly and patted Fred on his arm. 'You'll want to get unpacked no doubt, Fred, and then come and join us for a cup of tea and some Christmas cake.'

Picking up his bag once more, Fred looked up towards the landing in front of him and climbed the stairs. The door to his bedroom was closed. Immediately the memory of his last meeting with Jessie struck him. Sitting down on his bed, now neatly made up and covered with a paisley bedspread, Fred looked about him. Staring up at the ceiling, he took in the ornate coving at the edges, cracked in places, the heavy brocade curtains, already drawn against the winter chill, the shadowy pictures of Scottish landscapes from past centuries and the plain mahogany mirror which hung above his chest of drawers. All seemed so calm and unchanged that Fred, for a moment, felt he must have dreamed the whole interlude.

Then he saw the cheap white envelope tucked behind his copper shaving mug. It was addressed in scratchy black ink to *Reverend Black – Private.* Fred recognised the unformed handwriting immediately. It was Jessie's. Cursing the lack of light at this time of year, Fred lit the small oil lamp on his desk and, hastily tearing open the envelope, scrutinised the contents.

*My dear Fred*

*I didnae ken if I shud write tae ye but I hope you are feeling a wee bit better now. You will hae been happy tae see yer mither. I also wanted to say that I will never forget being with ye yesterday. Mebbe you feel sorry now but dinnae be. I'm nae sorry! From what you said to me, mebbe you feel the same? I am no' a fool though. You are so far above me in every way. But, Fred, I want to carry on my learning so that maybe one day I can make you proud of me. Please write to me to let me know how you are. Send your reply to Mrs Milne's house in Rose Street. She is happy to help.*

*With all my love*

*Jessie xx*

Ah, how should he reply? His mother's words still echoed in his head. To tell Jessie the truth would break her heart he feared yet he must not leave her to imagine they still had a future. The truth it had to be. He had to honour his father and mother in this most difficult of tests. He would write tomorrow and explain as best he could. But now he must rejoin Mary-Ann and Richard otherwise questions might be asked.

'Good to see you, Fred!' Richard stood up, smiling broadly as Fred entered the drawing room. 'And it is especially good to see you looking so much better.'

Richard returned to the sofa and patted the space beside him. 'Come, I have some news for you.'

Fred obeyed, hoping his expression gave nothing away but polite interest.

'As Mary-Ann has no doubt told you, we had an excellent sojourn with the Mackinnons in Inverness. So hospitable and kind. But there was a welcome addition to the party – William Russell. You recall I spoke to you about him recently and in particular the possibility of a post for you with him in Edinburgh.'

Fred leaned forward at the announcement and experienced both excitement and anxiety on hearing Richard's words. He would follow God's will. He could do no more if this was to be his path in life.

'It seems he is visiting various parishes around Scotland in search of a suitable assistant,' continued Richard. 'We talked some more about you and he would like to call in on his way back to Edinburgh to hear you preach. How does that sound?'

Fred sat silently for a few seconds to consider Richard's words. Sunday service was only a couple of days off. Would there be sufficient time to prepare such a sermon?

'You can do this, Fred,' reassured Richard. 'Be yourself. You must have many themes ready. You have spent long enough preparing for such a day.'

'Thank you, Richard. I will certainly give it my best effort. I am forever in your debt for your support and belief in me. I hope that Dr Russell will be as favourably disposed towards me as you.'

'And why should he not, Fred? I know you will put your heart into it and if William does not see this then the loss is his.' Richard smiled affectionately at the younger man.

Fred was not sure what he had expected Dr Russell to look like. His reputation and popularity had preceded him and Fred had imagined the cleric to be a tall and imposing, almost theatrical presence with a deep, sonorous voice – rather like one of the Old

Testament prophets he had studied. The middle-aged man to whom he was introduced was softly spoken and several inches shorter than Fred. His blue grey eyes looked mildly entertained and a hint of a smile lingered around his mouth. From the first Dr Russell appeared eager to know all about Fred, quizzing him about his studies, his home life and his hopes for the future. Richard had kindly allowed them to use his study for their conversation so they would not be disturbed. Fred, usually reticent and somewhat defensive of his background, found himself opening up to the mild mannered individual sitting beside him.

'Do you have a preference, Sir, for the topic of my sermon on Sunday? I am particularly interested in the common human predicament that affects us all. I understand I can be quite direct, but that is how I am.' Fred felt he had to warn Dr Russell, recalling the unfortunate reaction of Mr Ferguson at his inaugural address back in the autumn.

'I want you to be yourself, Fred, and am happy to leave the choice of subject to you. From what Richard has told me, you always make a strong connection with your congregation. That is what is important to me. If our parishioners do not feel we understand them or speak for them, then our Church will wither and die. It is not just about social niceties and appearances after all.'

On Sunday morning it looked as though St Columba's would be full. Word had got about that there was to be a visitor from Edinburgh and that Fred Black would be preaching again. Despite the bitter wind blowing straight in from the North Sea, many of the congregation initially stood outside taking the opportunity of greeting each other for the first time in the New Year. Then, as the bell starting tolling to alert them to the start of the service, the parishioners started to file in and take their places in the pews.

Fred had taken education and man's endeavours as his theme that morning. It was something very close to his heart. Where would he be without it? Climbing the stairs up to the pulpit,

Fred grasped the notes he had been working on in his free hand. They were for reassurance only. One he started to speak, somehow the words just came to him. He hoped his impassioned address would move the congregation and of course impress Dr Russell.

'The Lord helps those who help themselves', it is true but hope is a precarious sentiment and to make a start in one's life, to overcome the inevitable setbacks and disappointments, man needs to have optimism and a clear sense of direction. One's fellow man has much to contribute and for all that one might achieve materially, how much better does it feel if one's own good fortune has also benefitted others? You must never forget your roots, however far you rise in life.'

Fred's clear, stern voice rang out around the kirk. The parishioners sat in rapt attention.

'Remember, my brethren, we are all equal in the eyes of the Lord. None should think they rise above their neighbour and become better than they. There are many unfortunates in the world – too many – so one must, it is your holy duty, to reach out a helping hand whenever one can, so that others may benefit in some way from your good fortune. Remember it is easier for a camel to pass through the eye of a needle than for a rich man to enter the kingdom of God. What use material riches in this world if we face poverty in the next? '

Completing his sermon, Fred raised his head and stared out over the congregation. He deliberately chose to avoid looking at either Richard or Dr Russell. He had done his best and spoken from his heart. Suddenly his eye was caught by a small female figure several rows back towards the rear of the church. The bonneted head was bowed down but, with a start, Fred could immediately see that it was Jessie. For a moment he froze and it seemed as though there were only the two of them in the building. Would she raise her head he wondered? Before he could react further, however, Richard had stepped out to the front of the church and, raising his hand, made to speak to the assembled company.

'My grateful thanks to Reverend Black for his wise and thought provoking words.' He started. 'It has been my privilege to work with such a gifted young preacher and to guide him through his studies. There could not be a father more proud than I. We are indeed fortunate to have him to ourselves at present but we must not be greedy. Others must have the opportunity of hearing his valuable words and it is likely, therefore, before this year is out that our brother will be moving on to pastures new.'

There was an audible gasp throughout the congregation, with parishioners turning to each other to whisper their reactions.

'Fear not,' Richard continued, 'this will not take place for some time yet. Rest assured you will all have a chance to say your farewells and give Reverend Black your best wishes.'

Fred was taken aback by Richard's announcement. He had not understood anything was yet to be made public. Had Dr Russell already discussed the matter with the Reverend? Matters were indeed being taken out of his hands. On looking up again, Fred found himself drawn to the spot where Jessie was seated. No longer. The quiet dark-clad figure had already taken her leave. Had she heard Richard's words? A letter would not suffice. He must speak to her in person.

# CHAPTER 15

# A DIFFICULT ENCOUNTER

FRED REMAINED SEATED FOR SOME MINUTES AS THE congregation filed out of the church. Seeing Jessie so unexpectedly had proved a huge distraction. Rather than dwelling on his sermon and how it had been received, his thoughts now returned to the previous week when it seemed that all he held precious lay beside him on his bed. Had he really thought it possible to abandon his ambitions and plans for the sake of his heart? How weak is the flesh, he chastised himself ruefully. He felt he was being tested. Looking down, he caught Dr Russell's eye. Without speaking, Russell nodded and approached the foot of the pulpit to pay his respects. If only Russell were to read his thoughts at that moment, Fred considered bitterly, he doubted he would be so enthusiastic and positive

'Sir, I hope you were not disappointed?' Fred held out his hand to his colleague.

'Everything Richard has said about you is true.' William Russell reassured him. 'Clear and heart-felt and no-one could miss a single word you said. Well done!'

'Thank you, Sir, your approval means a great deal to me. I know Richard holds you in high esteem. I did not want to let him down.'

'Let us walk back to the manse, if that is agreeable to you? The air will do us good and we can discuss matters undisturbed. You seemed surprised when Richard made his announcement? I am sorry if it startled you. Perhaps we should have waited but I understood from Richard that you were keen to take up this potential post in Edinburgh? Not having second thoughts are you?'

William Russell stopped for a moment and turned anxiously to Fred.

'Not at all, Sir. You are correct in your understanding. It was just unexpected. I thought perhaps you had other candidates to consider?'

'It is true I have been visiting various parishes and have listened to half a dozen good preachers. But none came near to you in their delivery. Your background interests me as well. Since we broke away in '43 it is important that we retain our social and egalitarian principles. No, I would much rather have interesting, new blood than a safe candidate from down the road.'

'You are very honest in your appraisal, Sir,' reflected Fred. 'I appreciate that. I will try my utmost to do your faith in me justice.'

'Of that I have no doubt, my boy.'

After luncheon the Kelmans, Dr Russell and Fred retired to the drawing room to ponder on events and discuss practicalities. Having received fulsome praise from both William and Richard for his performance that morning, Fred was invited, as soon as he might, to visit Dr Russell and St Ninian's in Edinburgh.

'If you can spare him, Richard, I would like Fred to come and visit us in Edinburgh. It would be an ideal opportunity to introduce him to the elders and the church committee who would be considering his application. This will be a formality, have no fear! They trust my judgement and we are agreed on the type of candidate we are looking for.'

Fred looked earnestly at Richard and Mary-Ann. It was hard not to feel excitement at the prospect of going to Edinburgh and the opportunities that might open up for him there.

'Would that be convenient, Richard?' Fred queried. 'When might I go?'

'Of course, Fred, it is right and proper that you should visit first. I would suggest in a couple of weeks at the end of the month. Would that suit you as well, William?'

'Perfectly, thank you. I will make the necessary arrangements and let you know.'

The hall clock striking three o' clock reminded Fred that the day was progressing fast and he had yet to contact Jessie. Discussing his plans with his friends made him feel suddenly disloyal and two-faced. He felt a strong need to explain matters to her directly. Her understanding was important to him, he realised. Was he a hypocrite to feel so conflicted?

'Fred? You look miles away,' Mary-Ann's voice broke into Fred's thoughts. 'Are you happy with that?'

For a moment Fred wondered what she was referring to, then, coming rapidly back to the present, he reassured her of his complete agreement and appreciation of the plan.

'Thank you for the invitation, William. I look forward to the visit very much indeed.'

HAVING TAKEN LEAVE of the others, Fred found himself once again at his desk in his room, dwelling over what he should say to Jessie and what her response might be. He must be careful not to scare her away but equally he did not want to appear too intimate in his language. Pulling a sheet of writing paper out of the drawer, he dipped his pen carefully in the inkwell and set to writing the letter.

*Dear Jessie*

*I thank you for your sweet note which I found on my return from Strathmuir. Yes I am fully recovered now thank goodness. I was surprised to see you at St*

*Columba's this morning. You may have wondered at Reverend Kelman's announcement. I was sorry you heard it from him rather than me. It is important that I speak to you directly, dear Jessie. Can you come to the church on one of the parishioner days? They are Tuesdays and Thursdays between 2 and 4 in the afternoon. Please give your reply to Mrs Milne. I await your reply anxiously.*

*Yours, Fred*

Fred sat back and surveyed what he had written. He had made it as simple as possible and he hoped Jessie would be able to understand his request. Reluctantly, he had resisted from expressing more open affection. It would not make what he had to say any easier. Oh, that she were here with him now and he could try to explain and ask her forgiveness for letting her down. A vain hope. Fred placed his letter in an envelope, addressed it care of Mrs Milne at Rose Street and sealed it. He would rise early and deliver it himself. Thereafter he could do nothing but wait.

Despite his concerns and preoccupations, the days passed rapidly and it was only when Mary-Ann reminded him of his forthcoming visit to Edinburgh that Fred realised that he had yet to hear from Jessie. He must see her on either the next Tuesday or Thursday or else he would be unable to explain matters before his departure. Just as he was giving up hope of a reply, on the Wednesday morning Mrs Milne tapped on the door of his room where he was working on possible sermons to deliver at St Ninian's.

'Excuse me, Sir. May I come in? I'm nae disturbing ye?'

Her voice was low and her head peered round the half-open door with one foot on the threshold.

'No, no, come in,' was Fred's immediate response, as he turned in his chair to look at the newcomer.

'I'll nae keep ye but young Jessie says she can be at the kirk tomorrow afternoon at 2 o' clock. She disnae hae much free time, ken, so she cannae stay long.'

Already Mrs Milne was retreating out of the room, anxious that she should not be seen.

'Thank you.' Fred called after her.

Parishioner days were a regular occurrence at St Columba's. Often both Richard and Fred attended but on this particular Thursday, to Fred's relief, he was on his own. Richard had some church business to attend to and wanted to take advantage of Fred's presence before he went to Edinburgh.

'There should not be too many parishioners for you to see, Fred. There were several on Tuesday so it is likely to be a lesser number today.'

Fred felt uncharacteristically apprehensive as he walked into the vestry at a quarter to two. The sun was shining, lending a little warmth to the cold January air, and birdsong indicated that more clement spring weather was not far away. However, Fred was not in a mood to appreciate it. Closing the door he sat down at the heavy oak meeting table. Linking his fingers in front of him, he resisted the urge to chew anxiously at his thumbnail.

After a few minutes there was a soft knock on the vestry door and, just as he rose to open it, the door was pushed open to reveal Jessie. Despite all his previous intentions, Fred could not resist embracing the diminutive figure standing in front of him. He closed his eyes for a moment and bent his head down over her.

'My dear, I am so glad to see you. Thank you for coming,' he murmured.

Jessie stood stiff and unresponsive for a few seconds then drew back to look up at Fred.

'You wanted tae see me, Fred? You hae something tae say I believe?'

There was a jarring note of sarcasm in her voice that took Fred aback. But he bade Jessie sit and drew up another chair beside her. He could not have this conversation with a heavy table between them like a barrier. Her hands lay in her lap. Fred reached out one of his and laid it gently on top of hers. Whether this was to reassure her or himself he was unsure. Jessie continued to sit passively, her usually animated face a solemn mask.

'I wanted to explain to you in person, Jessie. Everything I have said about my feelings has not changed, please believe that. I told my mother about you. I wanted her blessing before we could continue. I so hoped she would give it but she wasnae happy. She has spent her whole life helping me get educated and she disnae want me to make any personal commitments yet. She has made many sacrifices and I cannae go against her wishes, Jessie. I am so sorry. Do you understand?'

Fred had leaned in close to Jessie as he was speaking, willing her to give him the answer he sought. His hand now gripped hers tightly and Jessie wriggled her fingers in an attempt to free herself.

'Oh I understand weel enough, Fred. I'm angry wi' meself an' a', thinking mebbe we would hae a future. I cannae say I am surprised. Why would someone wi' as much schooling as you want to get hitched up wi' someone like me – a wee fish-wife. It widnae do in yer polite society in Edinburgh, wid it?'

'That's nae the reason, Jess! I have never thought ye to be less than me. It is what is within that is important and you, Jessie, have courage and a good heart. In many ways ye remind me of my mother.'

Jessie snorted derisively, 'Weel, I'm nae yer mither, Fred, and I dinnae want tae be mitherin' ye! I hae plans too, ken. I cannae waste ony mair time holdin' yer hand.'

Her voice had started to rise with indignation causing Fred to hush her, nervous that any parishioners waiting outside might hear the altercation. This was not what he had hoped for when they met. Jessie stopped speaking and abruptly stood up, turning her back on Fred. To his anguish, he realised she was crying. Better they had never met, but it was too late for that now. He rose to his feet and let his hands rest lightly on her shoulders. She did not resist him.

'Forgive me, Jessie. I didnae want to hurt ye, please believe me. I will always be your friend and if ye ever need help ye must let me know.'

Jessie, wiping her eyes with the back of her hand, sighed deeply and nodded without turning round.

'Good-bye, Fred. I wish ye well. Remember me in yer prayers.'

# CHAPTER 16

# ST NINIAN'S

A GREAT SADNESS BROKE OVER FRED AS JESSIE TOOK HER leave. Every instinct urged him to call after her, to tell her to ignore what he had said, to keep her by his side. This could be resolved. But even as these thoughts rushed through his mind, he knew that it was not to be. He had to let her go. Cursing his weakness, Fred bowed his head in his hands and tried to find the words to pray for forgiveness. Had he done the right thing? Silently he implored God to give him the strength to bear this loss and that Jessie might be protected and cherished in her life in the way he was unable to do. She deserved better. He tried to read the meaning of their meeting, their friendship and now this sudden, sad fracture. But he did not have the emotional strength at present.

On his return to the manse, Fred realised that he must now ready himself for his departure for Edinburgh the following morning. It had been agreed that he would stay with Dr Russell for five days. In that time he would be required to preach at least once at St Ninian's, dine with Dr Russell, the kirk elders and prominent members of the congregation and, if time allowed, familiarise himself with the city.

'You will need a small trunk, I dare say,' announced Mary-Ann, as she poured him a cup of tea in her parlour later that afternoon. 'Richard will be happy to lend you one now but you will need to acquire your own should your move become permanent – which I am sure it will.'

'I doubt that I will present a very impressive figure, Mary-Ann. For too long I have been hiding myself away in this bonnie, silver city, where two of everything has sufficed. But I am certain more will be expected of me once I am in the capital.'

'You will impress whatever you wear, Fred. They are not inviting you to scrutinise your attire. Your modesty and economy will stand you in much better stead than if you appear as a man-about-town.'

'I did not mean that, Mary-Ann!' retorted Fred in embarrassment, stopping when he saw that Mary-Ann was smiling merrily at his discomfiture.

'Forgive me, Fred. I am only teasing. Let me not delay you any further. I am sure you wish to get on with your preparations. When do you depart in the morning?'

'The train leaves at ten. With the ferry crossings it will take the best part of the day but I hope to arrive in Edinburgh by four p.m. if there are no delays.' Fred peered out of the window. 'The weather looks settled. Let us pray it remains so.'

'Indeed, Fred. God speed!'

In the event Fred's prayers were answered and his journey to the capital, though long, was uneventful. The choppy grey waters of the Tay and the Forth did not succeed in unsettling his stomach but he was, nonetheless, thankful to set foot on dry land again. Finding himself on the platform of Waverley Station, amid the bustle of the crowd, Fred looked about him. Dr Russell had indicated he would try to come and meet him if he could but so far there seemed to be no sign of him.

'Porter, sur?"

Fred's musings were interrupted by a small man in a dirty peaked cap looking up at him expectantly.

'Porter, sur?' he repeated 'D'ye hae ither bags, sur?'

'Aye, I do, thank ye,' was Fred's response. 'In the goods wagon it'll be. A small trunk.'

Pointing to the rear of the train, Fred led the way followed by the porter pushing a small barrow, its metal wheels ringing on the platform surface. The doors of the goods wagon had been rolled open and among a jumble of portmanteaux, boxes, barrels and cases stood his black trunk bound in wood and metal and secured firmly with a wide leather strap.

'That's the one!' he confirmed, standing by as the porter wrestled Fred's luggage on to the barrow.

Fred decided he would take himself to the front of the station to see if there was anyone there. Failing that he would take a hansom cab. Melville Street was barely a mile from Waverley so it would not take long. Glad to be stretching his legs after so long spent seated, Fred walked briskly down the platform to the station exit accompanied by the porter, incoming travellers stepping aside to let them pass.

Outside several carriages were lined up awaiting business. Skinny horses moved restlessly on the wet cobbles, their hooves clipping the stone causing the harness and vehicle to creak in protest. Fred scanned the forecourt and, failing to catch sight of William Russell, shook his head and turned to the porter.

'I'll take a cab.'

He approached the nearest hansom and the driver climbed down from his perch to help the porter man-handle the heavy case on to the luggage rack.

'17 Melville Street, please.'

The driver then opened the door for Fred who, after pressing some coins into the porter's hand, climbed in and sat down.

Although the light was fading fast and he was mightily fatigued by his journey, Fred nonetheless felt a thrill of excitement as the carriage bowled up to Princes Street, past the Scott

Monument and headed west along the mile-long thoroughfare. Above his head towered the shadowy bulk of Edinburgh Castle, while rows of black chimney pots on the city roofs stood like sentinels silhouetted against the darkening winter sky. Peering through the window, Fred's eye was caught by the reflections in the glittering shop windows, the wide pavements and what seemed to be hundreds of passers-by jostling their way to their various destinations. Soon enough this scene was left behind as the cab turned into a quieter cobbled boulevard and about half way along drew up outside a handsome symmetrical town house. He had arrived.

Having paid the driver, Fred now found himself standing in front of an imposing black front door. Light spilled out from the fanlight overhead, illuminating the brass bell-pull, gleaming just to his right. Seizing it firmly, it announced his arrival throughout the house and within a few seconds the door was opened to reveal a middle-aged woman of medium height, dressed in sombre hues, her greying hair pulled back into a bun.

'Reverend Black, please come in,' she announced, a smile spreading across her angular features.

'Thank you. Good afternoon. I trust I am not later than expected? I was not sure whether to wait for Dr Russell at the station.'

'No, you were correct to take the hansom. Dr Russell has been called away to attend to a dying parishioner but he asked that I made you comfortable and showed you your room. I am Mrs Oliphant, the house-keeper. Mrs Russell passed away several years ago. God rest her soul.'

Fred held out his hand in greeting, and followed the house-keeper into the hallway.

'I will get Tom the boy to fetch your trunk in,' Mrs Oliphant continued. 'Let me take your coat, Sir.'

Having settled his things in his room, Fred returned to the first-floor drawing room where Mrs Oliphant had laid out a light afternoon tea. Pouring himself a cup Fred wandered over to the long windows that over-looked the streets. Apart from a few pedestrians and some passing carriage traffic, all was quiet. He marvelled at how protected and removed from the general hurly burly of the city streets it was possible to feel in such a residence. His mother's entire home would have fitted into this one room. Despite his earlier excitement, Fred now felt strangely disconnected and his thoughts turned to what Jessie might be doing at that moment. What would her reaction be to such a room he wondered?

'Excuse me, Sir,' Mrs Oliphant's voice behind him alerted Fred to her presence. 'As Dr Russell may be some time yet, I wondered what you might like to do until dinner is served. Dr Russell normally eats at seven thirty. Perhaps you would like to rest until then or you might like to take some air after your long journey.'

While the thought of reclining in a comfortable chair appealed greatly to Fred, his curiosity had been aroused by his surveillance of the street scenes since his arrival.

'Well, a short walk would do me good I daresay. Is St Ninian's close at hand? I would very much like to see it for myself.'

'Indeed, Sir, it is but five minutes' walk. Take yourself up to the end of Melville Street and turn right. I can point out the spire to you from the front door.'

'Excellent! Then that is what I will do. On my return, there will be time for me change and refresh myself before dinner.'

'Certainly, Sir. We will see to your unpacking while you are out.'

Mrs Oliphant's instructions were most accurate and just a few minutes after leaving the building, Fred stood in front of St Ninian's. The entrance, a simple set of double doors, was set back under a pillared portico in the classical style, while above it soared an elegant steeple, a large clock set into the lower portion. Five fifteen, Fred noted as he turned the handle to one of the doors and entered.

Now that the daylight had faded, Fred's eyes took a few seconds to adjust to the gloom. Normally the oval space of the body of the kirk would be flooded with natural light from many clear glass windows top and bottom, but at this hour the interior had to rely on strategically placed candles to provide some kind of illumination. As the front door closed behind him, it echoed around the building. The air was cold and musty and it seemed as though he were alone. Walking down to the altar, Fred looked up at the ornate wooden pulpit which rose imposingly to his left. In but a day or two he would be standing up there making his voice heard.

A light cough behind him startled Fred and he turned round to see who might be there. To his surprise he saw that he was not alone. In the third pew behind him sat a fashionably dressed woman in her forties. Her dark hair was covered by a dark green felt hat and her neck and shoulders were swathed in a russet sable collar. She sat motionless, her head bowed. Fearing he was intruding, Fred felt the need to explain himself.

'I beg your pardon, Madam,' he started apologetically. 'I believed I was alone. I am sorry if I have disturbed you.'

The woman raised her head, smiled at Fred and started to rise from her seat. She had beautiful dark eyes, he noticed.

'Please do not apologise,' the woman reassured him. 'I have been sitting here for some time. It is a place of sanctuary for me. One of my children is sick and it is causing me anxiety. I visit the kirk when I need some time for contemplation and prayer. It calms me.'

'That is most important,' Fred agreed, struck by her openness. 'We need to attend to our spiritual needs every bit as much as our material needs. I should explain, I am visiting Dr Russell for a few days. My name is Frederick Black.'

'Ah yes, Dr Russell, did mention that we might be having a visitor over the next few days. Let me introduce myself, Margaret Burnett.' And she extended a small, black-gloved hand to Fred. 'Would you like me to show you around our church?'

'That would be most kind, but only if I have not inconvenienced you.'

'Not at all. It would be my pleasure.'

While most the windows were of plain glass, Fred's eye was caught by a small stained glass window depicting a child with a small dog and his toys.

'That is charming,' he announced with enthusiasm.

Mrs Burnett turned to him and smiled sadly.

'Thank you. Yes, it is of great personal importance to our family. We lost one of our sons to measles five years ago. A great tragedy. We paid for this as his memorial. It gives me great comfort that it will endure long after I too have left this earth.'

She broke off speaking and looked down at the ground before continuing.

'Time is a great healer but a mother never overcomes a blow like that. Dr Russell was a great comfort to us. Having lost his wife around the same time, he understood how paralysing our grief was.'

'I am so sorry to hear this. It is a bonnie window. Thank you for taking me into your confidence. I will pray for you and your family.'

The two stood in silence for a few seconds, each with their own thoughts, when their contemplation was broken by the sound of footsteps. Looking up, Fred saw that the newcomer was no other than Dr Russell.

'William! You've tracked me down, I see.'

'Indeed I have. This is most timely. I am glad you have made Mrs Burnett's acquaintance. We are good friends and the Burnett family have given St Ninian's great support over the years. I hope that your paths will cross often once young Fred has made his move to Edinburgh.'

Mrs Burnett held out her hand again to take her leave. As Fred took it in his, it seemed as though her eyes held his just a fraction longer than usual.

'I hope so as well,' was Mrs Burnett's response. 'It has been a pleasure to meet you, Reverend Black. I hope we may see a lot more of you before too long.'

# CHAPTER 17

# CONSEQUENCES

WINTER SLOWLY RELEASED ITS TALONS AND THERE WAS A hint of spring in the air. Mornings were lighter and birdsong promised new beginnings. Cautiously, Fred began to think ahead to a new life in Edinburgh. The visit had gone even better than he had expected and his anxieties about the future had started to recede. There had been little time to dwell on the sadness and remorse he felt about Jessie and he welcomed the distraction.

William Russell had been a most solicitous host and had introduced Fred to several of his friends and colleagues. Despite his social reservations, Fred found himself enjoying lively discussions on politics, architecture and medicinal advances as well as the anticipated conversations on religion and philosophy. He was pleasantly surprised to find men many years his senior seemed interested in his opinions and demonstrated respect and admiration for his youthful achievements. On his return to Aberdeen, he could see much more clearly how he would fit into Edinburgh life in his new role.

William had indicated that the appointment would

undoubtedly be confirmed, but until Fred saw the official letter from the Free Church Council, he would not let himself believe it. However, just a couple of weeks later, Mary-Ann interrupted his early afternoon study with an urgent knock on his door.

'I believe it has come, Fred. Forgive me but I could not wait until you came down. Here, take it.' And Mary-Ann pushed a crisp parchment envelope into Fred's hand.

Breaking open the official seal on the back, Fred sat down again to take in the contents.

*Church of St Andrews,*

*George Street,*

*Edinburgh*

*Fifth of February 1861*

*Dear Reverend Black*

*Following your recent visit to us and having received only the most positive endorsements from Drs Kelman and Russell, it is with the greatest pleasure that, on behalf of the Church Council, I am able to confirm your appointment as assistant minister to the Reverend Dr Russell at St Ninian's Church, with effect from the First of September instant.*

*You have indicated your wish to accept this appointment but I would be obliged if you would please respond to confirm your formal acceptance within the next few days. Upon receipt of your acceptance we will give you full details of your duties and responsibilities as well as your stipend.*

*I remain, dear Reverend Black, your most obedient servant.*

*Reverend James Henderson*

'It is good news, is it not?' exclaimed Mary-Ann with a happy smile on her face.

'Aye, it is, Mary-Ann. The best. I still cannae quite believe it. I feel I should have struggled more.'

'Nonsense, Fred! You have had your struggles already, many years of them. So much hard work and application, you certainly deserve this. I am so proud of you! I can't wait for Richard to return home so you can tell him the good news. I think this calls for a wee celebration. I will have a word with Mrs Milne.'

At the mention of the housekeeper's name, Fred experienced an involuntary lurch in his gut. It was likely she would tell Jessie of this development and Fred, to his chagrin, knew that she would not share his joy and excitement at the news. Since their unhappy meeting at the Kirk, Fred had heard nothing from Jessie. Nor did he expect to. More than once he found himself on the verge of writing to her but reason prevailed and with a heavy heart he replaced the pen in its box and put his stationery away.

'Fred, what do you think?' Mary-Ann was looking at him expectantly. 'Lamb or beef?'

Fred considered Mary-Ann's offer.

'Some beef would be most welcome, Mary-Ann. Thank you.'

'A very good choice. I must not delay if I am to have time to make the necessary preparations.'

About an hour later Fred heard the front door open followed by Richard's voice calling out to his wife in his customary greeting. Fred had nearly completed his studies and, distracted by the news from Edinburgh, decided to join his friends downstairs. He knew that Mary-Ann would be waiting impatiently for him to tell Richard of his new appointment himself. Tidying up his papers and, picking up the letter from Henderson, he left his room and started to descend the staircase.

The door to Mary-Ann's parlour was ajar and Fred could see that the couple were standing close to each other. Mary-Ann was listening intently to her husband with a concerned expression on her face. Something made Fred stop and stand motionless in the hallway. Unwilling to be seen as an eavesdropper, he turned to the hall table and pretended to study some of the periodicals that lay there.

'He doesn't know what to make of it,' Richard was saying to his wife. 'They can't be certain yet, but Helen MacDonald says she noticed the girl was looking paler than usual and seems to be off her food. It may just be an infection of course. We're only just coming out of the winter and these things linger.'

'Oh I do hope so,' Mary-Ann responded. 'She seemed to have settled so well there. There was that unpleasant fellow she had to get away from back in the autumn but surely she would have more sense than to rekindle that relationship?'

Fred had heard enough. Leaning against the hall table he felt ice-cold fear flow through his body from head to toe, rendering him immobile for a moment. Then, just as he was about to retrace his steps back to his room, he heard his name called.

'Fred, don't be shy! Come and join us.'

Richard was holding the door open and smiled warmly at his young colleague. Fred felt physically sick and wondered how he would manage this encounter.

'Are you alright, lad?' queried Richard on seeing Fred's stricken expression.

'Aye, Richard, I, I… seem to have developed a bad head-ache. Too many hours peering at small print.'

Then, remembering the original reason for his arrival, Fred was thankful for the diversion. Following Richard back into the parlour he held out the official letter to the older man.

'Good news, Richard. I have just heard from the Church Council in Edinburgh. They have confirmed my appointment.'

'Wonderful news, Fred, though not unexpected. Many congratulations, my boy!'

Richard held out his hand to shake Fred's.

'Very well deserved, is it not, my dear?' turning to Mary-Ann.

'Indeed it is. I have already taken the liberty of saying we will enjoy a celebratory meal tonight.'

'Forgive me,' Fred interjected. 'My head-ache is troubling me so I will lie down for a short while, if I may, to see if it will pass.'

'Of course, Fred. We must not let a head-ache spoil your moment of triumph.'

As Fred lay on his bed staring up at the ceiling, the irony of Richard's words was not lost on him. It did not feel at all like triumph at this moment. He felt as though he were on a torture rack about to be pulled limb from limb. Was his guilty conscience playing tricks on him? He wanted to be persuaded that Jessie was merely ill or that she had had another liaison, but in his heart Fred knew that this was not the truth. He could not turn his back on her.

But then what of his career? The Edinburgh post was for a single man. He would have to turn down the appointment. What reason would he give? The truth? He would be done for. His mother's hopes, his father's support, all the help and care given him by his dear friends, the Kelmans. He could not let them down either. Unable to control himself, Fred let out a deep groan of anguish.

'Oh God, oh God, I am the wickedest man in the world. What am I to do?'

He should confide his fears to the Kelmans perhaps? That they cared deeply for him he had no doubt, but would they forgive him this betrayal? His heart sank at the thought of their disapproval and disappointment. He could not do it. No, he must bear this on his own. But he was not alone. He would ask God for guidance. He would walk to the Kirk to clear his head and order his thoughts.

Entering the church by a side entrance, Fred walked swiftly to a front pew and sat down, his hands grasped together on his lap. The handsome stained glass window above him denoting the Raising of Lazarus did not uplift him on this occasion. He was weak and cowardly and he suddenly felt out of place in such a hallowed location. Bowing his head, he attempted to pray.

'Dear God, forgive my weakness and my cowardice. I do not deserve another day of peace, miserable sinner that I am. Show me what I am to do, Lord. I had believed my path was set, but now I am full of doubt. Why was I not able to resist sin? Am I that feeble? I pray that You watch over Jessie Duthie and our child, wherever they may be. In penance, I swear that I will renounce marriage with any other and will dedicate my life to the ministry of others. Amen'

Still tormented, Fred sat motionless for a few more minutes, his eyes closed and his hands gripped tightly together. His breath was heavy and laboured as he contemplated what he had just said. Finally, his mind made up, Fred rose from the pew and left the church by the same anonymous side entrance.

He preferred not to disturb Mary-Ann and Richard on his return, so took care to enter quietly and made his way immediately to his first floor room. Alone with his thoughts, Fred decided to reply to Reverend Henderson's letter. Having taken this step, there would be less risk he would go back on his decision, he reasoned. Seated anew at his desk, Fred, smoothed a fresh sheet of writing paper, picked up his pen and started to write.

*St Columba's Manse,*

*Bon Accord Crescent,*

*Aberdeen*

*Twelfth of February 1861*

*Dear Reverend Henderson*

*I thank you most warmly for your letter dated the Fifth of February. I am very happy to accept your kind offer of employment as Assistant Minister of St Ninian's Church. It is a great honour for me that you feel I am able to assist Dr Russell in his holy work and I hope to live up to your expectations of me. I look forward to receiving further details in due course and in the meantime remain, Sir, your most obedient servant.*

*Reverend Frederick Black*

Under his breath, Fred read it back to himself, imagining Henderson and Russell smiling with pleasure and approval upon receiving it. They would have no idea of what was going through the writer's mind at that moment. His heart heavy and fearful that he had made the right choice, Fred folded the letter in three, placed it in an envelope and carefully addressed it. He would not catch today's post therefore he must wait one more day until his fate was sealed.

# CHAPTER 18

# LEAVE TAKING

DESPITE THE SHORT NOTICE, MARY-ANN MANAGED TO organise a fine dinner to celebrate Fred's good news. She succeeded in obtaining a tender piece of Aberdeen Angus topside which had been braised to succulent perfection. Anointed with mustard and horseradish, Richard pronounced this must be the king of meats. Notwithstanding his inner turmoil, Fred found he was hungry and shared Richard's appreciation of Mary-Ann's efforts. Raising his wine glass he turned to his hostess.

'Mary-Ann, I would like to thank you for this splendid dinner. This and indeed all your efforts with me are truly appreciated. Without you and Richard I know I would not be where I am today. Whatever may happen in the future, please know that I am forever in your debt.'

The three drank solemnly from their glasses and then replaced them on the white table-cloth.

'It has been our great pleasure, Fred,' replied Mary-Ann. 'As we have told you before, you are like a son to us. If we have helped in some way for you to achieve your goals that is sufficient reward. We are sure you will not disappoint us.'

'I can only agree wholeheartedly with Mary-Ann's comments,' added Richard. 'And remember our door will always be open to you. Do not become a stranger once you move to Edinburgh.'

'I would never do that!' exclaimed Fred. 'I hope that I may visit you and indeed that you will come to Edinburgh once I am settled.'

The door to the dining room opened and Mrs Milne entered to remove the dishes from the table. Fred looked up and, to his discomfort, caught her eye. To anyone else her expression gave nothing away but Fred could see from her stern gaze and pinched lips that she had something on her mind. Perturbed, he lowered his head and hastily made to finish the remains of the food on his plate.

'Excuse me, Mrs Kelman, I wondered if I should clear the table for ye?' Mrs Milne queried. 'I'm glad ye've enjoyed yer dinner. And if I may offer my congratulations to you, Reverend Black. Ye're awa' tae Edinburgh I hear?'

Startled at her direct approach and, wondering if he was imagining the underlying sarcasm in her tone, Fred was forced to look up again.

'Aye, thank ye, Mrs Milne.'

He was unable to say anything more and a brief silence descended on the group until Mary-Ann rose from her seat to assist Mrs Milne in clearing the table.

'You seem a little down-hearted, Fred,' commented Richard, once the two women had left the room. 'You'll be a bit apprehensive, I dare say, but that is to be expected. Once you get started you will find your feet very quickly, have no fear.'

Fred looked at his dear friend and mentor and for a fleeting moment considered taking him into his confidence. To be able to unburden himself would have been a wonderful solace but, looking at Richard's proud, admiring gaze, he knew he could not do this.

'Yes, I will be very sorry to leave Aberdeen. I have grown to love the city and its inhabitants. It has looked after me well and I will take many good memories with me.'

Fred paused and looked down for a few seconds before continuing.

'But naturally I am excited about my future in Edinburgh as well. And I am looking forward to working with William. It will indeed be a whole new world.'

The following morning, as he was starting work on his studies of the Old Testament prophets for that evening's Bible group, Fred was startled by the sound of his bedroom door opening and closing quietly behind him. Mary-Ann and Richard had announced at breakfast that they would be out for a couple of hours on parish business thus Fred expected to have the house to himself to work undisturbed. Turning round he saw Mrs Milne standing but a few feet from him. Her arms were folded tightly across her ample chest and her normally benign face looked severe. His heart pounding uncomfortably, Fred forced himself to acknowledge her.

'Good morning, Mrs Milne. I was unaware you were in the house. How can I help you?'

'Oh, it is'nae me I'm worried aboot.' There was no preamble or false pleasantries.

'Ye've mebbe already heard aboot Jessie?' Her direct gaze cause Fred to drop his eyes to the dark Turkey carpet beneath his desk.

'Jessie? No I hav'nae heard from her a few weeks.' He muttered. 'Nae' since my visit tae Edinburgh.'

Did his words sound as hollow to Mrs Milne as they did to him, he wondered?

'How is she?'

'Weel, if ye really dinnae ken, she's gang tae hae a bairn!'

'A bairn? Is it true? When?' Fred repeated, gripping his hands tightly to prevent them shaking.

'I dinnae ken. She will'nae say who the faither is, but I hae ma suspicions!'

Mrs Milne had taken a step towards Fred who now raised his hands in front of him as though in self-defence.

'You and your golden words! You're a lucky one, swanning aff tae Edinburgh withoot a care in the world, while she...'

Mrs Milne's voice had risen in her anger.

'She really cared aboot ye and she thought ye cared aboot her an a'. How could ye abandon her?'

'I do care about her,' Fred replied softly, 'But I have always been honest wi' her. I thought she understood the situation...'

'Honest? Honest? How can you sleep at night puttin' yersel' afore a pair lassie and her bairn? Weel, she may nae say onythin' but I hae a lang memory. Dinnae forget that among yer fancy friends in Edinburgh. Hypocrite!'

The final word was spat out with such venom that Fred's heart lurched in alarm but before he could respond, the house-keeper had turned on her heel and was gone.

Alone again Fred could not settle back into his work. His head was full of Mrs Milne's bitter accusations. What was he thinking? He could not ignore this. He had not yet posted his reply to Edinburgh. He must speak with Jessie first and take the risk. Writing a brief note to Mary-Ann explaining that he would be out until lunch-time, Fred picked up his door key and he left the room. In the hall he donned his heavy overcoat and woollen muffler and set his hat firmly upon his head. Satisfied he was ready, Fred left the house before he might change his mind.

He decided to walk to St Nicholas' Manse. It would take about twenty minutes but he could do with the time to assemble his thoughts. He was tired of hearsay and rumour and wanted to have the truth of the matter directly from Jessie. Passing St Columba's, Fred took a left turn down the cobbles of Mount Street. This was quieter than the route by Union Street and there would be less chance of his being seen. He made good time and could hear the St Nicholas bells striking the half hour as he approached the manse. With a flicker of trepidation, he opened the gate and walked up the tiled path towards the entrance.

Shortly after ringing the bell, the front door was opened by Mrs MacDonald.

'Reverend Black. Good morning. What a pleasant surprise! Was James expecting you? I'm afraid he is not here at present.'

'No,' explained Fred, lowering his voice. 'I am here to speak with Miss Duthie if you can spare her for a few minutes.'

'Jessie?' Mrs MacDonald looked surprised. 'I'm afraid you have had a wasted journey. She's no longer with us.'

Seeing Fred's expression of dismay, Mrs MacDonald suggested he come in so she could explain. Showing him into the morning room, blinds drawn against the sunshine, Fred was invited to sit down.

'I thought maybe you had heard already, Reverend Black? But clearly not. Jessie is indisposed and has gone to the countryside. In fact, let me be frank, she is expecting a child. As you can imagine this came as quite a surprise to us.'

Mrs MacDonald composed her features into an expression of concerned disapproval before continuing.

'We did not believe she would land herself in trouble in this way. She seemed determined to make a fresh start with her life. But there we are. But never fear we are not throwing her out, though I daresay many would. No, she has gone to live with another minister and his family near Alford. It is a quiet country place and Jessie will stay there until her child is born. Then we will find adoptive parents for it and she can return to us if she wishes. There are many God-fearing couples who sadly are unable to have bairns of their own and would love to give a fatherless child a good Christian home.'

On hearing Mrs MacDonald's words, Fred nearly cried out in protest but managed to control himself and was overcome with a fit of coughing.

'Reverend Black, let me fetch you a glass of water.'

'No need, thank you. I am recovered now. I was startled at your news. I came to tell Jessie that I have just been given a new appointment in Edinburgh and will go there in the summer. As I feel responsible for bringing Jessie to this neighbourhood I wanted to tell her myself. But it seems I am too late.'

'Why do you not write to her? She is fairly literate now, thanks to your efforts. I am sure she would appreciate knowing your plans.'

'That is a good idea. Do you have her address by any chance?'

'I do not, I'm afraid. It is near Alford, that much I do know. But if you write to her here, we will ensure that your letter is passed on to her. I believe James is planning on going to visit her later this week to check on her welfare.'

Mrs MacDonald waited for Fred's response to her suggestion with a small smile of encouragement.

'Aye, that will have to do. You will make sure she gets it though? I do not want to leave the city without hearing from her.'

'Of course, you have my word, Reverend Black.'

Fred returned home dejectedly. The adrenalin he had felt when he had made his decision to see Jessie had abated with the disappointment of Mrs MacDonald's news and was now replaced with a deep sense of sadness. This should never have happened. He longed to have Jessie beside him once again so that he could make amends. What must she think of him? He would write to her and give her the chance to keep her baby. Tell her that they would be married and he would forgo the move to Edinburgh. He thought of his own fatherless childhood and knew that he did not want that for his own child.

Fred was relieved to see that the Kelmans had not yet returned from their parish visits. He did not feel up to explanations at this moment. Returning his coat and hat to the cloakroom, Fred went up to his room to write immediately to Jessie.

*My Dearest Jessie*

Now he paused and looked at the blank sheet of paper in front of him. There was so much he wanted to say and to know. Their last meeting had not been a success. Why would she trust him now?

*You may be surprised to hear from me after our last meeting. Forgive me for letting you down. It will not happen again. I am writing as I have heard from both Mrs Milne and Mrs MacDonald that you are with child. I believe I must be the father. Therefore I must take responsibility. I realise I have been cowardly and selfish up until now, thinking only of my own future. Forgive me, Jess. I am just a scared young man, that is the truth of it, but I can only imagine how you are feeling.*

*What I want to say to you, Jessie, is that I will marry you if you will have me. I want to provide for you and our child. Please do not feel you have to give your child away. I cannot promise what life will hold for us but I swear I will be a good husband to you and a loving father to our child.*

*Please write soon as you can, my dear Jess, so that I can make plans for our future. I do not have your address in the country so am entrusting this to Reverend MacDonald who I believe will visit you from time to time. You may reply directly to me at Bon Accord Crescent.*

*I long to hear from you and send you all my love.*

*Fred*

Fred realised he would not hear from Jessie for some time. But as the days passed with no news, Fred grew increasingly agitated. He wished he could go to visit her and settle the matter once and for all but this, of course, was impossible. He hated the deception he was forced to endure and found it more and more difficult to discuss his move to Edinburgh with Richard and Mary-Ann with any enthusiasm. They must be wondering at his distraction and low mood, much as he tried to hide it.

Then one morning, Reverend MacDonald paid them a visit. Purely a social call he stated as he had been passing. Pleasantries were exchanged and he asked after Fred's planned departure for Edinburgh. Then, as the visitor stood up to take his leave, he spoke.

'By the way, young Miss Duthie has come to her senses at

last. She will let the bairn be adopted after all. A wise decision. We hope that she has learned from the error of her ways. What a business!'

Fred was unable to say a word. His heart felt leaden and he wondered if he would ever feel positive about anything ever again. There had been no mention of his letter and he was unable to question the Reverend MacDonald about it. Had Jessie received it? Helen MacDonald had promised him. Should he assume Jessie had decided she would be better off without him and without their child? Why would she not write to let him know? There was no way of knowing.

'Well, thank you for your hospitality, my friends,' MacDonald smiled at the assembled company. 'I must be on my way. I hope to see you, Fred, before you leave for Edinburgh.'

Fred nodded, the unspoken question filling his head. Then Mary-Ann and Richard accompanied the visitor to the front door and bade him farewell.

# PART TWO

# AULD REEKIE

# CHAPTER I

# A NEW LIFE

EDINBURGH – SEPTEMBER 1861

IT WAS LATE AFTERNOON BY THE TIME THE ABERDEEN TRAIN finally pulled into Waverley Station. Fred Black bade goodbye to his travelling companions and pulled his leather case down from the luggage rack above him. It landed with a thud on the floor of the compartment and he smiled apologetically.

'It nearly had my toes there!'

In truth he was relieved to have arrived at his destination only half an hour later than advertised. A sudden, fierce autumn storm had raged over the east coast the previous couple of days and there had been fears that all travel might be seriously disrupted. There had been talk of landslides and pools of water covering the tracks and of the sea being too high for the ferry across the Forth to leave the harbour. As a precaution, a telegram had been sent to Edinburgh to warn Dr Russell of his uncertain and late arrival.

Fortunately, such fears proved to be unfounded and now Fred found himself, a little after five o'clock, on the platform of Waverley Station looking about him. His trunk had been sent in advance so all that was required was to seek a cab to take him on the last short leg of his journey to Melville Street. With his bag gripped firmly in one hand, Fred set off down the platform towards the station exit. A sharp east wind blew, diluting the sickly smell of hops from the nearby brewery and the acrid taste of coal smoke which hung in the air. East Windy, indeed, thought Fred with a slight shiver. Surveying the hansom cab rank he saw he would have no difficulty in finding transport to his final destination. Approaching the first one in the line, he gave his address to the driver and climbed in. The driver clicked instructions to his horse and the carriage moved off down Princes Street towards the West End.

Amid all this change and activity, however, Fred had been unable to get the memory of Jessie Duthie out of his head. What should have been a triumphant and exciting time for him was in fact overshadowed with sadness and worry and a feeling of guilt that he had let her down. Her sad, tearful face, the last time they met, continued to haunt him. He had received no reply from Jessie to his letter and felt unable to insist on more news of her from the MacDonalds. He had no choice, therefore, but to turn his mind and thoughts to the new life which beckoned in Edinburgh.

Pulling up at the junction with Hanover Street, the cab paused for a moment and Fred glanced out of the window at the crowds on the pavement beyond. Suddenly, with a jolt of shock, his eye was caught by the figure of a young woman. Soft brown hair escaping from a cheap felt bonnet. An unadorned dark grey coat with a plaid shawl wrapped carelessly around the shoulders, she seemed out of place among the largely bourgeois pedestrians of Princes Street. Head down, she pushed her way doggedly through the throng. Fred leaned forward vainly to see her face. It could not be, could it? He must not let this moment pass. There might not be another opportunity. At any moment the cab would move on and Jessie, if indeed it was she, would be lost in the crowd.

'Driver, driver, forgive me!' Fred had opened the window and called out urgently to the coachman. Initially to Fred's frustration, the driver appeared to have not heard Fred's entreaty. Fred repeated his call and with relief saw the man turn his face towards him.

'Can ye pull over for a few moments, please? Ah've seen an acquaintance I am anxious tae speak tae.'

With some grumbling, the cabbie pulled his horse and coach over.

'Ye'd better nae dae a runner! I've yer trunk here, mind.'

'Dinnae worry, Sir, I'll nae be long.'

And Fred flung open the cab door and jumped out to join the crowd outside. Where was she? He was starting to feel foolish. But he had to be sure. Then some feet in front of him he caught sight of the woman, straightening her hat and looking about her. Excusing himself to other pedestrians, Fred pushed forward until he could reach out an arm to touch the woman's shoulder.

'Whit's the matter, man?'

Her response was immediate and indignant as she spun round to face Fred. Same height, same figure, same hair, but it was not Jessie. Of course it wasn't. Fred dropped his arm to his side and started to apologise.

'I beg yer pardon, Madam.'

'Are ye bein' sarcastic?' The woman's voice rose shrilly. Fred just wanted to disappear.

'No, not at a'. Ah thocht ye wis someone else. Sorry tae bother ye.'

'Ah well.'

The woman, mollified, sniffed and shrugged, and grasping the plaid shawl about her, started to move away. A few seconds later, she was lost from view. Mortified, Fred pressed back towards where the cab was still awaiting him.

'Sorry, it wisnae her,' Fred explained and climbed back into the security of the little hansom.

'Right ye are. It'll cost ye extra, mind. Ah've lost five minutes.'

This would not do, Fred, chastised himself. Once he was settled at St Ninian's he would try again to discover Jessie's whereabouts. But for now, he must try to concentrate on his new circumstances and his new responsibilities.

Forcing himself back to reality he looked about him. Though it was only a matter of months since his last visit, Fred was impressed anew with the elegant façade of the manse in Melville Street, far removed from the hustle and bustle, grime and smells of the Old Town just the other side of Princes Street. The hansom cab clattered to a stop outside and while Fred put a hand into his pocket for the fare, the driver jumped down to open the door. No doubt alerted by the activity outside, the front door opened to reveal William Russell, his hands held out in smiling welcome.

'Greetings, Fred my boy! We feared we might not see you today after all. Come in, you must be exhausted.'

With relief, Fred stepped over the thresh-hold into the tiled hallway. A small fire was burning in the grate giving some welcome warmth to an otherwise cold vestibule. Above Fred's head curled a mahogany bannister where the stairs led to the upper floors just visible through the metal spars of the staircase. Already his travelling bag had been taken up by the house-boy. For a moment Fred felt he could have done this himself, but he was interrupted by his host who beckoned him into a small parlour on the right.

'Mrs Oliphant will bring us some tea so you can catch your breath before dinner,' explained William, inviting Fred to sit down in one of the armchairs positioned on either side of the fireplace.

'Well, it is very good to have you here, after all this time. How are you feeling, Fred?'

'It is a great honour and responsibility, William, but I am most excited and looking forward to fulfilling your expectations of me.'

'I have no doubt of that, Fred. We will be able to discuss things at more leisure over dinner but tomorrow morning I would like to introduce you formally to the congregation at St

Ninian's. They are very much looking forward to meeting you, you will be pleased to hear.'

William smiled affectionately then his face grew solemn again.

'One sad change however I must warn about is in regard to the Burnett family. You may recall meeting Mrs Burnett when you were last here?'

'Aye, indeed I do. A most charming, sensitive lady. She had her worries I remember.'

'Yes she did and very sadly they were well-founded. Her little boy had scarlet fever and seemed to be recovering well, but then there was a seizure and his poor little heart could not cope. He died just a few days after you met her. It is tragic and has affected us all.'

William sighed and looked down at his hands.

'At times like this, despite one's faith, one can feel so impotent. It is difficult to persuade people that such cruel episodes must be accepted as the will of God.'

'Ah, no! That is heart-breaking. The poor woman - and her family. She had already lost one child I believe?'

'Aye. That too. Maurice and now George. The whole family are devastated and Margaret is taking it particularly badly. I go as often as I can to sit with her and talk to her, but she seems to be shut away in her own world at the moment.'

'Well, if I can help in any way, I would be happy to do so.'

'Thank you, Fred. I will bear that in mind.'

Later that evening, dinner having been eaten and the two men having talked until nearly eleven p.m., Fred finally bade his host goodnight and retired for the night. William's news about little George Burnett had greatly unsettled him and he felt so badly for the family and especially Mrs Burnett. Though their meeting had been brief, he had been struck by her sensitive demeanour and indeed her kindness towards him. Life was indeed cruel and unpredictable. At times it was difficult to read meaning into such events.

Unpacking the last of his personal effects, Fred took out the small red Morocco leather-bound edition of the Psalms that had been a parting gift from Mary-Ann. Inside the front cover, carefully inscribed in her elegant hand, Fred read her message

*To my dear friend Frederick Black, may he always be guided and protected by Your good words in this world and the next. Mary Ann Kelman – St Columba's Manse, September 1861.*

He wished she was just downstairs at that moment so he could unburden himself of his worries and concerns. But he would have to make do with his memories of her wise counsel instead. Opening the little volume at random, in the flickering light, Fred peered down and softly read out loud.

"*Lord hear my prayer and let my cry have speedy access unto Thee.*"

"And let me have Thy answer, Lord!"

Tucked into the back of the book, an off-white slip of paper caught Fred's eye - Jessie's last letter to him. Pulling it out, he scanned the lines.

*'..so that one day I can make you proud of me..'*

So honest and trusting. Oh, where are you now, Jess?

After staring at the page for a few more seconds, deep in thought, Fred finally refolded the sheet and returned it to its resting place. Closing the book and shutting his eyes, he mouthed a silent prayer before replacing the volume by his bed, extinguishing the candle and laying down to sleep.

She was standing directly in front of him, wearing the dress she had been loaned by Mary-Ann for the ceilidh. But there was no festive joy in her expression. Utter grief shattered her features, her eyes obscured by tears. She said nothing but held out the limp body of a dead baby.

# CHAPTER 2

# NEW COLLEGE

Awaking in shock, his heart pounding, at first Fred believed he was still in his old room in Aberdeen. In vain he sought out the familiar comforting furnishings of the past few years. In the dim light, alien shapes loomed into view. A fireplace with pale marble surround, a high mahogany chest of drawers, an upholstered armchair. Breathing heavily, Fred attempted to calm himself. Of course, he was now at Melville Street. It had been a dream, a bad dream. With so many emotions flooding through him it was not surprising. But the vision of Jessie had seemed so real. He could have sworn she had been in this room just moments before. He could have just reached out and touched her. And the child? What did this mean?

Sleep was now impossible. Fred threw off the bedclothes that covered him and stepped out of bed. Dawn was beginning to break and some welcome day-light had crept around the side of the wooden shutters. With a shaking hand, his heart still thumping, Fred sought out a match to light the little oil lamp on the desk. His first attempt failed and he threw the spent stub down in frustration. He needed some light in this room. The figure of Jessie was still far too real in his mind and he had to see for himself the empty room in all its utilitarian plainness.

Finally the lamp was lit and Fred sat down at the table to compose himself. Was he to be hounded by his imagination or his guilt wherever he went? He must seek her out to see how she fared. Without this certain knowledge, Fred knew he would never be free. Sitting at the desk, he closed his eyes and held his hands to his temples. How was he to achieve this? Then raising his head, Fred's eye was caught by Mary-Ann's leaving gift to him, lying on the bedside table where he had left it. A Bible, or a book of prayers, that would be fitting. Jessie had been his pupil after all. He would inscribe it in an affectionate but professional manner. Why should he not wish her well in her life? That would not raise suspicion.

The decision made, Fred now felt calmer. Outside the sun was rising and the coo of a wood pigeon echoed down the chimney. Although a fire was made up, it would only be lit when the temperature dropped substantially. Thus far September had been a mild month and the expense of fuel had been spared. Clad only in his night-clothes, Fred shivered and yawned. The longcase clock in the hall struck six, echoed almost immediately by the higher silver tones of the dining room clock. It would be a couple of hours before breakfast. He would return to bed and attempt to sleep.

Fred was awoken for the second time by the sound of Mrs Oliphant's voice greeting him and a harsh clatter as the shutters were folded back.

'Good morning to you, Reverend Black. How have you slept on your first night here? Well, I hope? Breakfast will be served in half an hour. Will you have one egg or two?'

Barely waiting for Fred's mumbled response, Mrs Oliphant departed as efficiently as she had arrived. Rolling on to his back and staring up at the pale blue ceiling above his head, Fred tried to recall the night terror he had experienced just a few hours before. He was determined to lay spectres to rest. He would speak to

William today and ask how he might be able to contact specific members of the ministry regarding an item he wished to return to its rightful owner.

'Well you would need to check the ledgers at New College,' was William's immediate response upon hearing Fred's question.

'I do not want to put you to any trouble, William. You have no doubt more important matters to attend to than helping me with my quest.'

'Well that is true, Fred, but I was planning on taking you there myself tomorrow, anyway. I will be happy to show you where to look. Alford you say? Not many in that area – maybe three or four.'

'That is most kind, William, but I insist you do not wait for me. It is sufficient that you have shown me where to look.'

Fred heard his own voice in amazement. Was he really such an accomplished liar that he sounded so totally at ease?

'I have some matters that I need to look into, Fred, so never fear I won't be looking over your shoulder.'

'That was not what I meant!' Fred feared he sounded too defensive but William merely smiled and changed the subject.

Thus on Monday morning, shortly after ten o'clock, William and Fred set off from the manse to walk the mile or so to New College. The weather had turned misty and the smell of hops from Youngers' brewery hung heavy in the air. Walking briskly up to Queensferry Road then along Princes Street before heading up the Mound, the two men made it to the heavy front door of their destination by twenty past ten. Fred glanced up at the soaring turrets above them. Though it was barely twenty years old, this building, representing the new Free Church, was already an unmissable landmark.

'We've made good time, Fred, so you won't be rushed in your research. I will present you to the staff and then leave you to your own devices. I'll see you back at Melville Street for luncheon.'

William greeted the dark-suited clerk in the entrance hall and introduced him to Fred.

'Good morning, Wishart. How are things with you today?'

The man nodded and smiled.

'This is my new colleague and assistant, Reverend Black. He would like access to the ministerial registers for a couple of hours. I hope you can help him find what he is looking for. No doubt he will be a frequent visitor to New College now that he is settled in the city.'

'Aye, certainly, Dr Russell. He will need to put his details in the visitors' book and if you would be kind enough to sign his application then I can issue him with his visitors' pass.'

'There you are, Fred. What could be simpler?'

After he had been shown into the cavernous Records Office, Fred looked about him. The vaulted ceiling was heavily timbered and decorated to resemble a medieval hall. For all that it was recently built, Fred felt a sense of destiny and history all around him. The red leather ledgers were lined up on solid wooden shelves, divided, he had been informed, by diocese and then alphabetically. He approached the nearest shelf and ran his fingers along the spines of the volumes. From Aberdeen, Orkney and Argyll to Dunblane, Dunkeld and Galloway, all of Scotland was there, even its most far-flung territories.

Fred wondered what it would be like to preach in Orkney, Shetland or the outer Western Isles. You would be such a hostage to nature, adverse weather and natural calamities, would you not? Would the word of God hold firm in such an environment? But in Orkney at least where the magnificent St Magnus Cathedral had been constructed more than seven hundred years earlier, it proved that faith was strong. One day it would be an honour to visit such a place. But for now Fred had a calling closer to home.

Peering more closely at the lettering on the spine of the ledgers, Fred found the volume A – E and carefully lifted it from its resting place. Judging by the dust on the top of the book, it had lain undisturbed for quite some time. Placing it on to one of the oak tables in the Registry, Fred pulled up a leather chair and sat down. Despite having studied for so long in Aberdeen, he was unfamiliar with many of the parishes in the countryside. Mrs MacDonald had been quite clear that Jessie had gone to the Alford area so it would be here he should start.

The heavy parchment pages smelt musty and were discoloured in places with dark damp spots. Despite this, fastidious handwriting clearly recorded each cleric and his tenure from the construction of his church to the present day. Fred gently pressed the pages open and ran his finger down the first column. There were three entries – Tullynessle, Keig and Cluny. The present incumbents were the Reverends Richard Grierson, James Anderson and David Gordon. He would begin by writing to them. All were remote country parishes where Jessie might be kept hidden until after her confinement. And if these failed to offer any clarity? There were three other churches somewhat further away in Tillyfourie, Monymusk and Lumsden. They would be his back-up Fred decided. Noting down the names and addresses he should contact, Fred's thoughts turned to Jessie's life since he had last seen her. Was she being well-treated? Empathy and understanding towards an unmarried pregnant woman were in short supply in too many Christian households, Fred reflected sadly.

'Sorry tae disturb ye, Reverend Black.'

Fred's ruminations were disturbed by the voice of Mr Wishart, the register clerk.

'I wondered if ye needed ony help wi' the registers? Did ye find whit ye were looking for?'

'Aye, thank ye, I'm nearly done now,' came Fred's reply. 'Just a few more minutes should do it.'

'Right ye are, Sir. I'll speak tae ye later.'

The interruption served to hasten Fred's actions and dipping the pen in the ink-well a second time, he finished writing down the information he had sought. Blotting the piece of paper, Fred waved it once or twice to ensure it was dry. Then with care the paper was folded in four and placed in his pocket. The heavy red register was returned to the shelf, no doubt to sit undisturbed for another decade, and Fred turned towards the exit.

'A pleasure to make yer acquaintance, Sir,' smiled Mr Wishart, handing him a small card. 'Keep it in a safe place and bring it with you every time you wish to use our facilities. I hope to see you again soon.'

'Thank you for your assistance, Mr Wishart. I wish you a good day.'

Stepping through the doors and down the steps to the street outside, Fred stopped to admire the panorama in front of him. The early mist had cleared and now, stretching above the rooftops of Edinburgh, over the waters of the Firth of Forth to the hills of Fife and Perthshire beyond, it was possible to see for fifty miles at least. It was one of the most beautiful and uplifting things Fred had ever seen. He could barely believe that he was now to live and work in this city. That he had won this opportunity. There and then he closed his eyes and threw his hands up skywards, thanking God from the bottom of his heart.

'Fred Black – what a coincidence! Preaching to the city now I see.'

Fred opened his eyes and to his surprise and embarrassment saw the stocky figure of Reverend James MacDonald standing smiling on the pavement in front of him.

'Reverend MacDonald! I did not expect to see you here. Forgive me, I was carried away by the view.'

'I'm down frae Aberdeen for a few days. Research and meeting with colleagues and such like. And you? I had heard you had left for your new post. How are you settling in, Fred?'

'Very well so far, thank you. It was a long journey but Dr Russell has been most kind and helpful to me.'

'And you are discovering the treasures of our wonderful New College I see?'

Fred did not want to be drawn into further conversation with his colleague. No doubt he was here purely coincidentally as he had explained, but, given his own reason for visiting New College, Fred was feeling increasingly uncomfortable in MacDonald's presence.

'Yes indeed, Dr Russell was kind enough to bring me this morning to introduce me to the staff. I am sure I will be returning often. But, alas, I must now return to the manse as there is much for me to do. I am sure you understand, Reverend MacDonald?'

'Of course, my dear boy. I have only a few hours here myself and will be leaving Edinburgh tomorrow. I will mention you to the Kelmans when I next see them. Preaching to the city indeed!'

Chuckling under his breath, Reverend MacDonald raised a hand in farewell and proceeded to climb the steps up to the entrance of New College. Fred, meantime, turned with relief to the street and began his descent down the Mound on his return to Melville Street. He wanted to write those letters without delay.

# CHAPTER 3

# LOST PROPERTY

FRED MADE GOOD TIME AND ARRIVED BACK AT MELVILLE Street by midday. He was still feeling unsettled by his unexpected meeting with James MacDonald. There had been something in the man's familiar manner towards him that had rankled. While he was the younger man and in no way self-important, he hoped, nonetheless Fred felt the minister from Aberdeen could have spoken to him in a more professional manner. But then again, Fred reminded himself, what was MacDonald to make of him standing on the steps of New College with his arms in the air? He was taking this too seriously – or perhaps it was his guilty conscience reading too much into the encounter.

Stepping up to the entrance of No. 17, Fred felt for the latch key William had given him the day before and let himself in. This gave him such a satisfactory feeling of belonging and achievement that he stopped for a moment in the hall to savour it. Then, remembering the morning's errand, he headed up the stair to his room. He would draft a letter before lunch.

His room was on the second floor and overlooked the back of

the building. It was larger than his accommodation in Aberdeen, with two windows overlooking a small drying green. A large copper beech stood majestically some distance away and beyond that was the mews serving the road. It would be quiet enough for work, study and prayer, Fred reflected gratefully.

Fishing into his jacket pocket, Fred withdrew the sheet of paper he had completed at New College. He laid it on his desk and smoothed out the folds. Should he write to all six possible manses or wait to hear from the three closest? Let that decision wait for now. Firstly he needed to decide what he was going to say by way of explanation. How should he introduce himself? After a couple of minutes' contemplation and satisfied that he had a credible reason for writing, Fred picked up his pen to draft the letter.

*My dear Sir,*

*I am trying to trace a Miss Jessie Duthie who I believe may have resided with you for a short while? She was a pupil of mine for some months when she lived in Aberdeen and I have some property of hers which I am anxious to return to her as soon as possible. If you are able to give me any information as to her whereabouts I would be most grateful.*

*I remain, Sir, your faithful servant,*

*Reverend Frederick Black*

Fred had just leant back to scrutinise his efforts when, in the background, he became aware of the muffled ring of the dinner gong. Luncheon was about to be served. Placing the drafted letter face down on his desk, Fred stood up and left the room.

The dining room was a handsome high-ceilinged room on the ground floor. Fred took in the portraits hanging on the wall. Stern and inscrutable, the earlier incumbents of Melville Manse stared out solemnly at him, hair, whiskers and attire changing with the decades. In due course William and perhaps even he would join them. The dining table was simply laid for two. Fred sat down at his place and shook out the heavy white napkin that lay on the table cloth in front of him.

'Good afternoon, Sir,' Mrs Oliphant greeted him. 'I have received word that Dr Russell will be late and you are to start without him.'

'Thank you, Mrs Oliphant, nothing serious I trust?'

'I'm afraid it is, but we are not sure if anything can be done. It concerns Mrs Burnett. Dr Russell told you about poor, wee George, I believe?'

'He did – I was so very sorry to hear it. My heart goes out to them all. Mrs Burnett is taking it very badly I understand.'

'Aye, she is, poor lady. And she's become a wee bit dependent on her medicine, I hear.'

'Her medicine? Is she sick?'

'No' sick in the normal sense. More in her heart and soul. It's laudanum.' At this point, Mrs Oliphant took a step closer to Fred and lowered her voice. 'Once it gets its claws into ye it is hard tae get away. My cousin ….'

Fred felt he did not want to hear any more and sought to bring the conversation to a close.

'I have heard of it, of course,' he interrupted. 'A very sorry business, Mrs Oliphant. Well, if anyone can comfort Mrs Burnett it must be Dr Russell. I will no doubt hear more when he returns. Might I have some soup now, please? My walk this morning has given me quite an appetite.'

'Of course, Sir, sorry to ramble on, but it is an upsetting business.'

Mrs Oliphant concluded the conversation and placed a bowl of Scotch broth in front of Fred.

'There is cold mutton and vegetables on the side board for you to help yourself and I will bring you the dessert later on. If you need anything further, please ring the bell.'

'Thank you, Mrs Oliphant. You are very kind.'

The housekeeper left the room and Fred turned to his soup, deep in thought. Troubles in life were no respecter of class or wealth, he contemplated. While his own mother had had a hard life of toil and poverty, she had not lost her only child and had him to comfort her in her old age. No doubt Margaret Burnett would gladly give up her fortune to have her two sons restored to her.

As he scooped up the last of the barley and carrot at the bottom of his soup plate, Fred heard voices in the hall and a moment later, William looked into the dining room and greeted him.

'Fred, my apologies. I was detained on a pastoral matter. I will join you in a few minutes.'

This was already turning into a more eventful lunch than he had anticipated. While he wanted to hear what William had to say, at the same time Fred was anxious to complete his letters to the Aberdeenshire clergy.

'I'm glad to see you started without me.' William had returned to the room and had seated himself opposite Fred. 'How did your visit to New College go? I hope you found what you were looking for?'

'Aye, indeed, William. It was all very well documented and I found several addresses which potentially could help me. Thank you very much for your help. Curiously,' Fred continued, 'I ran into James MacDonald, from Aberdeen, as I was leaving. I fear I may have made a bit of a fool of myself.'

'Really? How could that be?'

Fred related his encounter with the Referend MacDonald.

'I am surprised to hear it,' was William's response. 'Generally colleagues only come to Edinburgh once or twice a year. As you know yourself it is not the easiest nor shortest of journeys. Mostly it would be for the General Assembly in May. But perhaps he had other business to deal with. I would not concern yourself with it, Fred.'

The two men fell into a companionable silence as William crumbled a bread roll between his fingers and Fred finished the cold meat on his plate.

'Would you care to tell me about Mrs Burnett, William?' asked

Fred, after the house-keeper had departed. 'Or is it a confidential matter, in which case I beg your pardon.'

William sighed and replaced the soup spoon on his plate.

'Naturally it is a very sensitive matter, Fred, but I can rely on you to keep it to yourself. Poor woman. I am very worried. And her husband, David, is beside himself. She really feels life is not worth living. I so wish I could bring some lasting comfort to the family but so far, I regret to say, I am failing.'

William looked so sombre and sad that, for a moment, Fred feared he had reduced his friend to tears.

'Her moods change, so that her family finds it very difficult to support her. It is fortunate that the house is so well run by their staff that they keep everything functioning smoothly despite the troubles. But it is taking its toll on the other children who, I daresay, feel they have lost their mother. We must pray that better times are to come.'

'I am so very sorry to hear this, William. If I can be of any help, please let me know.'

'I will, Fred, thank you. But now you probably have work to do. I have kept you long enough.'

Later that afternoon, as the sun was beginning to sink lower in the autumnal sky and a dampness settled on the city, Fred completed his letters and helped himself to postage stamps from the inlaid Indian box on the hall table. Stepping out on to the pavement he turned right towards Princes Street. Office clerks and managers were starting to make their way home after a long day spent crouching over ledgers and files in the various legal and financial offices in the West End. Fred barely noticed them as he headed for the pillar box at the corner of Melville Street and Queensferry Road. In his hand he held six identical letters addressed to Aberdeenshire ministers who might, or might not, hold the key to his quest.

The letters safely posted, Fred noted it was not yet four thirty. He decided to extend his walk and visit MacFarlane and Reid in

Princes Street. Quizzing Mrs Oliphant earlier, she had confirmed that this establishment was the best source of good quality Bibles and prayer books, especially if they were to be a gift. He would seek one out for Jessie which, God willing, he would be able to present to her in person before too long. If he hurried, he would have time before it closed.

# CHAPTER 4

# CONFRONTATION

His letters safely posted, Fred allowed himself some optimism that finally he might be about to discover Jessie's whereabouts and at last make contact with her. He was beginning to feel more at home in Edinburgh and settled in his new life. His first sermons had been well received and William had said it would only be a matter of time until he might be asked to preach at other churches as well. When time allowed, he sought to familiarise himself with the city. Walking up to the brooding cliffs of the Castle, along the cobbled High Street to Holyrood Palace, then up to the Salisbury Crags, where, buffeted by the wind and unheard by anyone, he shouted his thanks to God for his good fortune.

But as time passed and a third week came and went without any news from Aberdeenshire, Fred once again felt himself falling into despondency. Until he received some news of Jessie, there would continue to be a nagging worry and an emptiness in his heart. One day after returning from his afternoon constitutional, Fred's hopes were raised by the sight of a letter addressed to him with an Aberdeen postmark. But on closer inspection, he recognised dear Mary-Ann's hand-writing and, indeed, it had been a warm and friendly letter enquiring after him and giving him local news of old friends and colleagues. He felt badly that he should be in any way disappointed to receive this. He would reply that very afternoon to show his appreciation.

Seated at his desk, reminiscing on his old life in Aberdeen, Fred became aware of activity and the sound of urgent voices in the hall. Rising from his chair, he walked across the room and opened his bedroom door a few inches.

'I am so sorry, Mr Donaldson, but Dr Russell is away for a few days. He will return on Wednesday.' The housekeeper's voice sounded apologetic.

'She needs some comfort and advice before then, Mrs Oliphant. Forgive me for disturbing you without warning but the Master is desperate. Only Dr Russell seems to be able to get through to her.'

'I am deeply sorry to hear that,' Mrs Oliphant continued. 'I wish I could help but…'

Fred stepped on to the landing and called down to the figures below.

'Pardon my intrusion but I could not help over-hearing. May I be of assistance? I am not Dr Russell of course but in his absence I would be happy to help if I can.'

Mrs Oliphant and Mr Donaldson stopped talking and turned their heads up to where Fred was standing. Now he started to descend the stairs towards them.

'May I be of assistance?' Fred repeated.

'That is very kind of you, Sir,' Mr Donaldson responded. 'It is the Mistress who is in need of support. Since young Master George's death ….'

'I am aware of the difficult situation, Mr Donaldson,' reassured Fred, not wanting to increase the man's strain. 'Please let me speak to her, or at least try. She should not be without spiritual solace until Wednesday.'

'Very well, Sir, would you be able to accompany me now?'

'Give me a couple of minutes and I will join you.'

It took the two men only a few minutes in the carriage before it turned into Charlotte Square and drew up in front of a grand porticoed house built in the classical style. For a moment Fred's courage deserted him as he stared up at this overwhelming edifice and wondered what kind of reception he would meet inside. Mrs Burnett had been most charming at their last and only meeting but much had changed since that day.

'Just wait there, Sir, and I will let Mr Burnett know you are here in Dr Russell's stead.'

The coachman came round to hold the horse's head as Donaldson jumped down on to the pavement. Then Donaldson approached the wide black door and disappeared inside. Fred tried to calm his apprehension and wondered if he would have been better to have left the whole matter to William. He was beginning to curse his optimistic enthusiasm that he would be able to calm this poor lady where others had failed. He turned his head away from the house and took in the spacious garden square opposite. Enclosed by black iron railings, within were planted bushy little rowan trees, their orange berries providing a bright note of colour on a grey day, while beneath them the grass was scuffed with curling yellow leaves. How pleasant to have such an amenity to enjoy at one's leisure, Fred reflected, far from anything difficult or disagreeable.

'You are to come in, Sir.' Mr Donaldson had returned and was now holding out his hand to aid Fred's descent from the carriage. 'Please follow me.'

On entering Fred found himself in a large square hallway. It was light enough thanks to the large semi-circular window above the front door and two side windows. Black and white marble tiles covered the floor and a handsome circular oak table stood at the centre on which were arranged a beautiful display of multi-coloured dahlias.

'Let me take your coat and hat, Sir,' invited Mr Donaldson

before leading Fred upstairs to the drawing room where David Burnett awaited him.

'Thank you for coming so quickly, Reverend Black.'

Mr Burnett took a step towards Fred holding out his hand in welcome.

'I was pleased to meet you the other day after service and I believe you met Mrs Burnett a few months ago before you moved here permanently and before .... our great loss.'

Mr Burnett stopped speaking and looked at the floor, pinching his lips tightly together.

'Indeed so, Mr Burnett. I offer my deepest condolences and am at your disposal.'

'Thank you, Sir.' David Burnett raised his head again and looked at Fred with brown eyes full of sadness. 'Come, let us sit while I explain how our situation is. Needless to say this is in the strictest confidence and must stay between us and Dr Russell. My wife has become addicted to laudanum. There is no point beating about the bush. The tipping point from occasional support to full reliance is easily reached, alas, and these last few months have proved most trying for her, poor darling. She is only able to cope by taking increasing draughts of the substance.'

Fred started to offer his sympathy but Mr Burnett held up his hand to stop him.

'Forgive me, but you must let me finish. I find it hard enough to articulate these words without breaking down. For short periods therefore she is calmed but the cravings come ever sooner and her agitation and distress, until she can next take a draught, grow ever more extreme. If I insist on preventing her access, she grows angry with me, which I find unbearable. Therefore I have to distance myself. Only Dr Russell has been able to reason with her. I do not know how she will react to your presence. Do not be offended if she refuses to see you. It is important that you know this. You are a young man and I daresay have not encountered such issues before?'

'Thank you enlightening me, Mr Burnett, and I am honoured

that you have taken me into your confidence. Rest assured not a word will pass my lips on the matter.'

'Thank you, Reverend Black. Now I will go and let my wife know you are here. Please make yourself comfortable while I am gone.'

Once again Fred was left alone with his anxiety and thoughts about the mission he had undertaken. Sitting on the edge of an upright sofa he looked about him. The drawing room was an elegant high-ceilinged chamber with long windows overlooking the square outside. The walls, painted a restful shade of duck-egg blue, were hung with gilt-framed paintings of the countryside and social groups. Everything about the room spoke to Fred of taste, money and social standing, from the intricate classical cornice around the ceiling to the languid portrait of a young woman in grey satin above the fireplace, who seemed to be appraising him coolly. Who was she, he wondered?

'She says she will see you. I have managed to persuade her. Please follow me.' David Burnett had returned and addressed Fred.

Fred stood up and did as his host requested. Now he found himself outside a closed door towards the back of the house.

'This is my study. It will be quieter and more private,' Mr Burnett explained. 'When you want to take your leave, please rejoin me in the drawing room.'

Then he knocked softly on the door, opened it a couple of inches and announced Fred's arrival to his wife.

Though Fred had resolved not to show any surprise or shock in front of Margaret Burnett, nonetheless her appearance today in comparison to his memory of her elegant and dignified presence only a few months ago, caused him to stop suddenly. She was sitting motionless on a low chair and appeared not to have noticed him. No attempt had been made to tidy her coiffure, which was dishevelled and fell in unkempt straggles on to her shoulders. The woman's cheeks seemed unnaturally pink and beneath her eyes were deep dark circles. She wore a loose fitting house coat which she held fast with one hand.

'Good morning, Mrs Burnett,' started Fred softly. 'Thank you for agreeing to see me. I apologise for Dr Russell's absence but he is out of town until Wednesday.'

There was silence from the chair opposite him – in fact no indication that she had heard him at all. Fred persisted.

'Do you recall our meeting at St Ninian's last spring? You were most gracious and kind to me. I was deeply saddened to hear about your loss. Life must seem very difficult at the moment. Is there anything I can do to help you now?'

Fred paused and looked expectantly at the distracted figure in front of him. He could hear his own words and found them lacking. If he were in her position, what would he want to hear, he asked himself?

'You must know that your husband is greatly concerned about you, Mrs Burnett. You have all suffered a great tragedy. He suffers as much as you but understands that life must go on. You have not left the house for many weeks I understand?'

Fred pulled his chair a little closer to the woman and leant forward urging her to engage with him. Was that a slight flicker of a reaction?

'You have made yourself ill now, which adds to his burden. And what of your other children? Are they also to lose their mother? Mrs Burnett?'

Yes, he was not mistaken. She had raised her head and was now looking directly at him. Emboldened, Fred continued.

'Hardship, grief, suffering - we all face these things – it is, alas, the human predicament. I want to help you, Mrs Burnett, but you must want to help yourself as well. George and Maurice you loved deeply of course and that will never change. But think of your other children and your husband David, they are alive and need you. They have lost their brothers and sons – are they to lose you as well? If you give up, then death has won. Be strong for your family's sake.'

Fred heard an intake of breath from the figure in front of him, then, catching him by surprise, she replied, slowly, clearly and deliberately.

'How dare you speak to me like that! How dare you! You cannot know how I suffer – every day! I wish I were dead sometimes. I fear that this will happen again and that I could not face. Do you understand me?'

Mrs Burnett stopped addressing him as she could no longer continue. Her sobs took over, her hands pressed to her face. Gradually there was silence apart from her ragged breathing. Fred was fearful he had gone too far and betrayed Mr Burnett's trust in his skills. Maybe he had made things worse. She was right, he did not know how she was suffering. Finally, he plucked up courage to speak again.

'Mrs Burnett, forgive my impertinence. You are correct. I cannot know the depths of your grief. I deeply regret adding to it. I only meant to help. Please accept my apologies. I will leave you now. Dr Russell will come and visit you after his return on Wednesday.'

Fred, chastened and shaken, started to stand up.

'Wait!'

Mrs Burnett had dropped her hands from her face and sought out a lace handkerchief to wipe her eyes and nose. In her grief, cheeks wet, nose reddened, Fred realised she was just a woman like any other, no better, no worse. A woman in pain. If only he could help her.

'No, you were right to say what you did. I am exhausted now but please come again. I give you my word I will be more composed on the next occasion.'

# CHAPTER 5

# CHARLOTTE SQUARE

Closing the door behind him, Fred found himself alone on the landing. The silence was in marked contrast to his recent exchange with Mrs Burnett and despite her apparent softening to his company, Fred was still uncertain what, if anything, he had achieved. She might have changed her mind when next he called. He hoped not. If he could restore some peace of mind to her and her family, he would rest more easily.

'Who are you?' came a young voice behind him, causing Fred to turn round in surprise.

Standing on the stair observing him with a grave expression was a young girl of about twelve or thirteen. She was clad in a plain dress of light grey wool, her feet buttoned into sensible black boots. The reddish gold hair around her pale face was pulled back smoothly into a long plait and her hazel eyes looked quizzically at Fred. At her feet, waving its tail against her skirt, was a small black and white cat.

'You look like a minister to me,' she announced.

'Aye, you are correct, Miss,' replied Fred, amused at her directness.

'Ministers always wear black and white even when they are not at work. It must get rather boring, does it not?'

'Not really. It makes life simple and practical. Let me introduce myself. I am the Reverend Frederick Black. I have been to visit your parents.'

'Hmm, I know Mama is not well,' the girl stated solemnly. 'Have you tried to make her feel better?'

'I hope so,' replied Fred, empathising with the child. 'But it will take a wee while. She is a very sad lady at the moment. I am very sorry that you have all had such a difficult time.'

Fred and the girl stood in silence for a few seconds.

'And what is your name, if I may ask?' continued Fred after a short while.

'Jane. Jane Eleanor Burnett.'

'That's a bonnie name.'

'Well, my brothers sometimes call me 'plain Jane' but I just ignore them.'

'They're wrong. I think they are just teasing you, are they not?'

'Maybe.' Jane paused. 'But mostly I'm called Janey.'

'Well, I prefer Jane, if I may call you that?'

'Certainly.'

And then the girl walked down the remaining stairs and extended a small white hand in greeting. The cat meantime remained where it was, observing them calmly through inscrutable yellow eyes.

'I am most pleased to make your acquaintance, Jane.'

'Thank you, Reverend Black. Will you come back to see us again?'

'I believe so. But now I must speak with your father before he thinks I have left without saying good-bye.'

The conversation at an end, Jane turned around and, with a nod of her head, walked back up the staircase until she and her pet had disappeared from view.

As he had been instructed, Fred now retraced his steps to the grand drawing room where Mr Burnett awaited him. The man had his back turned as Fred re-entered the room, so he cleared his throat gently to announce himself.

'Excuse me, Sir,' started Fred. 'I hope I am not disturbing you?'

'Not at all, Reverend Black. I hope my wife was gracious enough to speak with you?'

It was on the tip of his tongue to relate what had passed between them, but something held Fred back. He felt Mrs Burnett had confided her deep grief in him personally and he did not wish to discuss this dispassionately with Mr Burnett at this moment.

'She was indeed,' continued Fred. 'Understandably, she is still most distressed, but she was able to express herself. She was kind enough to say that I might return.'

'Well, I am very glad to hear that,' exclaimed Mr Burnett. 'It will mean less pressure on Dr Russell who I know has many parishioners to consider, many in more desperate circumstances than ours.'

'He certainly would not see it like that, Sir. You are all suffering and have equal need of our support. But if your wife is agreeable to speak to me as well as Dr Russell, I am happy to be of service.'

'That is most generous of you, Reverend Black. Please consider yourself a welcome visitor at any time.'

'I was also pleased to make the acquaintance of your daughter, Jane,' added Fred.

'Ah, Jane. She must have tired of her studies and come down in search of fresh stimulus. How did you find her?'

'Most polite and charming. You must be very proud of her.'

'We are, though I fear she finds home life trying these days. She was very close to her brother..... I find it difficult to know how best to speak to her. Her mother is better at it than I but at the moment ...'

'I understand, Sir,' interrupted Fred, anxious not to cause his host further distress. 'I am sure she is sympathetic to your situation. She seems very wise for her years.'

Behind the two men the carriage clock on the mantelpiece

struck midday. Fred was startled that so much of the morning had disappeared already and started to take his leave.

'We have taken up a lot of your time, Reverend Black. Would you care for some refreshment before you return to Melville Street?'

The invitation was lightly given and Fred, as sometimes happened, found himself considering the scene as if he were a by-stander. David Burnett Esquire, laird of Nether Airlie and master of N° 7 Charlotte Square inviting him, Frederick Black, a poor country boy, almost as an equal.

'That is most kind of you, Sir, but as Dr Russell is away, I feel my presence will be required at Melville Street. Perhaps another time if I may? I am pleased to have made your acquaintance, Mr Burnett. I hope there may be other opportunities.'

'You may be certain of that, Reverend Black. Can Jim take you home? I dare say the carriage is still available.'

'Thank you, Sir, but there is no need. I enjoy walking and some air will no doubt be of benefit to me before I hide myself away again with my books.'

David Burnett allowed himself a slight smile and held out his hand to his visitor.

'Until the next time, Reverend Black.'

By the time Fred found himself once again outside on the pavement, a heavy drizzle had started to fall. He began to regret turning down Mr Burnett's kind offer of a carriage ride home as he had no umbrella with him, leaving, as he had, in such a hurry that morning. No matter, it was less than half a mile to walk. Pulling up his collar and adjusting his hat, Fred set off. Preferring to avoid the busy main streets where he would have to dodge mud and manure and splashes from passing traffic, Fred took himself up Randolph Place, admiring the classical symmetry of the elegant New Town terraces.

He was about to cross Queensferry Street when he became aware of a young child wailing followed by the harassed tones of its woman attempting to hush it. The child clearly was not prepared to be mollified and merely increased its efforts.

'Yer a wee bissum so ye are, Davie Greig! I telt ye we'll be hame soon but ah'm nae carryin' ye. Gimme yer hand!'

The last order was shouted at the child and Fred raised his head to see the woman about to strike the little boy on the side of the head.

'Madam, excuse me! Can I help ye?'

At the sound of Fred's voice, the woman lowered her hand and defensively crossed both her arms across her body.

'Whit's it tae ye? Ah, a minister.' The last statement was said with a weary sigh. 'Am ah gang tae burn in Hell then?'

'I merely offered to help you, Madam,' Fred persisted.

'Weel that's mighty fine o' ye but I fear ah'm beyond help.' The woman laughed without humour, lowered her arms and pulled the child towards her.

'No-one's beyond help, Madam. Where are you headed? Can I help ye wi' the bairn?'

'None o' yer business. The bairn's fine. Jist a naughty wee bissum who willnae dae as he's telt.'

A picture of his mother bringing him up on her own in Strathmuir came to mind. Fred had no memory of her losing her temper with him but it must have happened.

'Mebbe he's hungry, Madam. The manse is nae far. Can we fix him a wee piece to keep him going?'

'Why are ye sae interested?' queried the woman, suspiciously. 'How do ye ken he's hungry?'

'All small boys are hungry, are they no'?' Fred attempted a lighter response. If she was determined to turn down his offer of help, he could not force it. After a few seconds, the woman seemed to relax a little.

'Weel, a wee bite o' somethin' wud be welcome, Sir, I cannae deny. But ah'm nae gang tae the kirk! I hae tae get hame.'

'Of course, Madam. Can I help ye wi' the bairn? Will he let me carry him?'

Fred bent down in front of the little boy who looked warily up at him out of dark brown eyes. Fred saw immediately that the child had not been washed properly for some time. His limp brown hair was matted, a long fringe hung over his forehead and his hands and fingers nails were discoloured with dirt. His drab clothing smelt of smoke and old cooking. When Fred put his arms out to lift him up, the child started to fret. His mother sighed in frustration.

'Davie, let the man carry ye. I cannae. Or ye'll be walkin'.'

Reluctantly Davie allowed himself to be picked up by Fred. Trying to ignore the thought that the child might have lice, Fred started to walk on. Perhaps they could clean him up at the manse? He was not sure what Mrs Oliphant might have to say about it? Or indeed the child's mother who might well be offended.

'Are ye in work, Madam?' asked Fred conversationally.

'I work wi' ma mither. We take in the laundry. Ma man died frae the cholera, two year ago. It's nae easy wi' a bairn.'

The woman announced these facts without any self-pity. Fred slowed his pace and turned to her.

'I am very sorry to hear this. God rest his soul. So Davie never knew his father then?'

'No, he wis jist one year old when his faither died. He wis a good man!'

'I do not doubt it, Mrs..?'

'Greig. Effie Greig.'

'Well Mrs Greig, I hope I may make your day a little easier. The manse isnae far – just in Melville Street. We'll get you and your boy somethin' tae eat, then you can get back home.'

Approaching the front door of No.17, Fred carefully lowered the little boy to the ground, before extracting his door-key.

'Sir, we cannae come in the front door. We'd better gang doon the stair.'

Mrs Greig was standing on the pavement and pointed to the steep, worn steps leading to the basement of the building.

'We're nae allowed upstairs,' she repeated to Fred, who

continued to stand at the front door with the little boy at his side.

'I am sorry, Madam. You are, of course, correct. Let us enter that way.'

And Fred, reprimanding himself silently for causing the woman any embarrassment, turned and led the way down to the back door. Pulling the bell pull once was sufficient for Mrs Williamson to appear and open the door, with surprise, to the newcomers.

'Forgive me, Mrs Williamson. These parishioners are in need of something to eat. I am sure we can spare something?'

From her expression, Mrs Williamson clearly had other thoughts on the matter but, faced with Fred's enquiring face and Davie Grieg's down-turned mouth, she gave in and ushered the mother and child into the kitchen.

'Thank ye, Sir,' called out Mrs Greig, as Fred turned to go back up the stairs. 'God bless ye!'

Alone again and standing in the hallway of Melville Manse, Fred stood for a few moments and dwelt on the day's encounters. The most recent was so much easier to resolve he reflected. Would that all human need could be satisfied so simply.

'Ah, Reverend Black, I thought I heard you come in,' Mrs Oliphant greeted Fred politely. 'I trust your morning was satisfactory?'

Without waiting for his reply, Mrs Oliphant added,

'You have a visitor, Sir. I've put him in the morning room.'

# CHAPTER 6

# AN UNEXPECTED CALLER

At that precise moment Fred wanted nothing more than to retire to his room to contemplate the encounters of the morning and dwell on how he might address Margaret Burnett in a more successful manner the next time they met. But he could already see the back of an unknown man through the morning room door, who, alerted by Fred's entrance, would no doubt be awaiting his imminent company.

'Thank you, Mrs Oliphant.' Fred acknowledged the housekeeper. 'I will be but a moment. Let me set my things down in my room and I will be with the visitor directly. Who is it?'

'Reverend Grierson, Sir. He said it was a personal matter.'

Grierson, Grierson? The name was familiar but initially Fred could not place it. Then it came to him. He was one of the Alford parish ministers he had recently written to. He felt a nervous spasm grip his guts as he wondered what the man might have to say.

By the time Fred returned, Reverend Grierson was facing the door. He was a short, red-faced man with grizzled dark hair, bushy eyebrows and flared nostrils from which protruded copious quantities of nasal hair. His waist-coat stretched over a rotund stomach, upon which his hands rested. Fred reflected that at that moment he resembled a somewhat aggressive toad.

'Reverend Grierson, I am sorry to have kept you waiting,' Fred commenced as affably as he could, extending his hand in greeting. 'I was out on a pastoral matter but you have my full attention now. Please sit down.'

And Fred indicated one of the upholstered wing-chairs set on either side of the fire-place.

'Thank you, Reverend Black. You will recall writing to me a few weeks back at my parish in Tullynessle, in connection with a Miss Duthie?' Grierson looked enquiringly at Fred before continuing. 'As I was in Edinburgh visiting family, I thought I would try to see you in person. It is a delicate matter better discussed face to face rather than committed to paper.'

Fred, who up until this point had been standing in front of the fire looking down at the man, now seated himself slowly.

'Thank you for taking the time to come and visit me, Reverend Grierson.'

Now Fred felt the need to explain himself.

'Perhaps I was not clear in my letter. Jessie, Miss Duthie, was a pupil of mine. She was working down in the harbour in Aberdeen as a fish-wife but suffered a violent attack by the man she was living with. My colleague Reverend Kelman and I became aware of this and felt it prudent to remove her from the danger she faced.'

Fred briefly felt guilty at bringing Richard's name into the matter but decided it lent greater credibility to his story.

'For a while she worked at their manse. It was at this time that, at her request, and with the Kelmans' support, I taught her to read and write. She was an able pupil.'

Fred paused in his explanation, watching Reverend Grierson's face closely for a reaction, before continuing.

'In due course, she changed employment and went to work for Reverend and Mrs MacDonald at St Nicholas' Manse. No doubt you will be acquainted with them? They do much good work for the unfortunates living and working around the harbour area. It had always been my intention to give Miss Duthie a memento, an award if you like, to record her diligence and progress. When I knew I was to depart for Edinburgh earlier this year, I sought her out to make good my intention. Sadly, I was informed she had already left the MacDonald household and gone to live in the country. I wrote to her then via the MacDonalds but, alas, heard nothing more. I regret I was unable to say farewell in person and would like to know how she is.'

Aware that his explanation had become somewhat lengthy and trying to keep his face and emotions under control, Fred stopped talking and glanced again at the minister. Grierson continued watching him intently but gave nothing away.

'Aye, well, it is a shame Miss Duthie did not take fuller advantage of the opportunities presented to her,' the minister pronounced solemnly, shaking his head from side to side. 'If she had, she widnae find hersel' in her present predicament. You ken she was expecting a bairn? She came to my colleague, Jim Anderson over at Keig, back in the summer. It was MacDonald who arranged it. He is a charitable fellow. He disnae like tae see the lassies on the street, despite their indiscretions.'

The visitor's disapproving manner riled Fred but he dared not show his irritation.

'A bairn? I had heard rumours but…' Fred's voice trailed off. 'Has she had the bairn? Is she alright?'

The haunting memory of his recent nightmare startled him and he feared that this foretold a tragic outcome.

'Have you seen her, Sir? I wish to know how she fares.'

Noticing Fred's worried face, Reverend Grierson stretched out a hand and patted Fred on the arm.

'I did see her during the summer. She was well enough to help Mrs Anderson in the house but nae since then. I heard she had a wee boy, jist a few weeks ago.'

'A wee boy,' Fred echoed softly. 'Is he healthy?'

'I believe so. I understand the mother went through a difficult ordeal and lost quite a lot of blood, but she is strong and has pulled through.'

Fred stood in silence contemplating Grierson's words. He hoped his face gave away nothing of the consternation he was feeling within. Then a thought occurred to him.

'Tell me, Sir, why did Reverend Anderson nae reply to my letter himself? I mind the name and am certain I wrote a letter of enquiry to him as well.'

'I understand Reverend Anderson does not want Miss Duthie disturbed or contacted. It is a difficult situation. She is low in spirits as she knows the child will be adopted. There have been many tears. Reverend Anderson wants her kept calm and not distracted or excited in any way.'

'And how can that help her?' Fred, despite himself, raised his voice in exasperation.

'I am inclined to agree with you, Sir,' replied Grierson. 'I felt you deserved a response from me at any rate. Particularly as you and Reverend Kelman have been so involved with her welfare in the past.'

'Must she give up her child?' Fred continued, his voice low and emotional. 'Is there no way she could keep the bairn? It seems inhumanly harsh to take him from her.'

'And how would she support herself and her child?' Reverend Grierson replied sternly. 'What kind of life could she offer him? We cannae be seen to be condoning her immoral behaviour. No, this may hurt her initially, but she will get over it. The bairn will hae a much better life in a settled God-fearing household with two parents. We hope she will hae learnt her lesson. She is fortunate to have been given this chance. Many in her position would be compelled to abandon their babes not knowing their fate – or worse.'

There then fell a silence between the two men with Grierson's disapproval hanging in the air. Fred dropped his gaze and stared at the ground in despair. While he now knew Jessie's whereabouts, acting on this information would compromise Grierson. Although the man seemed heartless in the face of Jessie's predicament, Fred nonetheless appreciated that Grierson had taken the time and initiative to reply to his letter.

'Reverend Grierson,' Fred started. 'Thank you for coming to see me. I have been considerably worried about Miss Duthie and I am shocked by your news. I wish I could do more to help her. I would ask you one further favour. I would be greatly indebted if you were able to give her my gift.'

'But I have told you, Reverend Anderson knows nothing of my visit,' Grierson replied, not attempting to keep the frustration out of his voice. 'The lassie is to be kept calm and undisturbed until her bairn has been adopted. Your gift would no doubt bring back sad memories and regrets over her past life. This is precisely why Anderson wants no contact. Ideas might be put into her head.'

'Man, you cannot deny her a Holy Book, a gift from a friend? She should surely gain solace from this?'

There was silence as Reverend Grierson considered Fred's request.

'Very well,' he conceded finally. 'She has little enough to cheer her at the moment. Let me have it and I will make sure she receives it.'

'Thank you, Sir! I am most grateful. Wait here please. I will be just a few minutes.'

Anxious to despatch his gift finally to Jessie, Fred took the stairs two at a time. Seated at his desk, Fred pulled out some brown paper to secure the package. He had started to wrap up the volume when he realised he wanted to say more to Jessie. Dipping his pen into the jar of black ink, on a single sheet of paper he scribbled rapidly,

*Jessie, I have not forgotten you. They have told me about your son. I so want to know more. If you can, let me know how you are faring. Here is my address - 17 Melville Street, West End, Edinburgh, Midlothian.*

*Forever in my thoughts*

*Yours aye, Fred.*

Then folding the letter as small as he could, Fred inserted it into the centre of the slim volume alongside the blue silk marker ribbon and pressed it shut. Wrapping it with brown paper he then bound it tightly with string and sealed his gift with a blob of red sealing wax. He had to trust that Grierson would be as good as his word and deliver the parcel safely. If prying eyes wished to look, then he would not make it easy for them.

Returning to the morning room, Fred held out the package to the visitor. Grierson took it slowly and turned it over in his hands.

'And what have we here, Sir?'

Seeing his guest looking at the parcel, Fred, for a fleeting, anxious moment thought Grierson might want to see the contents.

'A books of Psalms, Sir. A worthy and uplifting book which I hope will give her comfort. Now, even more than ever.'

To Fred's relief, Grierson merely nodded before slipping the volume into a brown pigskin attaché case.

'I am deeply obliged, Sir,' Fred commented feelingly. 'Please ensure Miss Duthie receives it as soon as possible.'

'That I will, Reverend Black. You may count on it. Well, I must away. I have taken up enough of your time.'

Reverend Grierson got to his feet and picked up the leather portfolio. Fred followed and led the way to the hall where he helped the man into his overcoat and handed him his hat and gloves.

'Thank you for coming, Reverend Grierson. If you have any further news of Miss Duthie I would be pleased to hear it. I will pray for her at this difficult time.'

Grierson gave a grunt of acknowledgement as Fred opened the front door. Stepping out on to the porch, Fred became aware of a hansom cab slowing down and approaching the house. As the window was pulled down he realised that the passenger was William Russell returned from his visit. In the confusion of the morning, Fred had forgotten that his colleague was due home that day. For an uncomfortable moment it appeared as if Russell and Grierson might come face to face but, to Fred's great relief, Grierson appeared to be in a hurry to depart. By the time the door of the hansom cab swung open, the caller had already stepped on to the pavement to make his way briskly towards Princes Street.

# CHAPTER 7

# IN MOURNING

DECEMBER 1861

AS 1861 DREW TO A CLOSE AND THE HOURS OF DAYLIGHT shrank, the stark beauty of Edinburgh continued to enthral Fred. He had already made several calls to the Burnett household in Charlotte Square since his first fraught visit a few weeks before and was heartened that Mrs Burnett seemed to be getting stronger and had agreed to see a doctor about her reliance on laudanum. Her grief was clearly still very raw and while she now spoke more willingly with Fred, often, when there was a pause in the conversation, he would see the woman staring sadly out of the window – silent and unreachable. He had learned not to be fearful of these lows but to wait quietly and patiently until, finally, Mrs Burnett would awake from her mournful reverie and turn apologetically towards Fred.

'Forgive me, Fred. I still find the waking hours an effort. You are very kind and indulgent of me.'

'There is nothing to forgive, Mrs Burnett. You are recovering, body and soul, from a great trauma. It cannot be rushed. It gives me great joy to see you come back to us.'

'Fred, I have a favour to ask. If it would not make you uncomfortable, please call me Margaret. You know so much about me now, it feels more fitting than 'Mrs Burnett'.'

'I would be pleased to...Margaret, but what would Mr Burnett say? I hope he would not think I am being presumptuous or over-familiar?'

'I have discussed this with him and he is quite agreeable. However, I think he would prefer still to be called Mr Burnett. But then he is much older than I!'

Margaret smiled and Fred was struck by how lovely she was when her expression lightened and her dark eyes sparkled in amusement.

Leaving Charlotte Square after one such visit in the middle of December, due to the darkness of the late winter afternoon, Fred decided to drop down towards Princes Street and walk home from there. After the warmth of Margaret's parlour, the cold air stung Fred's cheeks and made his eyes water. Dusk had fallen and the lamp-lighter was making his way methodically around the square. Smoke wreathed dreamily upwards from dozens of chimney pots infusing the air with the smell of coal. So wrapped up in his thoughts was Fred, that at first he did not register the urgent cry of the.news-vendor at the corner of Queensferry Road and Princes Street.

'*A Nation's Tragic Loss! The Prince Consort is dead! Read all about it!*'

Fred stopped immediately and listened again. What! Could it be true? Pray God he had misheard. The Prince Consort had been poorly but the last bulletin had been full of cautious optimism. Now Fred was standing directly by the vendor. No, there was no mistake. Prince Albert was dead at forty two years of age. Too young. The poor Queen! Fred reached into his pocket and handed over his pennies for a couple of copies of the Scotsman. He briefly scanned the headline before tucking them under his arm and striding urgently back to Melville Street to break the dreadful news to the household. Flinging open the front door, Fred stood in the hallway and once again ran his eyes over the front page. The announcement was stark.

> 'At ten minutes to eleven o'clock on Saturday night HRH the Prince Consort died at Windsor Castle. For some days previous to his demise, HRH had suffered severely from an attack of gastric fever but it was only on Friday evening that the disease assumed a form which gave cause for anxiety.'
>
> 'Alas for the Queen, who has lost the partner of her life – the first and dearest object of her affections. The death of the Prince Consort may be truly said to eclipse the gaiety of nations. His loss will be felt by the whole empire and it is no exaggeration to say that he will have an entire people for his mourners. A good husband, a good father, a wise Prince and a safe counsellor, England will not soon look upon his like again.'

Sinking on to a chair, still in his overcoat, Fred sat for a few moments to take in the tragic news. Then heading to William's study he pushed the door open without knocking.

'William, pardon the interruption. The saddest news!'

William had by now turned towards Fred, his face anxious.

'Fred, what is the matter, lad?'

'Prince Albert is dead!' Unable to say anything more, Fred held out one of the newspapers to his colleague.

'Last night. Poor man! And our poor Queen, she will be bereft.'

The whole nation shared Fred's disbelief and grief in the Prince Consort's demise. He could not remember a time when the tall, handsome German prince had not been at the Queen's side. For twenty years his energy and vision had propelled the country forwards and now suddenly he was no more. One morning, a few days later, William returned from a meeting of the Church Council and addressed Fred as they sat down to eat lunch.

'It has been decided that all churches will hold a memorial service at the very time of the Prince Consort's funeral on the 23rd. This is a most important and significant event as you can imagine, Fred. You and I will both preach a sermon which will be a fitting eulogy to a great man. It must be as if the Royal coffin were there itself. As preachers this will be our greatest challenge yet.'

In keeping with the sombre mood settled upon the whole country, Monday 23rd December dawned grey and chill. The cloud cover was low and the sun invisible throughout the day. Flags hung limply at half-mast on all public buildings throughout the city and muffled bells tolled solemnly. At St Ninian's, the elders stood at the church entrance to welcome the mourners who, soberly dressed in muted winter colours, were progressing towards the double doors.

Meanwhile Fred and William waited in silence in the vestry, going through in their minds, yet one more time, the words they were going to speak to the congregation. Beyond the vestry doors, the organ was being played softly, reminding those who entered to cease their conversations, bow their heads and make their own private prayers before the service started. Outside, as the church bell struck eleven o' clock, the doors to the kirk were closed and the elders took their seats. The general murmuring within the church ceased amid an air of expectation. It was time.

The two men had agreed that Fred would address the congregation first. Thus Fred stepped out from the privacy of the vestry and into the kirk. It was completely full. Without pausing, he continued his path to the pulpit and made his way up the steps to stand above the crowd. Looking out over the heads of the mourners, to his surprise and pleasure, Fred saw that in the third pew from the front, sat both David and Margaret Burnett together with their daughter Jane and their eldest son, Hugh, newly returned from Oxford University for the Christmas holiday. Looking solemn and pale, Margaret was nonetheless elegantly dressed and composed. Her head bowed slightly, she had one arm resting protectively around the shoulders of her younger child.

He would address his sermon as if to Margaret herself, Fred decided. The theme of life and death, love and loss would be pertinent to many in the congregation but to her in particular. For a moment Fred feared that Margaret's new-found mental strength might be sorely tested. But it was too late to make any amendments. He must take that chance. Looking up again, his eye was caught by Jane's solemn gaze. Fred nodded in acknowledgement then started his sermon.

As he progressed, his voice gained strength and purpose. He described Albert as an outsider who, with courage and purpose, had overcome prejudice to establish himself as a much loved and well respected Prince Consort. Those who are outsiders have a unique and valuable view on the world, he reminded the mourners. Their path is not easy, but giving up is not an option.

'And now we mourn him and feel his death so strongly. We feel an affinity with our dear Queen, for whom amongst us has escaped the loss of a loved one? We share her grief and desperation and we must remember that God himself led by example and gave his only son so that mankind might understand how much they were loved. From the greatest in the land to the humblest, we understand her loss. Let us bow our heads and reflect in private prayer on the nature of loss, to try to make sense of such events and ponder how we can retain our faith in the face of such difficult circumstances. We pray to God the Father to give us strength and purpose in our lives, to show us the path we must follow and to know that we will always be loved by Him and never abandoned.'

Below him, heads were bowed and shoulders shook with grief. Gulps, sniffs and brief cries could be heard throughout the kirk. Although there must have been over a hundred and fifty souls seated together, at that moment each was in a lonely world of their own, contemplating how weak and vulnerable they all were. As he descended the narrow stair from the pulpit, William was waiting for him. 'Well done, my boy!' he whispered.

An hour later when the last of the mourners had left the church, Fred and William started to walk slowly back to Melville Street. The air of the city was filled with the sound of church bells and in the distance, from the Castle esplanade, the muffled boom of the cannon. William turned towards Fred and laid his hand on his arm.

'You did very well there, Fred. Your words were most moving. You have a great gift to make your message personal. In fact I envy you.'

'Sir, you cannot say that. Your delivery is so powerful. I have much to learn from you.'

'We are always learning, Fred, that is true. But I want to say something to you now which I have been thinking over in my mind for some weeks.'

Fred, taken by surprise, stopped walking and looked at William with curiosity.

'In due course I would like you to take over from me at St Ninian's.'

For a few seconds, Fred found it impossible to respond. He had only just arrived in the city and now William was offering what he had dared not think about. How would he ever be able to fill his shoes?

'William, I am honoured but I trust that will be many years from now.'

'Of course, but I am no longer a young man and such matters need to be contemplated. We can talk about it further in the New Year but I wanted you to be aware of my thoughts. I hope you see that your future lies here, Fred?'

# CHAPTER 8

# IN THE BLEAK MID-WINTER

***'Earth stood hard as iron, water like a stone.' – Christina Rossetti***

KEIG, ABERDEENSHIRE – September 1861

JESSIE COULD NOT REMEMBER A PAIN LIKE IT. NOT WHEN Billy Smith had hit her in the face nearly breaking her nose, nor when she had a rotten tooth pulled. This was entirely different and seemed to occupy her whole body. When the baby finally announced its imminent arrival with a series of short sharp contractions, Jessie was initially relieved and glad the days of lumbering about carrying such an uncomfortable burden were nearly over.

She had been ambivalent about the bairn even though she could now see it clearly as a tiny separate human being, moving about in its confined space, tiny limbs poking up through the taut skin of her belly, then ducking back if she attempted to take hold of them. Jessie had not let herself get sentimental. If she could be sure it was Fred's child then perhaps she might have felt differently but as there was a chance it was not, she did not want reminding of that encounter.

Awoken by the pain, Jessie lay still for as long as she could bear it, both hands laid lightly against her body, rock hard as the contraction took hold again. That was when she called out. The sound came out from deep within her, profound and feeling as if it might relieve her of some of the agony.

'Mrs Anderson! Mrs Anderson! It's coming, the bairn is coming!'

After the contraction faded, Jessie, with the greatest of effort, gritted her teeth and hauled herself up to sitting. Looking down at her night gown she saw it was saturated with blood and a clear fluid. Panic-stricken, she called out again,

'Mrs Anderson!'

As a second contraction gripped her, Jessie was barely aware that the minister's wife had entered the room and was now standing in front of her.

'No need for so much noise, Jessie, it's jist the baby coming. I'll send for the mid-wife. Can ye walk, Jessie?'

Jessie shook her head. It had taken all her strength to sit up and now she felt suddenly nauseous and light-headed.

'I thought mebbe we would put ye in the next bedroom, it's a bit bigger but nae matter, we'll hae tae manage here. I'll get ye anither pillow and some towels.'

When Mrs Anderson returned, carrying an earthenware jug, she filled up the wash bowl with hot water and proceeded to wipe Jessie's face and neck gently. Then she proffered a glass of water which Jessie gulped down greedily.

'Try to breathe, lassie,' Mrs Anderson advised softly. 'Dinnae exhaust yersel'. I'm awa' tae fetch Mrs Massie in the village. I willnae be long.'

Jessie hardly noticed when the two women returned and Mrs Massie took charge. Everything was centred on her belly heaving and contracting, trying to expel the infant into the world. She screamed, she swore and gripped the mid-wife's hand so tightly that the woman called out in pain herself. The daylight faded, the door opened and closed, jugs of hot water were replaced and the pain continued. Dear God, when would it end?

'Push, lassie. It's ready to come. I can see its wee head. Come on, push!'

Jessie was feeling so weak that at first she felt this was an impossible request. She surely had no energy left. But then suddenly the momentum was such that she could not resist it. She had to push. And push. And finally with a last scream of effort she felt the tiny body slither out of her on to the bed.

For a desperate moment there was silence in the small, stuffy room, then suddenly the baby's cries broke into everyone's thoughts.

'A wee boy, Jessie!' Mrs Anderson's voice exclaimed in excitement. 'A fine wee boy!'

Jessie lay back on the pillows feeling completely drained. She was aware that Mrs Massie was still tending to her and, despite her exhaustion, wondered what the new-born looked like. As if reading her thoughts, Mrs Anderson was by her side gently placing the baby, tightly wrapped in swaddling bands, in her arms. Fearfully, Jessie received the child and looked down at her son. Immediately she saw two dark blue little eyes peering intently at her. The head was covered in a light dusting of dark hair, encrusted in drying blood, and the tiny red face had been cleaned carefully. Jessie lowered her face to the baby's and kissed him on the nose.

'Hello, wee one,' she whispered.

The baby thrived, thank the Lord. This was the coldest, hardest time of the year, when the wind whistled through the ill-fitting windows, causing the glass to rattle and snow flurries whirled outside, falling like white lace on the dark, frozen ground. Jessie had been allowed a fire in her room – not for her of course but for the bairn. Jessie could see he was a fighter from her first glance.

While she lay back exhausted and barely conscious, the baby held her firmly in his gaze.

She named him Jamie, after her father. *No, she didnae ken the baby's faither.* That drew disapproving looks, tightened lips and narrowed eyes. Despite their entreaties, Jessie declined to put any other name but hers and her son's on his birth certificate. She tried to forget that one day he would be taken from her. At first she thought she would try not to fall in love with the tiny creature but from the moment they placed him in her arms, she knew that would be impossible. As her milk came through, Jamie guzzled hungrily, only ceasing when he was full and fell back asleep immediately. Jessie brushed her lips over his downy head and closed her eyes, breathing in his sweet baby scent. She must remember this. It would have to last her a lifetime.

One day towards the end of January, when Jamie was four months old, Mrs Anderson entered the kitchen where Jessie was preparing vegetables for the evening dinner. Jamie was asleep in his crib beside the range, oblivious to the comings and goings around him.

'Jessie, sit down a moment. I would like to have a word wi' ye.'

'Aye..,' replied Jessie uncertainly, turning towards the kitchen table and sitting down slowly, one eye glancing towards her sleeping son.

'Jessie, my husband has asked me tae speak tae ye. Woman tae woman.'

Jessie blinked and swallowed nervously. She greatly feared what Mrs Anderson might be about to say and wanted to put the moment off as long as possible.

'Aye…,' she repeated, unable to say anything further.

'Jamie is a fine wee bairn and a credit tae ye, Jessie. I have grown very fond of ye both and I wish Jamie had his own faither here tae care for him. But sadly that is nae the case. He needs a faither, ye can see that can ye nae, Jessie?'

Jessie looked down at her hands and said nothing.

'*I can care for him, me'sel,*' she told herself fiercely. '*He's my son!*'

'Jessie?' Mrs Anderson was looking at her anxiously.

'Aye,' Jessie sighed finally.

'Jamie needs a family and security. That is the best for him. You must understand that, Jessie.'

'He has a family,' Jessie whispered. 'I am his family.'

'Aye, Jessie,' responded Mrs Anderson gently, 'You will always be his mother, but ye cannae give him the life he needs.'

'So what will happen, Mrs Anderson?' Jessie almost shouted out her question, tears filling her eyes. She wanted to weep in grief and frustration but knew that would not help her now.

'We ken a very kind, God-fearing couple who sadly lost their own bairn a year ago and cannae hae mair bairns. I promise they will love Jamie as their own and give him everything he deserves.'

'When?' whispered Jessie, feeling the desperation growing within her.

'Nae yet, Jessie, there will be time to say good-bye.'

On hearing this Jessie could take no more and, stifling a cry, stood up, picked her son up out of the crib and rushed from the room. She felt an overwhelming need to escape the house immediately. Wrapping the child in his crib blankets and clutching him close to her body, Jessie opened the front door and despite the blast of cold air which hit her, walked outside. Above her head, the silver-trunked beech trees surrounding the manse stood like motionless sentinels. Rooks cawed harshly as they roosted in the branches and in the distance stood the hill of Bennachie, its summit standing out against the pale blue winter sky.

Perhaps startled by the sudden change of temperature or sensing his mother's disquiet, Jamie stirred in Jessie's arms and started to wail plaintively. Jessie stopped walking and looked down at her son, shaking him gently to calm him. He would not be comforted however and Jessie, brought to her senses, sighed deeply and returned to the house. Carrying her son upstairs to their room, she laid him carefully on the bed. Stroking his velvety head she took hold of a tuft of the soft brown hair and delicately cut it with a tiny pair of sewing scissors. Wrapping it in a small piece of tissue paper, Jessie folded it up and tucked it into the Psalm book that lay on her bedside table. Then, before her son's cries grew even louder, Jessie settled herself in her armchair and put Jamie to her breast.

The worst of the winter had now passed and the sprightly yellow heads of daffodils were opening up around the edge of the manse garden. The wind still blew cold from the snow-covered Grampians but the sun shone for longer and daylight was returning, heralding spring. Jessie continued to live fearfully. After her conversation with Mrs Anderson in January, nothing more had been said. No official visits had been made to the manse and there had been no further mention of Jamie's future. Easter fell early that year and preparations for the spring festival were in full flow. Most of the practicalities fell to Mrs Anderson but she indicated to Jessie that she would need some more help from time to time.

'I have some errands I need to run today, Jessie. We bring eggs and daffodils to our parishioners, especially the elderly. It cheers them up. I could do wi' an extra pair o' hands that's for sure. If I get my daughter Maggie to mind Jamie, would ye come with me please?'

'Can Maggie no' help ye?' Jessie responded hesitantly.

'She's done it so many times afore, she would welcome a wee change. And besides an outing would be good for ye. You've been cooped up for too long, Jessie.'

Jessie could think of no further arguments but felt a deep sense of unease as she agreed to accompany Mrs Anderson. Putting on her coat and boots and wrapping a large shawl around her shoulders, she was just about to follow the older woman out of the front door when, on impulse, she turned back and looked into the kitchen. Maggie was sitting beside Jamie's crib reading a book and looked up as Jessie entered.

'I jist wanted to gie him a wee kiss,' Jessie explained, bending over and touching her lips to her son's cheek. 'God bless, my baby boy.'

The tour of the parishioners took about an hour and a half. Everyone was most welcoming and greeted Jessie kindly, one even asking after her bairn. Tea and shortbread were offered and by the time Jessie and Mrs Anderson returned to the manse, the sun was nearly down and a familiar chill had settled once again on the landscape. Nothing seemed different as they entered the warm hall of the manse but Jessie, anxious to allay her own fears, before even taking off her outer garments, rushed to the kitchen to seek out her son's crib. Maggie was no longer there and the crib was empty. With her heart pounding and a scream building within her lungs, Jessie raced upstairs to her room and flung open the door. Nothing! No fire in the grate, no snuffling bairn, no baby clothes. Gone!

'Far's ma bairn?' she shouted as she rushed back down the stairs, almost colliding with Mrs Anderson, who stood holding out her arms as if to catch hold of Jessie.

'Far's Jamie? Ye said I could say good-bye! Liar! Liar!'

'Jessie, Jessie, calm yersel'! This is no way to behave! This is for the best.'

'Ye promised I could say good-bye!' Jessie shouted again in desperation.

'It is harder to see the bairn taken by his new family. Trust me.'

'I'll nivvir trust ye again!'

Disturbed by the agitation and raised voices, Reverend Anderson's voice could suddenly be heard, deep and uncompromising.

'You forget yourself, lassie!' he turned on Jessie. 'You can count yourself fortunate indeed that we have taken you in, cared for you and found a good home for your bastard child. Many in your situation would not be so lucky. You should have thought of the consequences before you let yourself be seduced into intercourse. Now go to your room and calm yourself.'

Unable to say another word, Jessie ran upstairs. Throwing herself on to her bed, she screamed into her pillow.

# CHAPTER 9

# IMPROMPTUS

EDINBURGH – FEBRUARY 1862

FRED SAT AT HIS DESK SEEKING INSPIRATION FOR HIS NEXT sermon. He had already re-arranged the items in front of him a couple of times. The stack of fresh white paper, two pens and a silver ink well – a generous gift from William - his personal Bible and a treasured copy of the writings of Lancelot Andrews. After the praise heaped upon him following Prince Albert's demise, Fred knew that expectations were higher than ever. While the congregation of St Ninian's had always been good, William had informed him that numbers had swelled after the memorial service and it would be good to retain such approval.

Perhaps he should go for a short walk. The weather had been so bad recently, it had been well-nigh impossible to venture out of the house for very long. Fred was feeling the constraints of being indoors and was about to prepare himself to go out when there was a knock on the door.

'I am sorry to disturb you, Sir,' announced Mrs Oliphant, 'but Mrs Burnett is downstairs and wishes to speak with you,'

'Mrs Burnett? Is she well? I was not expecting her.'

'Perfectly well, I believe. But you can see for yourself.'

'Where is she now? I will be down very shortly.'

'She is waiting in the morning room, Sir. I will let her know you are on your way.'

Fred felt a mixture of anticipation and apprehension as he walked down the stair-case. He had no idea what the reason for Margaret's visit might be. Nothing bad, he prayed.

'Margaret,' Fred walked towards the seated woman, his hand outstretched. 'This is a pleasure indeed.'

Margaret was dressed in a dark green gown of heavy silk and a close fitting velvet jacket in a similar colour. A small hat trimmed with green and black lace was perched on top of her dark hair and she held a pair of black leather gloves in her left hand.

'Fred, I apologise for interrupting your morning, but I have an invitation which I hope you will be able to accept?'

She smiled at him, her head tilted to one side in query.

'I welcome your interruption. I was about to go out to clear my head but this is a much better solution. An invitation, you say?'

'Yes and I am sorry it is very last minute. We have tickets for a concert given by Clara Schumann tonight at the Assembly Rooms. It is to be a birthday treat for Jane. She is fourteen today. David was to come with us but he has just had word that there are some problems at Nether Airlie which require his presence. I tried to persuade him to go tomorrow but he was adamant he had to attend to it immediately. If the truth be known, David, for all his virtues, is not so interested in listening to classical music. It seemed a great pity if the ticket was to be wasted so I wondered if you might like to accompany Jane and me.'

'This is a most kind and generous offer, Margaret, but is there no-one perhaps more deserving than me? I have to admit that my own knowledge of concert music is very limited. I am more familiar with kirk music or the Scottish reels and folk songs we play back in my home town. I would not like you to think I am a complete Philistine!'

'Well perhaps it is time you were educated then!' laughed Margaret. 'Madame Schumann is playing a programme of piano pieces by Frederic Chopin. It is wonderful music. I am sure you will enjoy it.'

'Very well then, Margaret. You have convinced me. Thank you. I will let Mrs Oliphant know I will be out this evening.'

'That is wonderful, Fred. I am so pleased. I will ask the coachman to have the carriage ready by six o' clock. We only have to go to George Street so we will collect you at ten past six.'

By the time Jim the coachman slowed down in front of the Assembly Rooms, the pavements were already full of fashionably dressed citizens alighting from their carriages, milling around and exchanging greetings with each other. Inside the venue, huge chandeliers dazzled, reflected in the many mirrors hung around the foyer. The doors were open and warm, scented air wafted out on to the cold winter street.

Fred was uncomfortably aware that his attire left much to be desired. On entering the carriage only ten minutes earlier, he had immediately noted how beautifully turned out both mother and daughter were, from the ornate decorations they wore in their hair and the necklaces at their throats, pearls for Margaret and coral for Jane, to the satin dresses, lace gloves and intricate fans on their laps. He, by contrast, was plainly dressed, albeit in his best suit and a freshly laundered shirt. But when he started to apologise for such a social omission, he was immediately silenced.

'I think you look very handsome, Fred. Simplicity suits you. Do you not agree, Janey?'

Jane looked from her mother to Fred and nodded.

'He looks acceptable to me,' she said bluntly, fiddling with her fan.

Fred suddenly felt intolerably self-conscious as mother and daughter appraised him.

'That is very kind of you both but really my appearance is of no importance,' muttered Fred, more gruffly than he had intended. Then, in an effort to change the subject, he reached into his jacket pocket.

'Jane, I hope you will accept this wee birthday gift from me. Many happy returns to you!'

And Fred handed over a small rectangular package, carefully gift- wrapped with pink and green embossed paper. Jane took it, her expression lightening.

'Thank you very much, Reverend Black. That is very kind of you. May I open it now, Mama?'

'Yes my dear. I think we have time.'

Untying the coloured ribbon and removing the paper, Jane held up a framed print of Edinburgh Castle at night, looming mysteriously over the city.

'Thank you,' Jane repeated, holding it up to look at it more closely. 'I like it. It is rather unusual. It will hang on my bedroom wall.'

'Now we must go in,' urged Margaret, aware that the crowds had started to file into the Assembly Rooms.

Just as they were approaching their seats, Jane stopped with a gasp. Noticing her daughter's reaction, Margaret turned towards her.

'Whatever is the matter, Janey?'

'My fan, Mama, I have left it in the carriage!'

'Do not worry about that, darling, it will be perfectly safe.'

'But it is so hot in here, I will need it later I am sure of it!'

'You can borrow mine,' soothed her mother.

'But it is my birthday fan, I really wanted to be able to use it!' Jane's voice had started to tremble.

'There is no time to retrieve it, my darling. Please be sensible.'

Jane's shoulders drooped and she pinched her lips morosely.

'Shall I go, Margaret?' offered Fred, noticing the altercation. 'If I am quick I may catch the carriage before it returns to Charlotte Square.'

Margaret looked solemnly at Fred and then at her daughter and sighed.

'Very well, that is good of you, Fred. I am sorry to put you to the trouble. But if Jim is no longer there, you must return immediately. The concert will start shortly.'

Crossing the now empty foyer, Fred approached the exit, hoping fervently that the carriage would still be outside. They had left the coachman chatting to an acquaintance so there was a chance he had not yet left. As he left the building and scanned the street outside, with great relief Fred spotted Jim climbing up into his driving seat.

'Hey there,' Fred shouted out, waving his hand in the air. 'Mr Jim! Wait one moment please. It's Miss Jane's fan, she has left it in the carriage.'

By the time, Fred returned to the concert hall, silence had fallen over the audience. With as much care as he could, he found his way to his seat and handed the fan to Jane who rewarded him with a broad smile and mouthed her thanks. Margaret also looked up and nodded, smiling. He found he was sitting beside Jane, who sat erect and attentive on the red plush seat, her thin pale arms laid on each armrest, two slim silver bangles glinting in the candle light. To his shame, he fleetingly wished he were seated beside Margaret instead.

Ignoring the disapproving looks and turned heads of his neighbours, Fred seated himself as carefully as he could. The seats were not overly generous and Fred's six foot frame felt somewhat constricted. Anxious not to disturb further, he shifted with difficulty to find a comfortable position. What was Mr Chopin's music going to be like, he wondered? He must trust Margaret's opinion, otherwise it would be a long evening. He wanted to be worthy of her faith in him.

Suddenly there was a wave of loud applause and looking up, Fred saw a slight, dark haired woman, dressed in a crimson crinoline, walk slowly across the stage to seat herself at a highly polished grand piano. So this was Clara Schumann. Gradually the applause faded away as Madame Schumann raised her long pale fingers above the keyboard. Then, light as a feather, she started to play, her face transfixed by the music, her body swaying gently backwards and forwards. The music rippled as naturally as water, ebbing and flowing, louder, softer, gently and more forcefully. All was committed to memory, her eyes closed as she made the keyboard come to life.

Apart from a few coughs, there was rapt silence in the room. Fred started to relax and leant back in his chair, his vision concentrated on the petite figure on stage. The delicate notes whirled around his head and suddenly he felt a constriction in his gut and realised with consternation that there were tears in his eyes. The music spoke of such sadness and longing as if Mr Chopin's very thoughts were being expressed through the musical notes. Unbidden, it made Fred reflect on all the worries and conflicts of the past few months. So much still unresolved, while he sat in an over-heated concert hall among the well-to-do of Edinburgh, pretending to be a cultured gentleman.

'Are you alright?' whispered Jane in his right ear.

With a start Fred turned to look at her.

'Yes, indeed. I am listening to the music.'

'Why are you crying?' queried Jane, leaning more closely to him.

'Crying? No…,' Fred, in embarrassment, raised a finger to his eye. It was wet. The girl regarded him with mixture of curiosity and sympathy.

'Here, take this, if you wish,' offered Jane, holding out a small white handkerchief.

'No thank you, Jane.' Fred gently pushed Jane's hand away and turned his face back to the performance.

There was a small sigh from Jane as she tucked her handkerchief away out of sight and opened her fan instead. Flutter, flutter went the fan in the corner of Fred's eye. He wished she would cease. The spell cast earlier by the music had now been broken and Fred was brought unwillingly back to the present. Was Jane's fan disturbing others as much as him, he wondered? He glanced sideways to observe his neighbours but all seemed entranced by the music.

Looking the other way, he saw Margaret leaning forward slightly in her seat. On her lap, her fingers moved in time to the music. She seemed completely oblivious. Then just as Fred was about to return his gaze to Madame Schumann, Margaret looked up, caught his eye and smiled. His heart jumped in embarrassment at having been caught out. What might she think of him? Smiling back in return and hoping his demeanour looked calmer than he felt, Fred nodded his acknowledgement

'So, Fred, I do hope you enjoyed that?' asked Margaret brightly, once the applause and cheers had died down and Clara Schumann had finally taken her leave.

'I did indeed, Margaret. It was truly beautiful and most affecting. Thank you for inviting me. What was the music Mrs Schumann was playing so that I may remember it?'

'They are called The Impromptus, Chopin's Impromptus.'

# CHAPTER 10

# A FISHING EXPEDITION

April 1862

It was a Monday morning and Fred and William were finishing breakfast in the dining room. The low morning sun shone into the room across the table, causing Fred to shield his eyes and shift his chair out of its beam.

'I should'nae complain,' he said, smiling. 'When I see the bonnie spring light, I realise I've been cooped up inside for too long. If the fine weather holds, it will be good to spend some more time outside.'

'I couldn't agree with you more, Fred,' nodded William. 'Tell me, have you ever been fishing? As you may have already noticed it is quite a passion of mine.'

Fred had observed William studying his favourite angling books of a winter evening and spending time constructing the most delicate and intricate of flies. And it was impossible to ignore the glass cases of prize salmon specimens displayed in the drawing room and landing.

'I've nae done any fishing in my life, William,' admitted Fred, 'but I mind our neighbour in Strathmuir was a ghillie and he often went to help the fishermen on the Tay.'

'That is indeed a fine fishing river. I have been lucky enough to try it out once or twice, but mostly I go to the Tweed. My brother Robert is a doctor in Galashiels and I can stay with him. And now that there's a new station, it is easy to get to. I would rather spend my time fishing than travelling.'

'I didnae ken ye had a brother, William.'

'Aye, Robert is a couple of years older than I am. Sadly, he is also a widower so we enjoy each other's company when we can.'

'When did you lose your wife, William?' queried Fred. He was aware that William's wife had died but until now had not felt able to ask more.

William was silent for a few seconds.

'I did not mean to intrude,' continued Fred, concerned that he had upset his colleague.

'Not at all, Fred. I have come to terms with it but I still miss her greatly. Her name was Isabella. She died five years ago, of cancer. If I could have taken her place I would have done so willingly. In the end her death was a release.'

William stopped speaking and sighed.

'But enough of sad memories, Fred. We are going to plan a fishing trip so I can introduce you to the beautiful River Tweed. What do you say to that?'

'That is a very generous offer, William. Thank you, I would like that very much, providing you are patient with me.'

Robert Russell lived in an attractive red-stone villa on the outskirts of Galashiels. It was large enough to provide space both for his family and medical practice but small enough to be considered homely. Fred felt welcome as soon as he and William alighted from the pony and trap that had been sent to meet them at the station. With arms full of rods and baskets, the two men approached the front door. It was already open, with William's brother standing at the top of the steps, an excitable springer spaniel panting by his side.

'Welcome tae the both o' you!' Dr Russell held out a hand in greeting.

'Good afternoon, Sir, thank you for your hospitality.' Fred put down one of the baskets and acknowledged his host.

Then William and his brother embraced fondly before Robert led the way inside.

'Come away in and get yourselves settled.'

The spaniel pushed a cold wet nose into Fred's hand and Fred stroked the smooth brown and white head.

'He's a fine dog,' commented Fred, admiringly. 'What's his name?'

'Sam. Yes, he's a lovely fellow, right enough, and a very good companion.'

The tiled hallway was wide and full of natural light from the glass hall door. A large mirror reflected the newcomers as they entered the house. A handsome heavy pine staircase rose up in front of them leading to the first floor. On the wall hung a set of antlers.

'Leave your tackle there for the moment,' instructed Robert. 'I'll ask Laing to put them away shortly. Let me show you your rooms then you can come and join me for some afternoon tea.'

Outside the spring sunshine continued to bathe the house and garden with a golden glow. The wind had dropped and a few puffy clouds hovered gently above their heads. In the garden all was peaceful apart from the chatter of some hedge-sparrows and the cluck of a territorial blackbird. Conditions should be perfect for a day of fishing, Fred mused with satisfaction.

When he awoke the following morning, on looking out of the window he could see that it had rained overnight. Now however the sky was a clear washed-out blue and the garden glistened with dew and raindrops. As he came downstairs he encountered Robert Russell peering at the barometer in the hall.

'Hmm, medium high, but you should be alright for an outing today,' he announced, 'The river will be fairly full but it looks like the weather will stay dry for the time being. Better get a good breakfast though to give you some ballast.' And he chuckled as he led the way to the dining room.

Three places had been laid at a circular mahogany table and on the side-board were set three dishes of scrambled eggs, bacon and mushrooms.

'Help yourselves, lads,' encouraged Robert, handing a plate to Fred.

Twenty minutes later, the last morsels of toast and marmalade and sips of Ceylon tea were being consumed. In the hall the longcase clock was striking the hour. William sat up expectantly.

'Best we were off,' he announced. 'Do you think the weather will hold, Robert? I had my doubts last night.'

'Aye, the glass is looking good. The rain should hold off for now but mind you take care in the water. It will be in fairly full spate after last night's showers.'

Standing knee-high in the river, Fred braced himself against the current. William had warned him to be careful. Beneath the surface smooth stones were coated with slippery green weed which might catch the unwary angler out. Flipping the long, bendy rod back over his head, Fred then cast it forward again, and watched as it skidded, reel hissing, over the water to land several yards from where he stood. He tried this a few times, as instructed by William, until he was satisfied he was in the best position. Apart from the rush of the water and the uplifting sound of birdsong, there was silence. Fred breathed in deeply and shut his eyes for a moment.

The tug on his rod caught him unawares. Had he caught something already? A surge of excitement flowed through him and he straightened up ready for the encounter. In an effort to balance himself, Fred jerked one of his feet a few inches. Making contact with one of the smooth stones, his foot went from under him and, before he could right himself, Fred found himself floundering in the fast moving water as it rapidly filled his waders and saturated his jacket.

'Damnation!'

The expletive passed his lips before he could control himself. He did not want to let go of his rod, however, and tried to stand up unaided. His efforts only seemed to make matters worse and his annoyance started to be overtaken with something approaching fear. William was standing some fifty yards upstream and immediately became aware of Fred's predicament.

'Hold fast, Fred. I'm coming back to get you.'

Reeling in his rod, William waded back to the shore, placed the tackle on the bank and hurried to Fred's aid.

'Give me the rod, Fred, then get yourself upright.'

Fred tried to do as he had been instructed and attempted laboriously to raise himself up out of the unforgiving river. However, the weight of the water and the strength of the current made the manoeuvre difficult. He was already feeling very cold as the icy water soaked through to his skin.

'Take my hand, Fred,' William called out, raising his voice against the rush of the water. 'Can you pull yourself up now?

With extreme effort, despite his wet clothing dragging him down, Fred finally succeeded in standing up. At that moment, to Fred's alarm, William now also lost his balance and found himself on his knees in the water.

'Sir! Sir!' Came a shout from the bank. 'Can we help ye?'

Turning his head towards the sound of the man's voice, Fred saw two young mill-workers standing just a few yards away on the shore.

'Aye, that ye can, thank ye. But wait there, nae point you getting wet an a'.'

William had had to let go of the rod which now floated rapidly away downstream. Whatever might have been attached to it had grasped its opportunity to flee. And now the older man, both hands free, staggered to his feet and started to wade cautiously to the bank.

'We need to get these clothes off as soon as we can,' William announced. He was starting to shiver and Fred was overcome with concern for his friend and colleague. This was his fault. He should have been more careful.

'Do ye ken Bonniebank House?' William addressed the millworkers who were standing at the ready on the river bank.

'Aye, we dae. Off the Melrose Road?'

'Good man! Can ye get a message to Dr Russell as quickly as you can? We need the pony and trap without delay.'

To Fred's great disappointment it was decided that they would not risk another sortie to the river. A hot bath, a whisky toddy and an early night seemed to have revived them but Robert, after checking his guests over, advised against a further fishing expedition on this visit.

'There will be other opportunities, Fred,' consoled William, observing Fred's long face. 'I feel responsible for putting you at risk. The water was really too high to fish safely.'

'No, no, William, the fault was all mine. I was not paying attention. You had warned me and I let my mind wander. I am sorry to have spoilt your trip.'

'We will put it down to experience then,' smiled William.

In the event, they returned to Edinburgh one day early. Mrs Oliphant expressed surprise as Fred and William entered the house. Their rods were laid down carefully on the heavy oak chest in the hallway and William thrust a bag of clothing at Mrs Oliphant.

'These were soaked through and will need a good airing,' he instructed her.

'Did you not take your mackintoshes, Sir?'

'We did but not before we both fell over in the river. It was very high and in full torrent. Not our finest hour! We had to make our way back to my brother's soaked to the skin.'

'Oh no, Sir! And did you catch anything for your efforts?'

'Not a thing! Apart from a cold. They say there are plenty salmon in the river but I'm afraid they managed to escape our clutches!'

William laughed ruefully and then sneezed.

'Let us get you both into the warm otherwise you will be in no fit state to take the Sunday service.'

And Mrs Oliphant shooed Fred and William into the drawing room where a fire was burning noisily, logs spitting resin on to the hearth behind a cast iron fireguard. Removing the guard, she took a poker to the flames to settle them down.

'Warm yourselves here. What can I bring you? Some tea or maybe something a wee bit stronger?'

'That's an excellent idea,' laughed William. 'Fred, will you join me?'

William then broke off his conversation with a chesty coughing fit, causing him to bend over and cover his face with his hand.

'Perhaps you should let Dr Sinclair take a look at you?' suggested Mrs Oliphant, a little frown gathering on her forehead.

'Ah, no need. I'm strong as an ox! I would not want to waste his time. No, I will take a hot bath and get to my bed early. That should do the trick.'

# CHAPTER 11

# SUCCESSION

Fred seemed none the worse for his soaking in the Tweed. As a precaution he applied some eucalyptus embrocation to his chest and gratefully accepted the offer of a fire in his room overnight. But his gratitude was tempered by the fact that William continued to cough and sneeze and obstinately refused to see the physician, despite both Fred and Mrs Oliphant's entreaties.

'Thank you for your concern, Fred,' responded William, 'but I know what Sinclair will say. He will tell me to take to my bed and rest my voice for at least a week. I have responsibilities. My parishioners rely on me. I cannot afford to act the invalid.'

'Can I not take over for a few days, William?' Fred queried. 'The rest would do you good. I would be happy to help.'

'I do not doubt that, my boy. Thank you. I will not forget your offer but, God willing, I will be back to normal by the weekend.'

Going about his usual duties, Fred tried to ignore the sound of William coughing and retching. The coughing was particularly persistent at night which meant that William was getting little sleep. William continued to make light of it but Fred could see that his colleague was looking thinner and fatigued by the strain. On Saturday morning, he did not come down to breakfast as expected and Fred noticed Mrs Oliphant crossing the hall with a tray in her hands. A few minutes later she returned and entered the dining room as Fred was finishing a plate of eggs and bacon.

'Good morning, Reverend Black. I trust you slept well?' Mrs Oliphant addressed Fred politely. 'I have a message from Reverend Russell. He has not had a good night and does not feel able to get up so would you be kind enough to look in on him when you have had your breakfast? He has finally relented and agreed to see Dr Sinclair I am pleased to say.'

'Of course. I will go immediately,' said Fred, pushing back his chair and standing up.

Once upstairs, he tapped lightly on William's bedroom door and entered the room without waiting for a reply. The older man was lying back on several pillows, breathing heavily. His face was extremely pale and there were dark shadows under his eyes. The curtains were partially drawn and the room was stuffy and heavy with the smell of camphor oil.

'William, forgive me for disturbing you,' said Fred in a low voice, approaching the bed. 'Mrs Oliphant said you wanted to see me.'

'Thank you, Fred,' replied William hoarsely. 'As you can see I am not much use for anything at the moment.' Then he started coughing and turned his head away. Fred pulled up a chair and waited anxiously until William was able to speak again.

'Sorry, Fred. I cannot really say much. Would you please take the service tomorrow? I had hoped I would be better by now but it is not to be. I would be most grateful.'

'Of course, it is the least I can do.' Fred put out a hand in reassurance. 'Do you have a theme you wish me to follow?'

'No, I am happy to leave that to you. Give my apologies to the congregation and tell them I hope to be back before too long.'

Once again the effort of speaking caused William to break into another paroxysm. Fred stood up in alarm.

'Can I help you, William? Some water perhaps?'

At that moment there was a knock at the door and to Fred's relief it opened to reveal Mrs Oliphant with Dr Sinclair at her side.

'I'll take my leave then,' said Fred in parting. 'Please, do not worry about the service, William. Concentrate on getting well.'

As he walked down the landing to his room, Fred could hear the low rumble of voices, cut short by another bout of coughing.

There were expressions of surprise at St Ninian's on Sunday morning, when William Russell did not take up his usual place at the front of the kirk to welcome the congregation. Instead, Fred stood alone as the parishioners filed in to take their places. A few asked where William was but, mostly, they nodded their heads sympathetically at Fred before continuing into the church.

Fred had chosen 'Count Thy Blessings' as the theme of his sermon. It was all too easy to overlook, or take for granted, all the positive, happy things in one's life, pushed to one side by greed, ambition or envy, Fred told the congregation. Reflecting on William's illness, he asked them to thank the Lord for good health and kind friends.

'We must never forget to be grateful for all that we have.'

'Finally, please remember Reverend Russell in your prayers this week,' Fred addressed a hundred upturned faces. 'He has caught a feverish cold and his physician has advised bed rest for a few days. He apologises for being absent today but is hopeful that he will be back among you all again very soon.'

On his return to Melville Street, Fred looked in to reassure William and pass on the many good wishes for a speedy recovery he had received from the parishioners. William smiled and nodded his head wearily.

'Thank you, Fred. It is comforting to know that they are in such good hands.' William paused to catch his breath before continuing. 'I hope you remember what I said to you a few weeks back, Fred?'

Fred was startled by this reference.

'Of course, William, but you will recover soon and I look forward to assisting you for many years yet. I have much to learn before I can step into your shoes.'

William did not reply immediately but looked thoughtfully at Fred.

'That is my wish and hope as well but remember there will be others who would want to succeed me. Just because one is a man of God does not mean there is no ambition. Do not be dissuaded or discouraged. You have what it takes to be a memorable and influential preacher for this church.'

William stretched out a hand and took hold of Fred's arm.

'I have been here for twenty years and when my time is over, whenever that may be, I want to know that my life's work will be carried on by someone I trust and admire. Please go over to my bureau and bring me the piece of paper lying there.'

There was something in the tone of William's voice that filled Fred with doubt but he did as he was asked and handed the sheet of paper to William.

'Thank you, Fred, now read it to me please.'

*17 Melville Street*

*24th April 1862*

*I, Reverend Doctor William Russell, wish it to be known that, in the event of my demise, my choice of successor at St Ninian's Church is Reverend Frederick Black.*

*Signed: William Russell*

Fred stared at William with a heaviness in his heart. He did not want William to speak of such things.

'I am honoured, William, but I pray that situation is many years off. I …'

Fred was unable to go on.

'Think no more of it, lad,' consoled William, seeing Fred's distress. 'I will be on my feet again soon, have no fear. But I wanted the peace of mind that my thoughts on the matter are known. Now I must rest. We will speak again tomorrow.'

'Of course, William, I will pray for you.' Fred rose to his feet, 'Sleep well.'

The next couple of days seemed to see an improvement in William's health. The cough had eased and though he was still fatigued and remained in bed, he appeared to be sleeping better. Fred took the opportunity of spending more time with him and bringing him up to date with events in the parish.

It was therefore with shock and alarm that Fred was woken on Wednesday night by the sound of urgent voices on the landing outside his bedroom. He could make out Dr Sinclair issuing instructions and Mrs Oliphant's terse responses. But there was another voice he did not recognise. Stumbling out of bed and grabbing hold of his dressing gown, Fred opened the door and in as hushed a tone as he could manage, addressed the doctor.

'What is happening, Dr Sinclair, Mrs Oliphant? How is William?'

Now, as Sinclair and Mr Oliphant entered William's bedroom, the newcomer turned towards Fred. He was a youngish man about Fred's age and from his features, Fred immediately guessed at his parentage.

'Reverend Black, I am James, William's son.'

'Aye, I can see the likeness. How do you do?' Fred extended his hand.

'My father has taken a turn for the worse, alas. I arrived a couple of hours ago from Newcastle.'

'But I understood he was getting better,' replied Fred, staring in disbelief at William's son. 'We spoke just a few hours ago.'

'And so I had believed as well, but Sinclair fears my father's blood may have been contaminated with whatever infection ails him. He is fading.'

Fred let out a cry of grief.

'No, it cannot be! Let me see him!'

Without waiting for a reply, Fred pushed open the door to

William's room. The embers of the fire gave off some warmth and an oil lamp illuminated the bed in which William lay. Waiting in the shadows were Dr Sinclair and Mrs Oliphant. The housekeeper gave a little shudder of grief and sought to quell her tears. Sinclair indicated the chair beside the bed and invited Fred to sit down.

'Speak to him, Fred. It will give him comfort. I believe he can still hear you.

Fred did as he was told and leant forward over the bed.

'William, it is me, Fred.'

Fred stretched out his fingers and laid them very gently over the pale, still hand that rested on the eiderdown. For quite some time there was only the wheezing sound of William's rapid, shallow breathing and Fred feared he was too late. Then, with obvious effort, William opened his eyes and turned his head towards Fred.

'Dear Fred, your company warms my soul.'

'Do not speak, William, you will tire yourself.'

'Ah, it is too late for that. But I am not afraid of death. I know I go to a better, fairer place in Heaven and will be reunited with my dear Isabella. I am just sorry to be leaving you too soon, Fred. And I am truly blessed to have lived long enough to have found you as my successor.'

William then paused and tried to catch his breath. Beckoning to the others in the room to come closer, he whispered urgently, while gripping Fred's hand.

'Here is my successor, note my wishes. God bless us all.'

Then he fell back on the pillow and closed his eyes. His lips had taken on a bluish tinge and, as the sound of his breathing grew weaker, Fred leant closer to the dying man. William's hand still held his and, very gently, Fred raised it to his lips.

'May you rest in peace, my dear friend.'

# CHAPTER 12

# BREACH OF CONTRACT

THE WEEKS THAT FOLLOWED WILLIAM'S SUDDEN DEATH filled Fred with despair. For the first time in his life he began to question his faith and his future. William had been adamant that he should succeed him but to find himself so unexpectedly alone this early in his career, shook Fred to his very core. The once life-filled manse, so full of activity, plans and discussion, was now stilled. How could he replace his mentor in the minds and hearts of the congregation?

The funeral had been a heart-felt and emotional affair. William was much loved it was clear. St Ninian's had been completely full, with mourners standing in the aisles and at the entrance. These included Richard and Mary-Ann Kelman, who, to Fred's gratitude and relief, had made the journey south from Aberdeen.

'*This is a heart-breaking loss for us all,*' Richard had written in his letter to Fred on hearing the news. '*As you know, William was one of my oldest friends and someone to whom I could always turn. After less than a year in his company I am glad, Fred, that you will have also come to know what a good and kind man he was. Mary-Ann and I will of course come to attend the funeral and to support you.*'

The sonorous voices of those who eulogised and remembered William filled the church with their heartfelt sentiments. Then Fred took his turn at the pulpit and could not help his voice breaking as he praised his colleague for his kindness, encouragement and acknowledged how much he would miss him.

After the service, a small sad group of mourners accompanied the coach bearing the coffin the short distance to the Calton Cemetery. Two of William's sons, James and Edward had chosen a simple rectagonal grave-stone of polished pink granite to remember their father by.

**In Loving Memory of the**

**Reverend Doctor William James Russell, DD, (1802 – 1862)**

**Minister of St Ninian's Church, Edinburgh.**

**Loving husband of the late Isabella (1810 – 1857),**

**much respected father of James, Edward and Andrew**

**and friend of many.**

**May his soul rest in eternal peace. Amen.**

Later, sitting in the Melville Street drawing room with Richard and Mary-Ann and James and Edward Russell, Fred found it difficult to speak. William's third son, Andrew, had been unable to attend as he was posted to Calcutta with the East India Company and it had been impossible for him to make the long journey back to Edinburgh in time. The group sat as though frozen, studying their hands or gazing distantly into the fire, each alone with their private thoughts. Occasionally, one would take a breath as though about to say something but then thought better of it. The longer the silence continued, the more it felt irreverent to break it. Finally Mrs Oliphant broke their reverie by summoning them to eat.

'You need to have something, Madam, gentlemen. It has been

a long, hard day for all of us.'

Despite his doubts and sadness, life had to go on. William would not have wanted it any other way. Thus, Fred found himself sharing the duties at St Ninian's with the Reverend James Henderson. Henderson, who had formally appointed him to his post, had been one of the first of William's colleagues to introduce himself and Fred was glad of his support and quiet confidence at this most trying of times.

It had been agreed that a six week period of mourning would be granted before the necessary task of seeking William's successor began. The Church Council had been made aware of William's preference for Fred but it had been explained to him that, despite this, the post would be advertised and applicants interviewed. This would include Fred. He recognised that if he were unsure, now would be the time to make his decision. If he were appointed as the next minister of St Ninian's there could be no turning back.

He was in urgent need of wise counsel. Were his doubts and fears temporary? How would his mother and indeed his father, who had invested in his career, react to him missing such an opportunity? And what would Jessie have to say? Fred was ashamed that she had occupied his thoughts less of late. Partly due to William's demise and partly due to the continuing silence on her part.

His thoughts turned to a conversation he had had with Richard Kelman. The Kelmans had stayed in Edinburgh for a couple of days following the funeral and had spoken to Fred about his future, so unexpectedly changed from the previous year. He had confided William's wish to them and expressed his own doubts. As always, Richard spoke calmly and supportively to Fred.

'You have had the greatest shock and sadness. We all have but you especially. It is completely understandable that you have doubts and feel weak and ill-prepared. But William would not have spoken to you as he did, if he did not truly believe you could do it. You must remember this, Fred.'

Mary-Ann regarded Fred with sympathetic concern.

'My dear, Richard is right,' she added. 'You must not doubt your gifts and what you have to offer. You are being tested but you will come through it stronger and an even better person. Trust me, Fred.'

Then she approached Fred and put her arms around him. For a moment Fred felt like a small boy again and had to suppress an urge to cry.

At the beginning of June, shortly after submitting his formal application to the Church Council, Fred was surprised to be summoned to an unexpected meeting at New College by Reverend Henderson. Normally, James would have spoken to him directly as they saw each other nearly every day at the moment, but on this occasion, the request came by letter bearing the Church Council crest. There was no further explanation so it was with some puzzlement that Fred set out for his rendezvous. Walking up the Mound and considering the looming façade of the College, Fred tried to anticipate what might await him.

On entering the room, Fred smiled genially at the five men seated in front of him. James Henderson was of course well known to him and the other four he had encountered several times since his arrival in Edinburgh. He was, therefore, taken aback when none of the men stood up, smiled or even extended a hand in greeting. A shot of cold apprehension flowed through him as he crossed the room and sat in the single chair indicated to him.

'Gentlemen?' Fred started conversationally. 'How can I be of assistance?'

There was a moment's silence as the five men looked at one another before James Henderson assumed the mantle of inquisitor and addressed Fred.

'Reverend Black,' he started, forgoing any informalities. 'In the light of your application for the position of minister at St Ninian's, I regret that we have received new evidence which causes us to have grave concerns as to your suitability for the post.'

Fred could not help himself. He felt his mouth fall open in shock and surprise. For a moment he was unable to speak. Evidence? Concerns? Were his qualifications lacking? Had one of his references been unacceptable?

'James, Reverend Henderson, I do not know what to say. I believe I completed the application correctly to the best of my knowledge. In what way might I be unsuitable?'

Rather than reply, Reverend Henderson merely stretched out his hand in which was held a letter. Even in his shocked state, Fred could see that the handwriting was his own. Slowly and disbelievingly, he cast his eyes down to read the contents.

*My dearest Jessie*

*You may be surprised to hear from me after our last meeting. Forgive me for letting you down. It will not happen again. I am writing as I have heard from both Mrs Milne and Mrs MacDonald that you are with child. I believe I must be the father. If this is the case I must take responsibility. I realise I have been cowardly and selfish up until now, thinking only of my own future. Forgive me, Jess. I am just a scared young man, that is the truth of it, but I can only imagine how you are feeling.*

*What I want to say to you, Jessie, is that I will marry you if you will have me. I want to provide for you and our child. Please do not feel you have to give your child away. I cannot promise what life will hold for us but I swear I will be a good husband to you and a loving father to our child.*

Fred could not read any further. For a moment the room darkened and he thought he might faint. There was a rushing in his ears and briefly he found it difficult to breathe. Where had this come from? It was from him to Jessie. Clearly, she had not received it and now his behaviour was laid bare for all to see.

No-one spoke. A plain brown clock ticked steadily on the wall and outside could be heard the raucous shriek of an aggressive herring gull. Fred could hear the beat of his heart and his own rapid breathing, then the clearing of a throat on the other side of the table.

'Well, Reverend Black?' finally came the reminder from James Henderson.

'Aye, it is my letter. I dinnae deny it,' whispered Fred. 'But how do you come to have it? It is private.'

'Speak up, please. We need to be able to hear what you have to say.'

Reluctantly, Fred repeated his admission.

'That may well be the case,' responded Henderson grimly, 'but it is very much our business. The new minister of St Ninian's has to be above reproach. You were William's choice but this changes everything.'

Fred sat in silence, his head bowed. This was his punishment, he could see that now. How could he have thought he could walk away from Jessie without any consequences? He was an arrogant fool. Aware that the men in front of him were awaiting his reply, Fred reluctantly raised his head to face them.

'Every word is true. She meant, means a lot to me but I have received no reply from her. I believed she did not want me. How did you come by this? I gave this to Mrs MacDonald. She promised Jessie would get it!'

Suddenly, an image of Reverend MacDonald's amused face on the occasion of their last meeting at New College, rose up in front of Fred. At the time he had wondered at the man's over-familiar manner. Now he had his answer.

James Henderson's disapproving voice broke into Fred's thoughts.

'I am not at liberty to say how we are now in possession of this but, as you do not deny you wrote it, that detail is irrelevant.'

Combined with losing William so recently, the frustration, grief and uncertainty Fred had been feeling for so long now came rushing to the fore. He could not fight it any longer.

'Sirs, I have let everybody down!' he cried out. 'I will resign my post and be done with it. I am truly sorry to have misled you.'

As he started to stand up, Reverend Henderson, who until so recently had been his close colleague, indicated firmly that he should sit down.

'Reverend Black, calm yourself. We are not finished here. We will let you know when you may depart.'

Then the five men in front of Fred turned in towards each other and muttered urgently in low voices. Fred could do nothing but clench his teeth and listen to his pulse thud relentlessly in his neck. All those years of study, work, expectation to be obliterated in a few minutes. Then Reverend Henderson turned his gaze once again towards Fred.

'We will consider your offer of resignation. It is not something we can accept or refuse here and now. William Russell clearly wished you to succeed him. A dying man's wish. Whether he would be so generous if he knew of this letter is another matter, one we need to discuss. You will have our answer by the end of the week. You may take your leave now, Reverend Black.'

The five men glanced coldly at Fred then rose and turned their backs. The meeting was at an end.

# CHAPTER 13

# ENGAGEMENT

STUMBLING OUT OF NEW COLLEGE AND INTO THE EARLY summer sunshine, Fred was completely oblivious to his surroundings. On this occasion, the far-reaching views that generally so impressed him had no impact and he hurried, head down, back to Melville Street, more than once nearly colliding with passers-by who looked askance at the grim-faced young man who had just passed them.

For the rest of the day Fred avoided human contact, having requested that Mrs Oliphant leave a tray for him at meal times. He had no energy for conversation of any kind and decided to take refuge in his room until his inner turmoil eased. That night he barely slept. What would William have thought, he wondered? His humiliation was complete. How could he continue in this city now? Even if the Council did not accept his resignation, he would now almost certainly be passed over by one of the other candidates.

The next morning, as he sat at the breakfast table, Mrs Oliphant came in with a letter.

'Good morning, Reverend Black. I hope you are feeling better this morning? This was just delivered for you – from Mrs Burnett. The coachman is waiting outside for your reply.'

At the mention of Margaret's name, Fred looked up in surprise. He had not had any direct contact with the Burnett family since the funeral. The Burnetts had both attended but Fred had managed only the briefest of exchanges with them after the service when they expressed their condolences. The thought that they might also have knowledge of his shame filled him with despondency. Noticing his hesitation, Mrs Oliphant gave him a quizzical look as she waited for him to take the envelope. Without a word, Fred took the letter from her and opened it.

*Charlotte Square*

*3rd June 1862*

*My dear Fred*

*Some information concerning you has come to my notice recently. I would be grateful if you were able to visit me as soon as possible as a matter of great urgency. I will be at home today if this is convenient.*

*With warmest regards*

*Margaret*

Folding the letter, Fred returned it to its envelope and put it in his pocket.

'Please let the coachman know I will be with him directly,' he instructed the house-keeper. 'I will be but a few minutes.'

As he climbed the stairs to his room, the shame and embarrassment he felt was almost too much for Fred to bear. Fleetingly he thought that he might just pack his bags and flee back to Strathmuir. But what would that solve? He would have to live with the disappointment and disapproval of his mother for the rest of his life. No, he could not be a coward as well. He must face up to this.

The splendid house in Charlotte Square always looked its best in the morning as the easterly sun bathed the sandstone façade with a golden glow. Even after several visits, Fred found it hard not to be overwhelmed by such grandeur. Donaldson greeted him as he climbed down from the carriage and walked up the steps to the front door.

'Good morning, Sir. A pleasure to see you again. Mrs Burnett is waiting for you in her parlour. Let me take your coat.'

Seated alone with Margaret, Fred remembered the first visit he had made back in the autumn when she had been so ill. Seeing her now, sitting poised and coiffed on a low chaise longue, filled him with both pleasure at her recovery and apprehension for what she might be about to say. Fred felt unable to relax and sat uneasily at the edge of his chair, his knees pressed tightly together and his hands folded on top of them. It was impossible to tell what Margaret was thinking. There was a kindly expression on her face though her eyes seemed to be narrowed in some kind of concern – but perhaps that was his imagination.

'Thank you for coming so promptly, Fred. I am sorry David and I were not able to see more of you after Reverend Russell's funeral but there were so many people I am sure you were kept very busy. How are you?' She stopped speaking and looked sympathetically at Fred.

A small part of Fred was relieved. She wished to express her commiserations in person. It was typical of her to show concern and solicitude after such a tragic event.

'I am heart-broken, Margaret, and still mightily shocked. I can still barely believe it. It all happened so quickly and so unexpectedly but life must go on.'

Fred looked up at her and smiled feebly. Margaret did not return his smile but continued to watch him with concern.

'Yes I can see that. You have my and David's deepest sympathy. William will be greatly missed for a long time.' She paused before continuing. 'Actually, I have asked you here today on another most delicate matter. What you will hear may shock you but I must ask you for total honesty.'

Fred's earlier relief receded and was replaced once again with a deep sense of unease and foreboding.

'I will always be honest with you, Margaret. You should not doubt that for an instant.'

As Fred was speaking, Margaret stood up and crossed the room in a few paces. Pressing the heavy door shut with a click, she turned and for a moment leant against it, surveying Fred. Then she returned to her sofa and addressed him.

'You will be aware that David is an elder of St Ninian's and that we have both been patrons for many years. Although not members of the Church Council, our views and opinions are taken into account in serious matters which might affect the congregation.'

Fred nodded slowly at the preamble. Margaret continued.

'We had a visit yesterday afternoon from Reverend James Henderson.'

'Ah!' Fred was unable to stop the gasp of regret that passed his lips.

'Let me finish please, Fred. Rest assured you will have ample time to respond to what I have to say. Henderson brought with him a letter. He told me they had shown it to you and that you admitted you were the writer. It seems you have promised marriage to a young woman and that she appears to be carrying your child?'

Fred bent forward and placed both hands over his ears. His humiliation was complete. If Margaret knew, then there was no hope for him. He was done for. His eye was caught by the patterned Indian rug beneath his feet and how radiantly the colours shone where the morning sun hit it. It looked like a maze and he felt as though he himself were at the centre of it, stumbling and lost, while outside life went on as normal without him.

Margaret's voice broke into his despair and he realised he would have to reply. He could not hide this any longer.

'You must tell me the truth, Fred, if we are able to help you.'

Slowly Fred straightened his back and looked directly at Margaret.

'You'll nae want to know me, far less help me, when you hear the truth.' Fred took a deep breath before continuing. 'I deny nothing. I said as much to Reverend Henderson. This is something which happened when I was still in Aberdeen. I dinnae regret it. I only regret that I wasnae able to honour my offer to Jessie. She deserves better. I havnae heard from her since our final meeting last year. I have tried to find her, believe me. But the fact that this letter is now in the hands of the Church Council must mean she never received it? And she is unaware of my proposal? And the bairn is to be adopted.'

Fred ceased speaking and covered his face with his hands. If Jessie had not received his letter, she would have truly thought he had abandoned her. It was unbearable.

'I willnae bring disgrace on St Ninian's, Margaret, nor on William's memory. I have already offered the Council my resignation which they will no doubt accept.'

Fred slumped back in his chair and passed a hand over his mouth to stifle a groan.

For a few seconds there was silence. Then in a low, quiet voice, Margaret spoke again.

'You will not resign, Fred.'

Fred looked up in disbelief at Margaret's certainty. He could not find any words in reply.

'You will not resign, Fred,' she repeated, emphatically. 'David and I have spoken with Henderson and the rest of the Council and they have agreed.'

'What do you mean, Margaret? It is impossible for me to continue. I have let everyone down, I have sinned. There must be many, far better men than me who would be worthy of the post.'

'That may be the case, Fred, but no-one else has your humility, your devotion, your experience of real life. Yes, you are flawed but that gives you a greater understanding of man's psyche. You do not set yourself above others. And besides, **I** need you here, not buried somewhere in the countryside where your talents and gifts will go unappreciated.'

Fred sat upright and stared at Margaret, trying to comprehend what she was saying and why she would say such a thing.

'As I have said, Reverend Henderson paid us a visit yesterday and we spoke at length about the situation. We do not believe you are a libidinous man. You are a young man who has made a mistake but this should not blight your entire career. David supports me in this and we are prepared to act as your guarantors. We have agreed to endow St Ninian's with a considerable sum provided they do not accept your resignation and agree to you becoming the next minister, as I understand Reverend Russell wished.'

'Margaret, I cannae let you do this! I'm nae worth it.' Fred was aghast. 'You should let me go and forget about me.'

'Fred, it is done. The Council have agreed and have given me the letter. I cannot let you go. Do you not understand this?'

No, he did not understand anything. At that moment all he wanted was to be away from this place, away from the compassionate gaze of the beautiful woman sitting opposite him, talking in riddles. Then she stood up and crossed to where Fred was sitting. Stretching out a pale hand, very gently Margaret touched his cheek.

'Dear Fred, you have been my saviour. When I was at my darkest, I believed I had nothing to live for. But your compassion and patience showed me that there was still light. I will forgive you almost anything.' She paused, staring intently at him. 'But, there is one condition that must be met….'

Fred felt as though he were hypnotised by her proximity, the urgency in her low voice. For a moment he was unable to speak.

'Ah, of course, anything my dear Margaret. How can I refuse you after your kindness and generosity?'

Fred looked up at his benefactress in puzzlement, wondering what her condition might be. He would be forever in her debt if she succeeded in delivering him from such ignominy. Margaret returned to the chaise longue and sat down slowly. Leaning forward and fixing her gaze on Fred, she spoke.

'In four years' time, when she has turned eighteen, you are to marry our daughter, Jane.'

At first Fred believed he had misheard Margaret's words. This could not be the condition.

'Your daughter? Jane?' Fred gasped. 'But she is a child still. How can you think of it?'

'She will not be a child in four years' time. You will have a long engagement. There will be time to get to know each other better.'

Fred stared at the calm, resolute woman in front of him and tried to understand. Why would she want this for her daughter? As if reading his thoughts, Margaret spoke again.

'Jane is an unusual girl. Very intelligent and enquiring. Not like other girls of her age. She is not interested in fashion and gossip. As your wife she would have the intellectual balance and respect she needs.'

'But I can offer her so little. I am a poor minister. In many years' time I may make my mark, God willing, but Jane is accustomed to a life of comfort and ease and financial security. Does she know about this?'

'Not yet, but when the right moment presents itself, her father and I will speak to her. I know she is fond of you.'

'But....'

Margaret stood up and held her finger to her lips. Opening up a small mahogany writing bureau she withdrew an envelope and held it in front of Fred.

'Once you and Jane are married, I will return this to you. Until then you will succeed William Russell at St Ninian's and fulfil his dying wish.'

# CHAPTER 14

# NEW SCOTLAND

KEIG, ABERDEENSHIRE – June 1862

'JESSIE! JESSIE!' MRS ANDERSON'S VOICE SOUNDED increasingly urgent.

Jessie pulled the bedclothes over her head in an effort to block out the unwelcome intrusion. Mornings had become intolerable since Jamie had been taken. Briefly, just before waking fully, she enjoyed a moment's peace of mind before the painful reality of her life encroached on her once again.

'Jessie! Reverend Anderson wants to leave within the hour. Ye must get up now and eat your breakfast.'

The door opened abruptly.

'What a lazy quine ye are! I hope ye are packed?' Mrs Anderson stood by Jessie's bed, her arms folded in exasperation.

'We've been through a' this before, Jessie. Ye cannae bide here any longer.' Mrs Anderson's tone had softened. 'You must return tae Aberdeen. The MacDonalds are expecting ye. Ye are lucky they have kept a position open for ye. Ye'll be able tae start over.'

Jessie dreaded the return. Everything within her fought

against it. She had tried to put it off as long as possible but now it had to be faced.

'There is naethin' fer me there.' Her voice was muffled. 'I've lost ma bairn. I hae nuthin'.'

'Listen, Jessie,' Mrs Anderson leant in towards her. 'Ye must be strong. If ye dinnae, ye'll be sent to Cornhill. Ye ken fit that means?'

Aye, she did. The so-called Royal Lunatic Asylum. Once you went in you did not come out. She was not a lunatic. Just very sad and so tired with this life she found herself in. Summoning all her strength, Jessie stood up and faced Mrs Anderson.

'Aye, I do. I ken ye want tae help me. I'll get dressed and be doon the stair shortly.'

For a moment the two women regarded each other sadly, then Mrs Anderson held out her arms and drew Jessie to her.

'Be strong. Dinnae give up.'

Jessie found herself weeping hot tears which stung her eyes. She held on to Mrs Anderson for a few more seconds then pulled back.

'Thank ye, Jean. Thank ye for being so kind tae me. I've been lucky.'

'Now, now, enough o' this or Reverend Anderson will be displeased wi' the both of us.'

Mrs Anderson stood up dabbing her eyes with her forefinger.

'I'll take your bag downstairs. There's some breakfast waiting for ye.'

And she turned and left the room.

Lumphanan Railway Station was some ten miles away. It would take Reverend Anderson at least an hour to get there in the gig. The train departed at eleven thirty so he was anxious to leave promptly with Jessie and her luggage. He would not be coming with her on the train, he had told her. An unnecessary expense. Once in Aberdeen she could walk the short distance to St Nicholas' Manse. All being well she would be there by lunch-time.

With a final look around the room where so much had happened to her, Jessie picked up her coat and hat and a small well-worn personal bag. Inside was her purse, a handkerchief and the psalm book Fred had sent her together with his letters and the fragile lock of Jamie's hair. She would take no chances with these precious possessions and would not let them out of her sight.

Out of the window the Vale of Alford lay before her in early summer perfection, a peaceful palette of blue, grey, green and yellow. New growth in the fields would, in a few months' time, turn into fields of oats and barley while at the edge of grey stone dykes, bright splashes of yellow broom and white meadow parsley brought some dainty detail to the panorama. Despite everything, Jessie knew she would miss the beauty and tranquillity of this place. She stood at the open window for a few seconds and breathed in the fresh country air. A ride in a pony and trap amid such surroundings might be considered a pleasure but Jessie felt it would be wasted on Reverend Anderson.

By the time she came down the stairs, Jessie could hear the minister outside already fussing over the pony. There was porridge and eggs set out in the kitchen which Jessie ate as quickly as she could before returning to the hall. Mrs Anderson approached her holding two packages wrapped in grease-proof paper.

'Here's some food for your journey, Jessie, and some shortbread for Mrs MacDonald. Tell her we hope tae see her and the bairns at some point in the summer. Oh, and I want ye tae hae this.'

Mrs Anderson lowered her voice and glanced towards the front door before pressing a sealed letter and a five shilling note into Jessie's hand. Jessie looked at her in surprise.

'The letter's a reference for ye. It may be useful at some stage. Put it all awa' now and dinnae lose it. Nae need for my husband tae see.'

Jessie did as she was told and stood facing Mrs Anderson.

'Thank ye,' she whispered, pulling her bag closely to her. 'Thank ye fer everythin'.'

'Good luck, Jessie lass. You deserve to be happy.'

Once again Mrs Anderson put her arms round her and gave Jessie a quick hug.

'There's no time for sentimentality, Jean.' A man's voice broke the moment.

Reverend Anderson stood at the door, puffing impatiently.

'We want to get you on that train, Jessie, so we need to get going now. You've said your good-byes I take it?'

Jessie nodded and, biting her lip to stop it trembling, she turned away and walked outside to the pony cart.

As she expected, Reverend Anderson had little to say to her during their journey to Lumphanan. He sat stiff and disapproving and did little to disguise his relief at being rid of her at last. As he drew up in front of the station building, he turned to Jessie.

'Remember you've had a second chance, lassie. I dinnae expect to hear any more bad news about you. I hope that is understood? I pray that God will show you the righteous path from now on.'

He stared at her briefly, his small blue eyes unblinking and his fleshy lips pursed tightly together. Then he jumped down and went round to retrieve her valise. Meantime Jessie hitched up her skirts and climbed down to the ground. Reverend Anderson handed over the case and, with just a curt nod of his head by way of farewell, clambered up again on to the gig and turned the pony's head in a homewards direction. Jessie stood still for a couple of minutes watching them disappear into the distance, then, hearing the warning hoot of the approaching locomotive, she hurried to purchase her ticket and walked on to the platform for the Aberdeen train.

Anxiety started to hit Jessie after the train left Banchory. The thought of returning to St Nicholas' manse filled her with revulsion and dread. She could not go back there. The house was not a place of sanctuary – the very opposite. But what choice did she have? She had turned these thoughts over and over in her mind the past few weeks, even appealing to Mrs Anderson to let her stay with them, but to no avail. She had been unable to reveal her true reasons. She dared not. No-one would have believed her, as MacDonald had scathingly reminded her on that hideous day.

The hills of Donside had been left behind and now farmland lay on either side of the rail track. Culter, Milltimber, Bieldside – the train stopped briefly at each village. There was a slamming of doors and the bustle of temporary activity as passengers got on and settled themselves for the short journey into the city. It would not be long now before both she and the locomotive reached their destination.

Soon enough the solid, grey houses of Aberdeen came into view as the train made its way steadily past backyards, gardens, parks and workshops. At twenty minutes to one, it finally steamed its way up to the buffers and came to a shuddering, hissing halt. For a moment Jessie sat in a daze, as around her fellow passengers grabbed hold of their luggage and exited on to the station platform.

Her head was whirling. What should she do now? Slowly she stood up, picked up her travelling case and followed the crowd on to the station concourse. With reluctant steps she moved towards the exit. Outside the sky was a fresh blue and the summer sunshine sparkled off the granite facades. The familiar whiff of the fish market hit her nostrils and suddenly it felt as if the past couple of years had been an illusion.

Then out of the corner of her eye Jessie spotted a large poster, one of many, pasted up on the walls of the station. Something about it made her pause and drew her to it. Underneath the images of sea, fields and happy smiling people were the words:

> 'A New Life Beckons! In Nova Scotia, Canada!
>
> Space, Fresh air and Opportunities for all Hard Workers.
>
> Domestic servants, agricultural workers and skilled tradesmen particularly welcome.'

Putting her case down, she peered more closely at it. Where was this place?

'Ye interested in goin' tae Canada then?' A voice at her shoulder caused Jessie to jump and turn her head. A young man was looking at her intently.

'Ma cousin's bin there nearly ten year now,' the speaker continued. 'Land's really cheap. A settler can own a farm there for less than he wid hae tae pay in rent at hame. Nae straight awa' ken but wages are guid and ye can save. I'd gie it a go mesel' but ma mither's auld noo and it wud break her heart if I left.'

Jessie listened with growing interest.

'How did yer cousin get there then? It wid be a lot o' money?'

'He sailed frae Glasgow. Took a few weeks mind. I dinnae ken how much it cost him. A few bob I dare say!'

Glasgow? She could go to Glasgow. Mrs Anderson's gift would get her there and then....

The sound of the St Nicholas clock chiming the quarter hour interrupted the conversation and the young man started to move off.

'Weel, I must get back tae ma work. Guid luck tae ye. Better than this cauld place onyhow!'

'Aye, thank ye. Mebbe I will.'

Her heart racing, Jessie realised she would not get this chance again. Her bag packed, some money in her pocket. But she had to decide now. If she did not arrive at the manse within the next half hour, the MacDonalds would wonder where she was and maybe come looking for her. How much would a train ticket to Glasgow cost she wondered? Approaching the nearest ticket booth, she addressed a bored looking clerk who was checking a ledger.

'Excuse me, the next train tae Glasgow please?'

Looking up at her briefly, the ticket seller jabbed a finger at the notice board behind her.

'Ten past one, lassie.'

In the background the St Nicholas clock struck one o' clock and Jessie swallowed nervously.

'And how much for a third class ticket tae Glasgow please?'

'Return or single?'

'Single.'

'Twa shilling.'

It was time to make her mind up. Then Jessie turned away to extract the precious note given to her by Mrs Anderson and handed it over to the ticket seller.

'Right ye are. Platform 4. Ye'll hae tae change at Stirling, mind.'

Carefully Jessie took the ticket and counted out the change she had been given – three shillings – which she returned to her purse. If she took this move there would be no going back. As she pondered this, a tall figure in black hurried past, brushing into her on his way. He looked back briefly and Jessie's heart lurched. A minister - but no-one she knew. Now she was certain she could not return to St Nicholas Manse. And there would be no use in thinking of returning to her mother in Dundee. After the incident at the mill she dared not show her face again there. No, she had to be brave and find her own future. Once she was in Glasgow she would have time to plan.

The hands on the huge black and white station clock moved slowly round. The train would leave in five minutes. After all her indecision, Jessie suddenly felt a rush of panic lest she miss it and started to run as fast as she could towards Platform 4. She nearly lost sight of the locomotive in the cloud of steam emitted from the engine, as it drifted back to envelop her. Hearing the shrill sound of the parting whistle, Jessie reached out for the nearest door and flung herself inside.

# CHAPTER 15

# AFTERMATH

FRED STARED AT THE PIECE OF PAPER HELD BETWEEN Margaret's slender fingers and then looked up at her face. Her dark eyes watched him intently causing Fred to turn away. There was no doubt she was in deadly earnest. All Fred could think about was Jane's pale, solemn face, her thin body and gauche, immature manner. A child. And she was to be his wife? The thought repulsed him.

There was a strange stillness in the room as if time had slowed down and it came to him that his whole life would hinge on this moment. He was aware of his own breathing, the slight rustle of the satin fabric of Margaret's gown and the gentle tick of the French clock on the mantelpiece. It was as if, at that moment, there was nothing beyond that room and that he and Margaret stood at the epicentre of their world.

Fred was the first to break the silence.

'May I have some time to reflect, Margaret? Your proposal has taken me by surprise.'

Margaret did not respond immediately but her eyes narrowed slightly.

'Yes, Fred, of course. But I hope you will not disappoint me.'

Looking directly at her, Fred knew there could be only one outcome but he felt unable to make that commitment immediately.

'Thank you.'

'Well, I expect you have duties to attend to. I apologise if I have taken up too much of your time.'

The dismissal was cool and sudden and within a few minutes Fred found himself on the pavement, surveying the street in front of him. He had declined Margaret's offer of the carriage. He would walk to St Ninian's, he decided. He hoped the peaceful, timeless interior of the kirk would calm him and help him to think.

Inside the church, seated quietly on a pew, Fred bowed his head and tried to pray. After failing Jessie, he had made a promise to God that he would not marry anyone else. But now, after speaking with Margaret, he saw he was trapped. How could he honour that promise now? If he did not agree to her proposal, then his professional and personal life would be over. Margaret would not get over such a rejection and he could not risk sending her back to the drug-induced purgatory from which he had rescued her.

'Dear God, what is Thy Will?' He appealed. 'I have sinned, I am weak. I have tried so hard to follow the right path but truly now I feel lost. How can I best serve You? Give me a sign, I pray. Amen.'

Oh, that he could speak with William now. If he could have shared this predicament some of the weight would have been lifted from him and he might be able to see more clearly and calmly. The memory of the older man was still so strong and it felt as if he had lost his father all over again. Suddenly a huge wave of sadness and regret swept over Fred and he grasped his face in both hands seeking to block out both the daylight and his tumultuous thoughts.

He remained thus for some minutes until he heard the scraping sound of the main door opening. Doubtless a member of the congregation. Was there nowhere he might be alone? It would not do for them to see him so distraught. Taking a deep breath, Fred sat upright and tried to compose himself.

'Reverend Black, I am sorry to disturb you.'

It was the voice of one of the elders, Mr Gillies. He had been a good friend to William.

'I am just fetching some Church papers,' he continued.

'Not at all, Mr Gillies. I was just leaving. A short period of contemplation you understand, after William…'

Fred kept his face averted and thought how he could make his escape.

'Of course. We all miss him a great deal.'

Fearing he would once again be overcome with emotion, Fred stood up hastily, his head bowed, and made to leave.

'Forgive me, I must away now,' he muttered.

Mr Gillies nodded in sympathy as Fred passed him and headed for the exit.

The manse was silent when he returned. Mrs Oliphant was no doubt out running errands. Fred discarded his coat in the hall and was about to head to the study when he noticed a letter propped up against the vase of cut flowers on the hall table. It was addressed to him in black ink in deliberate, careful handwriting. Aware his heart rate had quickened, Fred picked it up. Initially, the Glasgow postmark threw him. He knew no-one there. Then he looked at it again. It had been so long, he did not want to let himself believe that this was the reply from Jessie he had been waiting for. He held it up closely to his face. It was indeed her hand-writing. He looked at his name and address on the front of the envelope and wondered where and when Jessie had written it. What had been going through her mind? Why now? And why was she in Glasgow?

He continued to the study, sat himself at his desk and picked up a letter knife. There was a single sheet of paper inside the envelope. There was no return address, only the name of the city and a date one week earlier. Fred opened the letter and started to read.

*Glasgow, 22 June 1862*

*My dearest Fred*

*After all this time it is hard to know where to start but I wanted to write to you before I went away. Thank you for the psalm book and your message which Reverend Grierson passed to me. I knew then that you still thought about me which made me so happy. The last time we met I was hurt and angry and believed you did not care for me at all. Maybe I should not say this but I really loved you and I thought you felt the same way too. I never knew if we could really be together but sometimes I had hoped. You made me feel better about myself. I felt safe with you.*

*Sometimes I picture you so clearly and other times I cannae even remember your face which makes me very sad. But I do mind your voice and I think of that when I lie in bed at night trying to sleep. When I heard you had gone to Edinburgh I knew then we had no future and I felt so alone. But I want you to know that I understand why you had to go. I would probably have done the same in your shoes. I just wish we could hae said our farewells properly.*

*It is hard to speak about the bairn. He was the sweetest wee boy. I called him Jamie after my father. I loved him - I will <u>always</u> - even though I knew I could not keep him. They took him from me at Easter when he was just six month old. He was adopted but I dinnae ken where he is. They said it was for the best but my heart is broken and will <u>never</u> mend. That is why I must get away.*

*I was due to go back to the MacDonald's at St Nicholas but MacDonald is a <u>bad</u> man. Not what he seems. I do not want to say any more than that but I could not return so I have a chance to go to Canada to make a new life. I am afeart about what is in front of me but there is nothing here and my son is gone so it cannae be worse than that.*

*I so wish things could have been different between us, Fred. I will never forget you and I hope you will never forget me.*

*With my love always*

*Jessie*

Fred found he was having difficulty reading the last couple of paragraphs. His vision had become blurred and this made the writing indistinct. Holding his head in his hands he wept.

'Oh, Jessie, Jessie! What have I done tae ye?'

Should he go to Glasgow and seek her out? Where would he start in a city of tens of thousands of people? Maybe she had already started her voyage to Canada?

After a few minutes, his head throbbing, Fred raised his head and started to return Jessie's letter to its envelope. Something was impeding its movement. Fred extended a couple of fingers to see what was there and drew out a tiny packet of tissue paper. Barely daring to breath, he unfolded it to reveal a tiny tuft of brown baby hair.

It felt as though he had received a body blow to the stomach. Seeing this tangible evidence of a new young life, his son, who he had let go and would now probably never know, was more than he could bear. Fred found himself gasping for breath and grappled with the top button of his shirt. Then, rushing over to the sash window he hauled it open as quickly as he could before gulping in breaths of fresh air like a drowning man. He stood like that for several minutes, staring down at the street below as folk went about their everyday business, oblivious to the haggard young man at the upstairs window.

Finally, calming himself, Fred pushed Jessie's letter deep within his jacket pocket. He knew there were decisions to be made that could not be put off much longer, but at that precise moment he had an overwhelming urge to escape the present for an hour or so. Leaving the study and entering the drawing room, Fred approached the deep mahogany cabinet in the far corner, in which William kept his selection of malt whiskies. Before he could change his mind, Fred unlocked the cupboard and picked out a bottle of Glenlivet.

Pouring a slug into a cut glass tumbler, Fred took the drink and sank down into one of the deep armchairs by the fireplace. The fumes of the spirit hit his nose and made him cough. Then he raised the glass to his lips and drank. Then another gulp and another, until the tumbler was empty and he replaced it carefully on the table beside him. Fred was aware he now felt light-headed but his earlier turmoil had receded somewhat. It would be a temporary state of affairs but for now he welcomed the warm embrace of the whisky in his body. He knew he should return to the study to let Margaret have his answer before the day's end but the temptation to allow himself a small refill and the temporary comfort it would bring was too great.

In fact, Fred was awoken by Mrs Oliphant's voice a couple of hours later, still in his chair.

'Sir, Reverend Black? Are you unwell?'

Fred roused himself with a groggy start. The sweet smell of the residue of whisky in the glass beside him rose to his nostrils making his stomach turn. He turned his face towards the house-keeper.

'I am sorry, Mrs Oliphant. No excuses. I felt the need of a dram. I have a lot on my mind and it will not let me rest. It will not happen again.'

'There is no need to apologise, Sir. You are quite entitled to some relaxation after the few weeks you have had. You took your post I see? Not bad news I hope?'

Fred wondered if the housekeeper was trying to catch him out but her expression seemed quite open and natural with a gently concerned look in her eyes.

'Everything is as it should be, thank you,' he replied firmly.

# CHAPTER 16

# FATE

Although Mrs Oliphant had merely nodded politely before leaving the drawing room, Fred thought he might be observed if he remained downstairs. There would be less privacy in the study. He would feel self-conscious and find it hard to concentrate. Accordingly, he retreated to his room where he splashed some cold water over his face and neck in an attempt to refresh himself. Then, seating himself at his desk, he commenced his reply to Margaret. He would keep it brief and formal. Margaret only wanted his assent. She knew he was a man of his word so flowery emotions were uncalled for.

Fred wished he knew what Jane would feel about this arrangement and he felt a pang of pity for her. She was like an immature plant who had yet to bloom. To have her future set up for her in this way was as if the plant had been cut prematurely with the hope that it would, nonetheless, blossom indoors, deprived of soil and sunlight. He did not want to be the cause of her future unhappiness. He could not have two women on his conscience.

*17 Melville Street*

*29th June 1862*

*My dear Margaret*

*Following our conversation yesterday, I am honoured that you consider me a suitable husband for your daughter Jane. You will understand that I was taken by surprise by your proposition but now, having taken time to reflect, I would be most happy to accept her hand in marriage. I have only one request to make, which I am sure as a parent you will agree with. It is important that Jane is not against the idea of marrying a poor minister so many years older than she is. I promise I will make every effort to make her happy but I need to know that she is receptive to this match.*

*I remain faithfully yours,*

*Frederick Black*

Fred held the letter in front of him and scrutinised the words again. In sending this reply, his fate would be sealed. He had so many regrets. He would always hold Jessie dear in his heart and his punishment was knowing that he had failed her and the bairn. But there was no undoing that now. He must accept the life that had been offered to him and make every attempt to be a good husband to Jane. He would do his duty. Folding the letter, he pushed it into an envelope and sealed it with the St Ninian's crest. Then, before he could change his mind, Fred put on his coat and set off for Charlotte Square.

Two weeks passed before Fred heard from the Burnetts. He tried to put the matter out of his head and concentrated on parish duties. Until he was formally instated as William's successor, Fred worked alongside a locum, preaching, welcoming parishioners to St Ninian's and attending to the many pastoral needs of his congregation. It seemed no-one was aware of the unsettling encounter Fred had had with the Church Council and he was relieved and thankful to be treated with the same affection and enthusiasm by his parishioners as before. But as the days went by and he received no summons from Margaret, Fred began to wonder if they had had second thoughts. If so, where would that leave him?

Summer had come finally to Edinburgh with long hours of daylight stretching far into the evening. Fred liked nothing better than to take himself off after dinner and walk through the city, alone with his thoughts. Striding through the Princes Street Gardens, he climbed the Mound to the High Street then down to Holyrood Palace and the craggy grandeur of the Salisbury Crags, lit up with chrome yellow gorse filling the air with its warm coconut scent.

Fred stood and contemplated the vista stretched before him. Looking at the strip of blue water to the North of him that was the Firth of Forth, he thought of Jessie's plans to emigrate. In high summer, with barely a whisper of wind, it all looked benign enough, but he knew very well the ferocity of the sea at other times. He then wished with all his heart that, at that moment, Jessie was standing safe next to him, perhaps leaning against him, his arm around her shoulder, as they stared outwards together.

It was after one such evening outing that Fred returned to the manse to be greeted by Mrs Oliphant.

'Ah, Reverend Black, I wasn't sure when you would be back. You have just missed Mr Donaldson from the Burnetts. He hoped to speak with you but he has left you a wee note.'

In her right hand she held a small envelope such as might be used for an 'At Home' invitation. Fred took it, murmuring his thanks.

'How long ago?' he queried. 'I may have passed him in the street?'

'Oh barely ten minutes, I would say, Sir.'

'Thank you, Mrs Oliphant. Well, I will attend to this in the morning. Good night to you.'

Fred was invited for two days hence at 5 p.m. The card was

formally printed with the date and time filled in in Margaret's hand. On the back she had written a brief note.

*Thank you for your letter, Fred. David and I are very pleased. We have spoken with Jane and she is looking forward to seeing you again. And please do not concern yourself about your ages. David is 13 years older than I am. In time it will seem nothing at all. M.*

When Fred was first shown into the drawing room at Charlotte Square, he was surprised to find no-one there. Part of him was relieved that he had more time to recover from the nervousness he felt and part of him wished the encounter to be over with as soon as possible. He glanced in the large gilt mirror hung on one wall to check that he presented a respectable image.

Fashionable dressing was not in his nature and he had spent more time than he would have liked deciding what to wear. The weather was close and stuffy so his usual formal evening wear would have been uncomfortably hot. However his lighter clothing seemed creased and shabby by comparison and Fred grew increasingly agitated as the appointed hour drew nearer. In the end he decided against a waistcoat but tied a magenta silk cravat around his neck and put on a dark dress coat. A little sandalwood pomade in his hair and a splash of eau de cologne on his freshly shaved cheeks revived his confidence a little.

And now as he stood alone recalling his first encounter with David Burnett in this room nearly a year ago, he marvelled at how life had unfolded for him since then. Lost in reflection, Fred was startled to hear Jane's voice behind him.

'Good evening, Reverend Black, or may I call you Frederick?'

Fred spun round and was momentarily lost for words. Jane stood in front of him with a tentative smile on her lips and her eyebrows raised as she awaited his answer. She was wearing a summer crinoline of pink sprigged cotton and a white lace shawl draped over her narrow shoulders. Her waist looked tiny which emphasised her slight frame. Her auburn hair was caught up in a thick coil which made her look older and her ears were decorated with two tiny emerald pendant ear-rings. A similar gem hung around her neck and contrasted with the milky paleness of her skin.

'Good evening, Jane,' stuttered Fred, aware that he sounded awkward. 'Of course, Frederick, or even Fred, that is what most folk call me.'

Jane approached him with her hand held out. Fred took it gently and raised it quickly to his lips.

'You are looking very bonnie this evening, Jane, if I may say so.' Fred dropped Jane's hand and straightened himself up. 'That is a colour which suits you very well.'

He stood still unable to think of what to say next and was relieved when Jane walked towards an upright sofa and sat down.

'Come and sit down, Fred,' she requested calmly, and Fred inwardly admired her composure. Where were Margaret and David he wondered? Should they not be there to chaperone their daughter? As if reading his thoughts, Jane continued,

'Mama and Papa will join us shortly. Mama said I should have some time to speak to you on our own.'

'Ah, I understand. That is wise of them. Thank you.'

Fred sat down at the other end of the sofa and placed his hands on his lap.

'Your parents have spoken to you about ....us, I understand?' he continued. 'I am concerned that the idea is agreeable to you, Jane. I am maybe not what you had in mind as a husband, if you had even thought about such a thing?'

Fred stopped abruptly. He felt he was gabbling and had maybe said too much.

'They have, Fred. Thank you. I trust my parents completely to make the right decisions for me. I have no experience in such matters and I know they only want the best for me.'

Jane now looked solemn and momentarily the initial confidence she had shown seemed to desert her. She looked down at her hands and started to fiddle with the lace edging of her shawl.

'I will look after you, Jane, I promise,' Fred leant towards Jane, an earnest expression on his face. 'You must be open with me. If this is not what you want, I will accept this. I want you to be happy.'

'Thank you, Fred.' Jane lifted her head and looked straight at Fred, her hazel eyes bright. Then, before he could react, Jane lunged forward and kissed him on the mouth.

'Now we are truly engaged,' she whispered.

Shocked by Jane's unexpected embrace, Fred felt unable to move until the drawing room door opened slowly and David Burnett appeared in view followed by his wife. With some relief, Fred stood up and walked towards them.

'Good evening, Fred. I am glad Jane has been keeping you company,' David Burnett greeted him. 'We hope this will be the first of many happy meetings between us. Margaret and I are delighted to welcome you into our family, Fred. I think this calls for a little celebration.'

Mr Burnett pressed the bell by the fireplace and shortly afterwards Donaldson appeared carrying a silver tray on which were four glasses and a bottle of Dom Pérignon. The butler then proceeded to open the bottle and fill each glass with the sparkling golden liquid.

'This is a very good vintage,' announced David. 'I have been keeping it for a special occasion such as this. Fred and my darling, Jane, here's to you both. Let us drink to your long and happy life together.'

After they had raised their glasses and sipped the champagne, Margaret took Fred to one side.

'I feel truly blessed today, Fred. Thank you for making me so happy again. I know you and Jane will make a very good match. We will make the formal announcement at the weekend.'

The following Saturday, Mrs Oliphant left a copy of the Scotsman on the dining table for Fred to read after finishing his breakfast. Fred had mentioned the betrothal to the housekeeper the day before. If she had been surprised, she did not show it but merely congratulated him warmly, saying that it was 'lovely news'. Pushing his plate to one side, Fred picked up the newspaper and opened it, turning the pages over until he came to the Register. Ah, there it was.

*The Engagement is announced between*

*Dr Reverend Frederick Black DD of Strathmuir, Angus*

*And*

*Miss Jane Eleanor Burnett*

*Only daughter of Mr and Mrs David Burnett*
*of Charlotte Square, Edinburgh and*
*Nether Airlie, Perthshire*

In a strange way until he had seen it printed officially, part of him felt he could pretend it was all a figment of his imagination. But now there could be no hiding from the fact and from his decision. In formal black script the facts were laid out for all to see.

Fred was about to put the paper down and make a move to get on with his day, when his eye was caught by another headline which caused his stomach to lurch in panic. All other thoughts were forced from his mind as he looked in horror at the dozen or so stark words in front of him.

PASSENGER SHIP SINKS OFF THE
COAST OF NOVA SCOTIA

GREAT LOSS OF LIFE

IMMIGRANTS SEEKING A NEW LIFE PERISH

Jessie! Where was Jessie headed? Might she have been aboard? He had no way of knowing. Frantically he scanned the article for further information. The shipping line would publish a manifest as soon as possible and a full list of casualties would be known after the rescue operation was completed. Fred shut his eyes and prayed that it might not be so and that Jessie had been spared. She of all people deserved a new life. Not to have it snatched from her in this terrible way. Should he seek out a passenger list or should he believe that she was not involved? Dear God, was there to be no respite?

Fred was not sure how long he spent staring at the newspaper. The print seemed to dance in front of his eyes and he had to lift it closer to try and make sense of it. He was certain that God was taunting him. At the very moment of his public betrothal, his first love might be condemned to a watery grave at the bottom of the Atlantic. His stomach turned over once again and he wondered if he might actually be sick from fear. He looked again at the sheet of newsprint in front of him.

> SS Caledonia hit dangerous rocks in thick fog off the coast of Nova Scotia. It is believed that there were one hundred and twenty passengers on board, none of whom have yet been accounted for.

The shipping line had an office in Leith. He would go there immediately. He could not rest until he knew the truth.

'Mrs Oliphant, Mrs Oliphant!' Fred stood in the hallway and called out to the housekeeper.

'Reverend Black, whatever is the matter?' Mrs Oliphant regarded him with a concerned look.

'I must go out for a while this morning. Something urgent has arisen that requires my immediate attention. It will probably take a couple of hours.'

'Very good, Sir. Shall we expect you for luncheon?'

'I cannot say. Just leave me some cold cuts and some cheese. That will suffice. I do not want to put you to any unnecessary trouble.'

'It will be no trouble, Sir. I hope your errand is successful.'

'Thank you.'

Fred hoped he had not sounded too abrupt but he was

finding the polite exchange difficult to maintain in his current frame of mind.

He hailed a hansom cab in Princes Street and some twenty minutes later found himself in front of the Anchor Line shipping offices on the Leith waterfront. A sign had been erected which had just two words on it - *SS Caledonia* – and already a queue of anxious faces was lining up in silence. Fred joined them and saw to his frustration that the answer to his quest would not be immediately forthcoming. The shipping clerks in their booths were doing their best but clearly none of the visitors had received satisfaction to their desperate enquiries.

After half an hour or so, Fred finally found himself face to face with an Anchor Line employee.

'Are you next of kin, Sir?'

Fred was taken aback by the question.

'No, but I believe a close friend of mine may have been on board.'

'I'm sorry, Sir, but it is strictly next of kin, otherwise this will take a' day.'

Unaccustomed fury rose in Fred.

'Sir, have you no humanity? The lady in question is very close to my heart and I need to know. She has no other family.'

There was a pause while the clerk considered the situation.

'Very well, what was her name?'

'Jessie, Jessica Duthie.' Fred's voice came out high and strained.

'Where was she travelling from?'

'Glasgow, I believe.'

'And what is her occupation?'

'Domestic servant.'

The clerk ceased his questions and looked at the manifest in front of him. He pulled a finger down a list of names then stopped.

'Well, there are a couple of Duthies here.'

'And their first names?'

'Only initials in steerage.'

'Let me see!' Fred lent over the counter and grasped the ledger from the man.

*Duthie, B.* He read, and then, there it was, *Duthie, J.*

He grabbed hold of the brass rail in front of him, lest he fell to the ground. His mouth was so dry he found it hard to speak.

'Do you know if there are any survivors?'

The clerk regarded him sadly.

'We received a telegram an hour ago. There are no survivors, Sir.'

Fred did not want to hear any more. Unable to say anything, he turned around and pushed blindly towards the exit.

'No survivors, no survivors,' he muttered to himself as he stumbled down the steps on to the quayside.

The lead weight of nausea within him now rose in his gullet and he turned and vomited on to the cobbles. Above him, the sun disappeared behind a dark cloud.

# PART THREE

# LEGACY

# CHAPTER 1

# GOLDEN WEDDING

NETHER AIRLIE, PERTHSHIRE – July 1916

'MRS BLACK, WE ARE READY TO SERVE LUNCHEON. SHALL I call the family in now?'

Jane was standing in the dining room at Nether Airlie, staring out of the long windows towards the majestic walnut tree that dominated the front lawn. She had been coming here all her life. To this wonderful old house with its history and its memories. It was hard to take in that she was no longer the little girl of history, nor the young woman on honeymoon, nor even the new mother. She was here with Fred and nearly all the family to celebrate their Golden Wedding. How was it possible so much time had passed?

'Mrs Black?' Agnes, the housemaid repeated herself and Jane turned around and back to the present.

'Of course. Thank you, Agnes.'

It had been her elder brother, Hugh, who had suggested they celebrate their anniversary at the house. Initially Jane had demurred. The war was on. Would it not seem inappropriate to be celebrating when so many had lost so much? And of course their dear boy would not be there. The family had not gathered together since his memorial service last autumn. Then perhaps it was time to replace such a sad memory with a happier one, Hugh had mentioned gently. Robert would not have wanted them to pass such an occasion by, he was sure.

Robert had been so determined to sign up. Initially it looked as though his poor eye-sight might save him, but, to Jane and Fred's great disappointment and Robert's exhilaration, he had finally been accepted into the Royal Scots as a private. He had proudly turned down a commission, stating that he knew nothing of soldiering and would learn from the bottom up. That was typical of him, Jane thought with tenderness. So full of integrity, passion and fair-play. He would have brought so much to whatever he chose to do in life.

But it was not to be and Jane would never forget the heart-chilling moment when the letter telling them of his death was delivered last year. Robert had been killed instantly by a shell at the Battle of Loos on the Western Front. He was only twenty two. Somehow, she had thought their sweet, kind, gentle boy would be protected. God knows they had prayed enough. She would always remember the last time they saw him on leave for a precious ten days. So young still and full of life. His eyes sparkling and his lopsided grin as he hugged her and chided her for worrying so. Then he had turned, hoisted his knap-sack over his shoulder and was gone.

Since his death, all Jane's previous energy and zest for life seemed to have abandoned her. It was to be expected, the doctor had reassured her. She had had a huge shock and she truly felt her heart had been fractured beyond repair. She had her other children of course and she thanked God for them every day but, in a strange way, their happiness and achievements only served to emphasise what Robert had been forever deprived of on a muddy, bloody field just a few hundred miles away.

Robert's passing had also dealt Fred a dreadful blow but it

was typical of him that he should be concerned with how much she was suffering rather than thinking of himself. When friends and well-wishers commiserated at his loss, Fred stated staunchly that he could at least look his parishioners in the eye as an equal when he consoled them.

"Our soldier boys are not dead: they are already with Christ which is far better than the longest and the best life on this earth,' he said firmly, his eyes bright with tears.

Hugh had persevered with the idea of a celebration and when word of it came to the rest of the family Jane had realised that it would be futile to resist. Thus on this bright July Sunday the whole family were gathered together under the same roof. It had been a long time since the old house had accommodated so many people and it was joyful to see. Hugh was right, Jane mused. Robert would have loved this. How he would have laughed and joked and embraced everyone with his good humour.

The dining room looked beautiful. Agnes and Mrs McCrae had done a marvellous job. The large oval mahogany table shone with a warm lustre and the silver cutlery and crystal glasses sparkled in the bright summer light. At the centre of the table was a large bowl of sweet-peas, Jane's favourite flowers, picked only that morning in the garden, the blue, white, pink and purple blooms filling the room with their sweet, peppery fragrance.

Most of the grandchildren were to be fed in the kitchen where Agnes and Mrs McCrae had laid out a festive feast on sturdy stoneware with homemade lemonade poured into tumblers and paper bags of boiled sweets as an after-lunch treat. However, Jane's oldest grand-daughters, Anne and Joan, Alexander's girls, were going to join the grown-ups in the dining room. At thirteen and sixteen, they looked so charming in their drop-waisted muslin dresses and hair especially crimped for the occasion.

'Come and sit beside me,' Jane insisted to her grand-daughters, as the family drifted into the dining room and started to find their places.

After a delicious summer lunch of Tay salmon served with new potatoes and peas from the kitchen garden, followed by a bounty of luscious red strawberries and double cream, Fred tapped his glass a couple of times to calm the hub-bub and rose to his feet. As voices fell silent, expectant faces turned towards him and Jane smiled affectionately as her husband started to speak.

'It is strange that, after so many years preaching from the pulpit, this is perhaps the most important speech of all for me to make,' he announced. 'How do you sum up fifty years of marriage? If you had told me as a young man, when I was studying and trying to make my way in the world, that I would be here today in this beautiful room surrounded by the most precious people in my life, celebrating half a century of love and companionship with my dear Jane, I would not have believed it.'

Fred paused for a moment and sipped a glass of water before continuing.

'I wish to pay a heartfelt tribute to my dear wife, who has been my friend and soulmate for fifty years. Without her by my side and the support of the Burnett family I know I would not be where I am today. Jane has been my mainstay, intellectually and emotionally, throughout. Please raise your glasses in a toast to my darling wife.'

Jane stared up at her husband in loving surprise. He had never been a man for heartfelt statements, even in private, but here he was publicly praising her. She put a hand to her cheek and realised she was blushing like a girl. Around the table the family drank from their glasses amid calls of 'To Mother!' and 'To Jane!' Then Fred indicated he wished to continue so glasses were replaced on the table and voices calmed.

'Without doubt the most important gift Jane has given me is our family. You know how much you mean to us but I want to salute each of you today. Alice, Alex, William, Janet, Richard, Sophia and Charles.'

Fred nodded lovingly at each of his children as he addressed them in turn. Then he stopped speaking and held his glass aloft, staring beyond it.

'And, of course, Robert,' he finished.

Jane watched anxiously as her husband seemed to sway slightly. Robert's absence could not be ignored by any of them. In a softer, less assured voice Fred continued.

'In truth I would have rather been a humble dominie in my wee home town if Robert could have been spared to us.'

The family fell silent as they each remembered the young man who was so dear to them all.

'Well said, Father!' Alexander spoke first and then turned to the others. 'To Robert, may he always rest in peace.'

'To Robert!' echoed the others.

Aware that the mood had changed and that her husband now looked drawn and tired, Jane stood up and went around to him, putting her hand on his shoulder.

'Do you think you should rest now, dearest? Let me take you upstairs.'

'No need for that. I don't want to break up the party. It has been a marvellous occasion, my dear. Thank you. I will be refreshed in an hour or so.'

'Let me see you comfortably settled, Fred. It would reassure me. Then I can return to our guests.'

Once upstairs, Jane could see that Fred was looking troubled. Before she left she wanted to try and calm him and put her own mind at rest.

'What is the matter, Fred? I hope you have enjoyed yourself?'

'It has been a very special occasion but I cannot stop thinking about Robert. You know, I sometimes think that his death was my punishment.'

'No, Fred! What do you mean by your punishment? Why should you say such a thing?'

Fred took Jane's hand and looked at her sadly.

'My dear, I am not as blameless as I might appear. There have been things in my life – before I met you…'

'Dearest, you cannot blame yourself for Robert's death,' Jane spoke urgently. 'It was the war. You have been the best of husbands to me and the best of fathers to the children. You have nothing to reproach yourself for.'

'Ah, I wish I could agree with you, my sweet Jane.'

'Please stop this talk, Fred! You are tired and must rest. Mrs McCrae has made a special anniversary cake. We will wake you when it is to be cut.'

'You are right, dearest. I am overwrought. You are so wise and caring. I am blessed to have you. I will try to sleep now and join you later.'

Mrs McCrae proudly brought the cake into the drawing room as the clock struck five. A spontaneous round of light applause broke out as the cook entered and placed it on a table set with small plates, forks and napkins. It was a two tier confection covered in white royal icing and on the top tier were the intertwined initials F and J.

'You are truly talented, Mrs McCrae,' praised Jane. 'Thank you so very much for this marvellous effort.'

Then turning to her eldest son, she said,

'Alex, go and see if Father is awake and let him know the cake will be cut shortly. Mrs McCrae has done us proud.'

'Of course, Mother.'

As he left the room, the younger grandchildren started to file in to join the ceremony. One ventured close to the cake and dared to place a tiny finger on the pristine icing.

'No, no, Elise! We must wait for Grandpapa,' her sister admonished her.

Suddenly, Alex burst into the room, startling everyone who turned in surprise, wondering what the commotion was.

'Call the doctor! I cannot wake Father. I think it may be a heart attack.'

# CHAPTER 2

# WATER COTTAGE

PENN, BUCKINGHAMSHIRE – 1919

FRED'S HEART ATTACK WAS THE TURNING POINT. AS JANE anxiously nursed her husband back to health through the autumn of 1916, she realised that his strength would not allow him to return to the pulpit however much he and his congregation wanted it.

'Am I to lose you as well, dearest?' Jane had appealed to him. 'It is time to hand over to someone else.'

The Church Council had accepted Fred's retirement with sad understanding. He had been at St Ninian's for so long it was difficult to imagine anyone else in the role. In due course, however, the Reverend Donald Murray was appointed as his successor and a handsome monument commemorating Fred's half century of service was erected in the vestibule of the kirk. A smooth grey stone plaque, on which Fred's profile had been carved into a circular medallion, and inscribed below were the words:

**In dear and honoured memory of**

**Reverend Doctor Frederick Black DD**

**Minister of this congregation**

**1862 – 1916**

**A Great Preacher and an Inspirer of Youth**

**A lifetime of service and much loved**

Then, after an equally long time at Melville Street, Jane had been faced with the daunting prospect of finding a new home.

'Come and stay with me and Emily and the children,' exhorted Alex. 'We have plenty of space and it will be a pleasure to have you.

Alex had just taken up a new appointment as a writer with the Spectator in London and had recently moved to England with his family. Until the war was over a house had been rented in the village of Penn in Buckinghamshire. Safely out of reach of the Zeppelins that were wreaking havoc in London, it was peaceful and attractive with its red brick and flint houses, a pretty duck pond, a village green and the ancient Norman church with its square steeple, so different from the austere grey kirks they knew in Edinburgh.

Leaving Scotland had been a huge wrench but with Alex's family now in the south it made sense, finally, to come and join them. For two years Jane and Fred were made very welcome and it had been a joy to find themselves at the heart of family life. They would be forever grateful to Alex and Emily for sheltering them so kindly, but now Jane wanted to find somewhere of their own. She longed to unpack her own furniture and personal possessions and create a peaceful retreat for herself and Fred before his health declined further. If they were to move it should be done before he became too weak. And then, fortuitously, Water Cottage came into their lives.

Water Cottage was set back from the road in a row of identical houses. Built a century earlier for estate workers, they were now let out to the general public. Jane had fallen in love with the house the moment she saw the For Let board and urged her husband to come and take a look at it. It would not be available for long she was sure. They were shown around one damp autumn day in late September. The sun tried weakly to shine through the heavy mist and the unkempt garden smelt of wet earth and decaying vegetation. It must have been lovely once, Jane reflected, noting the untidy, overgrown hollyhocks and blowsy, tangled rose bushes on either side of the garden path. That could be a project for the spring – if they secured the property.

They moved into Water Cottage early in November 1919. Jane felt it was not a moment too soon. Fred's strength seemed to be waning and, while the cold winter weather had the world in its grip, he spent more and more time in bed, reading and sleeping. One morning, Jane heard her name called out urgently by her husband. On hurrying upstairs she found him in a state of some distress.

'What happened to Jamie?' he queried suddenly, grasping her by the wrist. 'Was he killed as well?'

Jane was perplexed. Jamie? He had mentioned this name before and it was as though he wanted to tell her more. Although weak, Fred seemed to be in control of all his faculties but, when pressed, he had retreated.

'Who is Jamie, my darling?' Jane asked quietly, hoping that this time there might be an explanation.

Fred looked at her as though seeing her for the first time. A fleeting look of fear and confusion passed across his face.

'Robert was killed, dearest. Remember?' Jane reminded him sadly. 'Was Jamie a friend of his? I don't recognise the name.'

With tears in his eyes, Fred shook his head.

'Of course, Robert, my poor boy.'

'Can I fetch you anything, Fred?'

'No, my dear, nothing thank you. Let me sleep and come back later to read to me if you will.'

Still puzzled by her husband's question, Jane returned

downstairs to the sitting room at the back of the house where she had started to sort out balls of knitting yarn. It was not the most interesting of tasks but something she had been meaning to do since they moved in. She had enjoyed knitting for the war effort but now her worsening eyesight meant that too many dropped stitches made it more of a chore than a pleasure.

The loud rattle of the front door knocker startled her and she stopped what she was doing and looked up. Would Gladys get that, she wondered? Then she remembered that the maid had gone down to the village for some provisions. Laying down a ball of lemon yellow wool, Jane got up stiffly and walked into the hall. Beyond the small circle of stained glass in the front door she could see a figure waiting somewhat impatiently, moving from side to side. The temperature had remained below freezing for the past few days and no doubt the visitor wanted to be on his way as soon as possible. He was just about to knock again when Jane opened the door. The postman smiled and held out a white envelope bearing an unfamiliar brown stamp with the King's head on it.

For a moment Jane was revisited by the awful memory of the letter advising them of Robert's death. There had been so many envelopes bearing bad news in those days, far too many, more than the country and its people could really bear.

'I've been told to make sure the gentleman lives at this house,' the postman explained. 'This has been chasing him around most of the country. Dr Black, is it?'

'Yes, this is the right place,' said Jane, taking the letter from him. 'He's indisposed at the moment but I will make sure he gets it.'

'Thank you. Please sign here, Madam, just to confirm it's been received,' and the man held out a small wooden pencil and an official printed pad, indicating the space beneath their address.

Jane signed the piece of paper and handed the pad and pencil back to the messenger. Aware of the icy air rapidly pervading the hallway, she was anxious to close the door and get back to her cosy parlour as soon as possible.

'Thank you, I'll see Dr Black gets this,' she repeated, closing the front door.

Stepping back into the hall, Jane glanced down at the envelope in her hand. It was then she noticed that the unfamiliar stamp was in fact Canadian. Her curiosity awoken, she peered at it again. The postmark was dated some three weeks earlier on the 4 January 1919. Who could this be from? As far as she was aware they knew no-one in Canada. A retired cleric perhaps? An old friend of Fred's? She turned it over to see if the reverse offered any clues as to its sender. It did not. The original address was the manse in Melville Street. This was clearly the last known residence the correspondent had had for Fred as two other addresses had been scored out before the letter was finally handed to Jane at Water Cottage.

Instinctively she did not want to leave it on the round brass tray on the hall table. She would wait and then go up later to see if Fred was awake and if he was up to reading a mystery letter. The doctor's warning came back to her. Fred was much weakened by his heart attack and must avoid stress and worry at all costs. If not there was every chance he might have another attack, which he might not survive. Jane placed the letter on the small rosewood table by the door and returned to her wool sorting. Picking out the various colours and textures of yarns she found strangely calming, as she wound them and tucked them into the large basket by her feet.

From time to time her eyes flicked over to the letter. What might the contents be? If it were an old friend, it would surely cheer Fred. But if it were bad news, it would cause unnecessary distress. Perhaps it would be better if she opened the letter and then read it to him. Jane was not in the habit of opening other people's post but reassured herself that this was necessary for the welfare of her ailing husband. The clock on the mantelpiece struck midday. Jane completed her last ball of wool and put it away. She had come to a decision. She would open the letter and, if good news, take it up to Fred after lunch. It would be an interesting diversion for him.

Picking up the letter, she went over to her writing desk and sat down. Pausing for just a couple of seconds, she lifted the ivory-handled letter opener Alex had given her for Christmas and slit open the envelope in one deft movement. Carefully she extracted two sheets of white paper and laid them in front of her. The letter was dated the 2nd January and was written neatly in black ink. The writer lived in Halifax, Nova Scotia. Jane's curiosity increased and she turned to the end of the letter to discover their identity. Jessie Richardson. It meant nothing to her and she had never heard Fred mention such a person throughout the whole of their long marriage. Then she started to read.

*My dear Fred*

*You will no doubt be very surprised to hear from me after all this time but I have often thought of you and wondered how you are and how your life has been? I do not know if this letter will ever reach you or indeed if you are still alive but I hope you are and that you will be able to read this. I have hesitated many times about writing to you but now that I have not long left to live, it is important to me that I write to you while I still can. We are both very advanced in years, so whether or not you receive my letter is in God's hands.*

*Things in the world are so different now especially after this dreadful war which has brought so much misery and destruction to so many people. Although it was a long ago I often think about our old life and the short time we had together. I can truthfully say I have never forgotten you. Although it was so hard to leave you, without meeting you and getting to know you I would never had the life I have had.*

By the time she had read the first couple of paragraphs, Jane wished she had not opened the letter. This was clearly a private matter and she knew reading more would upset her. But she felt compelled to continue. Now Fred's references started to make sense. But who was this person and why had she never heard of her? Had her parents known? So many questions. Her first thought was that Fred must give her an explanation. But what would he say? Was their semblance of a happy marriage a sham? The idea was unbearable to her. Jane was aware of her heart racing and a nauseous feeling rising in her stomach.

When she finally came to the end of the letter her mind was made up. She would not read it to Fred nor give it to him. What she had just read should never be made public. Fred was revered and loved and their union was held up as an example to all the family. She stood up and walked over to the fire which was blazing vigorously in front of her. For a moment she hesitated. Then she folded the letter, replaced it carefully in its envelope and, opening her wooden sewing box, put the letter inside and shut the lid.

# CHAPTER 3

# ISABEL

London – March 2016

Isabel Thom pushed the door to her flat open with her shoulder and dropped her bags on the floor with a sigh. What a shit day! She was so tired she didn't even have the energy to pick up the junk mail which lay scattered on the door mat. Her lesson observation hadn't gone well - the kids playing up as they knew they were being watched. Marion Smith, the head-teacher, had smiled sympathetically at Isabel when giving her feedback at the end of the day.

'You need to be consistent and firm, Isabel. You can't be good cop one minute and bad cop the next. But I'm sure you know that really. Don't worry. It'll go much better next time.'

Isabel wasn't so certain. Each day she felt her self-confidence ebb further and she was having difficulty finding the enthusiasm and energy she once had.

Opening the fridge door, Isabel was faced with a box of Ferrero Rocher - which she hated - a carton of eggs and the remains of a feta and broccoli quiche. Half a bottle of Sauvignon Blanc nestled up against the semi-skimmed milk and a carton of orange juice. She pulled out the piece of quiche, poured herself a glass of wine and sank on to the sofa just as the 6 o'clock news started.

She was awoken by the sound of her phone ringing from her bag. Bugger! The wine had taken the edge off her tension and she had begun to relax for the first time all day. She really could not be bothered talking to anyone else this evening. A bath and an early night beckoned before everything started all over again the next day. There it was again. What could be so urgent on a Tuesday evening? With a sigh Isabel opened her eyes and got to her feet.

There were two missed calls from her brother David in Edinburgh. And then a voicemail. What was going on? He never rang her spontaneously. They always agreed a time when they would both be able to chat freely.

*I hope he's alright?*

'Dave? I got your message. You alright?'

There was a slight pause before her brother responded in a tone quite unlike his usual jokey, chatty manner.

'Iz, are you at home?'

'Yes, what's going on?' Isabel felt a chilly apprehension creep across her.

'It's Dad. He's had a heart attack.'

'What? When? How?' Isabel heard a screech of alarm and realised it came from her.

'He came back from work this evening and said he felt really bad and went to bed,' David explained. 'Mum said his face was grey and she had never seen anyone look so ill. She called the ambulance and they said he had had a heart attack. He's gone to hospital. Mum's with him now. I said I'd let you know then I'm going over later to give her a break.'

'Is he going to be alright?' Isabel realised she was trembling. 'He'll be alright, won't he?

'Hopefully, Iz. It's too early to say. He's in intensive care at the moment.'

'Where is he? The Western General?'

'Yep.'

'Oh God, David, this is awful. How's Mum?

'Very shaken, as you can imagine. But he's in the best hands. We just have to wait and hope.'

'You'll let me know as soon as you hear anything?'

'Yes, of course. Try and get some sleep.'

'Fat chance!' Isabel stared at the ground. 'Look, I'll let school know and come up as soon as I can.'

'OK. Keep me posted. I'd better get over to the hospital now.'

'Give Mum my love and tell Dad I'm thinking of him.'

'Yeah, will do.'

As she had anticipated, Isabel found sleep almost impossible. Despite a second glass of wine and soaking in a hot bath, she could not settle. She tried to resist the temptation to keep looking at her phone. It was the middle of the night, she would know soon enough. She must have fallen asleep eventually because when she awoke she could hear her neighbour was already up and padding around above her head. For a brief moment she had forgotten her brother's news and then, like a sledgehammer, it hit her again. Dad! Scrambling out of bed she grabbed her phone and stared at the screen. There was a text from David. '*Call me*' was all it said.

Isabel could barely recall the next twenty four hours, it all seemed so unreal. From the shocked, muted conversation she had had with David when he told her their father had died at twenty past two in the morning, to the sympathetic email from her head-teacher saying she could have a week's compassionate leave. She hadn't been able to cry, yet. She just felt frozen, numb. It was only when she looked out of the window as the Edinburgh flight winged out over the Firth of Forth before coming in to land that Isabel realised with a great heave of emotion how much she missed her home town. Below her, as they flew low over Cramond, sheep looked like grains of rice on a green background, the bunkers on the golf course appeared as little scoops of sand and the causeway resembled a row of matchsticks jutting out of the sea.

*I will never see Dad again. This was not supposed to happen. He was far too young to die.*

Then she remembered their last meeting. He had asked her if she wanted to go to the printmakers' workshop with him like she did when she was younger. She had only been up for the weekend and had already made arrangements to meet some old friends. So she had declined. She would go next time, she had said. She should have gone then. There would never be another chance. She wept now, behind dark glasses, feeling stupidly self-conscious.

She remained in her seat until the last moment. Then, moving like a very old, tired person, she stood up and reached for her bag in the overhead locker. Mouthing her thanks to the cabin crew as she left, she walked up the gangway into the scented, artificial brightness of the terminal building. Thankful she didn't have to wait for any luggage, she made her way, head bowed, to the exit. Isabel spotted David immediately. All six foot of him, black jeans and a short leather jacket over a tee-shirt. It was his uniform all year round – Dave didn't seem to feel the cold, which was lucky if you lived in Edinburgh. He raised his arm in greeting and mouthed a sad smile.

'Thanks for coming to meet me.'

Isabel hugged her brother. They didn't usually hug each other much. They didn't really need to, each was confident of how close they were to each other. But this was different. Nothing could be taken for granted now.

'Of course, you silly creature! What do you think?'

Then David took her bag, slung it over his shoulder and led the way out of the terminal to the multi-storey car-park.

They drove in silence. Darkness had fallen and it had started to rain. Outside the streets and pavements glistened in the glow of the streetlights and Isabel found the rhythmic hum of the car's windscreen wipers quite hypnotic and oddly comforting. Twenty minutes later they turned off Ferry Road and drew up in front of the family house. It was the sight of their father's car that set Isabel off.

'Oh Dave, this is awful!' she wailed. 'I just want him back.

I never said goodbye or anything.' And she buried her face in her hands.

David reached a hand out to hold her shoulder.

'I know, Iz, I know. But we need to keep it together for Mum.'

Isabel nodded and patted her pockets for a tissue.

'I don't look too wrecked do I?'

'You're fine. Come on.'

Letting themselves in, Isabel called out a greeting.

'Mum, we're here!'

Standing in the hall she paused and breathed in the distinctive aroma of her home. She would know it with her eyes shut. Hers smelt of home cooking – but in a good way. And then there was the haunting background smell of turpentine and oil paint that came from her father's studio on the first floor. For a moment everything felt normal. But then their mother appeared from the living room, her hands clasped, looking like a small pale wraith. She seemed to have shrunk and Isabel had an overwhelming desire to protect and comfort her. Without taking off her coat, she walked up and put her arms around her.

'Mum, I'm so sorry!'

They stood like this for several seconds. Her mother said nothing but with one of her hands stroked Isabel gently on the back.

'Why don't you two go and sit down. I'll make us some tea,' suggested David, approaching the two women.

'I should be doing that.' Their mother's voice was faint and shaky.

'No, Mum, you shouldn't. I know where everything is.'

Isabel shrugged off her coat and, taking her mother gently by the arm, walked into the large bay-fronted living room where so much family activity had taken place over the years.

'He's at the undertaker at the moment, if you want to see him.'

Isabel was taken aback at the directness of her mother's suggestion.

'Ah, have you seen him?'

'No, not yet. David was at the hospital when we ....heard. I thought we might go together, if you want?'

Isabel stared at her mother. Really this was the most surreal conversation. Everything around them seemed exactly the same. She was still finding it hard to take in that Dad had really gone, that he was not going to walk in at any moment and she would hear his familiar, confident voice greeting her.

'Can I think about it please, Mum?'

'Yes, of course, darling… How long can you stay?'

'Well, I've got a week off but that can be extended. Depends when the funeral is…'

Speaking the word brought fresh tears to Isabel's eyes. She was trying so hard to be calm.

'Sorry, Mum.'

'The funeral? I've not really thought about that yet. But we might have it at St Ninian's, my great-great-grandfather's old church? Dad's good friend, Andrew Duncan is the minister there and he's already been in touch.'

# CHAPTER 4

# MATTHEW

**Thom, William, unexpectedly on**

**March 16th 2016**

**Beloved husband of Rachel and**

**Adored and adoring father of**

**David and Isabel.**

**Funeral to be held at**

**St Ninian's Kirk on**

**Saturday 26th March at 2 p.m**

ISABEL STOOD LISTLESSLY IN FRONT OF THE MIRROR. Her dark hair emphasised her pale, drawn face and the smudges of fatigue under her eyes. Outside it was a grey day, with the kind of low light that drained colour from everything. Isabel observed herself in the plain wool dress. Too sombre - something was missing. It echoed how she felt but she knew Dad hadn't been dark and dismal – he had been full of life and colour and humour.

And she wanted to honour this. Reaching into the top drawer, Isabel pulled out the multi-coloured silk scarf her father had given her for her 25th birthday. Italian, he had told her, cost a packet!

'*Oh, Dad, how are we going to get through this?*'

Isabel held the scarf to her face and allowed herself the release of warm tears. Then she wrapped it around her shoulders and pinned it in place with a small silver brooch. Better.

At half past one, five of them were sitting silently in the living room, awaiting the funeral cars. David had come over before lunch bringing his aunt and uncle directly from Waverley Station. No-one had much of an appetite and many of the M&S delicacies remained untouched. Isabel had volunteered to make mugs of coffee for everyone which they now held in front of them, sipping the hot liquid cautiously. There was a buzz on David's phone.

'That's them now,' his voice broke the silence.

Trying to stop her hands shaking, Isabel stood up.

'I'll get your coat, Mum.'

The two cars were parked outside. Incongruously large black limousines. The drivers had got out and were waiting to help the family into their seats. David slipped into the front while Isabel sat with her mother in the back. Once again the sense of unreality she had experienced over the past few days hit her. It was almost dreamlike, as though she were looking down on the tableau from above. Isabel placed her hand on her mother's but there was no response. It was as if her grief had frozen her reactions. Isabel left her hand there for a few more seconds then removed it as the cars moved off very slowly.

Isabel and David stood on either side of their mother at the entrance to the church. The pale oak coffin was already in place before the altar, a large spray of blue, white and yellow spring flowers the only decoration. On the altar two large beeswax candles had been lit and the 2nd movement of Mozart's Clarinet concerto, one of her father's favourite classical pieces, filled the church with its serene, mournful sound. Tears started to well up in Isabel's eyes and she was glad she had decided to forgo any eye make-up. If she kept her head bowed and concentrated very hard on the floor, she might just get through this. As she walked into the church, her mother's arm resting lightly on hers, out of the corner of her eye she could see dozens of people gazing sympathetically at her. She would have liked to respond but didn't trust herself to hold it together at that point.

With relief Isabel found herself at the front of the church. The original uncomfortable wooden pews were nowhere to be seen and the congregation now sat in semi-circles on chairs upholstered in a vivid purple. Leading the way, Isabel took a seat in the front row and picked up the order of service. There were going to be two hymns. She wouldn't be able to sing, she just knew. Even in much happier times, hymns always brought a lump to her throat. It was half way through the second verse of *How Great Thou Art* that Isabel finally broke down. The tears came first, then the sobs. The misery just came pouring out and there was nothing she could do to stop it. Her mother took her hand and gripped it tightly in hers until the service finally came to an end.

The reception was held at the Roxburghe Hotel. The venue was a little stuffy maybe, but it was convenient and the service was excellent. A long trestle table covered in a stiff white cloth had been laid out with plates of sandwiches and sausage rolls on one side and miniature cup-cakes and flaky pastry concoctions on the other. Four young women with unnaturally bright expressions were lined up to serve cups of tea or coffee. On the other side of the room, Isabel could see her mother deep in conversation with several of her father's colleagues, one of whom, from time to time, patted her gently on the arm. There were so many people. Isabel had no idea her father had been so popular.

'*Mum looks exhausted,*' she thought anxiously.

'You look as though you could do with a cup of tea?'

Isabel turned to see a tall young man about her age, with short sandy-coloured hair and a light beard, smiling sympathetically at her. He was casually dressed in a checked shirt and a dark coat and held a cup of tea in one hand.

'Or something stronger?' he added, nodding at some of the guests who were holding glasses in their hands.

'I was really sorry to hear about your dad,' he continued. 'He taught me drawing and painting at the art college. He was one of my favourite tutors – really encouraging. He had a great sense of humour too.'

'Thank you. Yes, he did.' Isabel allowed herself a small smile.

'Matthew Duncan,' he held out a hand.

'Isabel,' she replied in acknowledgement. 'Thanks for coming. I'm really touched by how many folk are here.' Isabel turned and scanned the room. 'There must be at least sixty people.'

'I'm not surprised. He was a really popular guy.' Matthew looked solemn. 'It's been a big shock to everyone. How are you bearing up?'

For a horrible moment Isabel felt herself welling up again. Swallowing, she looked down at her shoes and noticed the decorative velvet ribbon on one had come undone.

'Not so good.' Isabel returned her gaze to Matthew. 'It's difficult at the moment. Sometimes I forget for a bit and then it all comes back.'

'Yeah, sorry, didn't mean to upset you.'

'No, it's OK. Thanks for asking. So what kind of art do you do?' A change of subject was urgently called for.

'Well,' Matthew considered for a moment. 'Abstract landscapes I suppose you could call it. If you're interested I've got some work in a mixed show at the moment down in the Lawnmarket. The Lawn Gallery?'

Isabel hadn't heard of it but then she'd been away from Edinburgh for a few years.

'It's on until the end of the month if you want to look in.'

'Yes, I'll try. That would be nice. I'm here for the week.'

'I'd like to do it full time,' Matthew continued, 'but that's not possible at the moment. So the rest of the time I teach at James Gillespie's – my old school would you believe? Oh, and my dad did the service today. He knew your dad quite well.'

'Ah, he did it really well. Very personal. Mum said he knew Dad from the Conservation Society or something like that. They both had bees in their bonnets about ugly modern developments apparently.'

Despite herself Isabel found herself laughing at the memory. Then over Matthew's shoulder she could see David beckoning her.

'I'm sorry I've got to go now. It's been nice to meet you, Matthew.'

'Likewise.' Matthew smiled at her again. An attractive smile. 'Maybe see you again next time you're up.'

As the day of her departure drew nearer, Isabel realised she was not looking forward to returning south. Even though Dad was no longer around, she at least felt connected to him while she was in Edinburgh. And she was dreading returning to the class-room. Teaching took a lot of energy and positivity and she just couldn't find it in herself at the moment. The day before her flight south, she remembered about the exhibition at the Lawn Gallery. She was curious to see what kind of work Matthew did. Perhaps she could persuade her mother to come with her?

'I just don't think I have the energy at the moment, darling,' had been her mother's response. 'You go. It'll be a nice distraction.'

A girl with close cropped dark hair and a single gold nose ring was sitting at the front desk, peering at her computer screen, when Isabel walked in. On the wall was a poster advertising the exhibition *Nature Exposed – a deconstructed look at the Scottish landscape*. Apart from a middle-aged couple at the far end of the room, she was alone. The receptionist raised her head, smiled and, without being asked, handed Isabel a price list.

'Is it OK to take photographs?' Isabel queried.

'Sure, but no flash please.'

The gallery was made up of two interlinked spaces brightly lit by strategically placed spotlights. There seemed to be three artists showing but Isabel wanted to look at Matthew's work first. She spotted his bio on the wall and surreptitiously took a photo of it. The painting next to it was a small square abstract in earthy hues, as if viewed from the air, with recognisable images from the landscape superimposed – a small house, a group of trees and what looked like a standing stone. Isabel liked it and checked it against the price list. *Dreaming of Orkney - £500.* She didn't know much about pricing in the art world but it seemed reasonable. Unfortunately, still out of her range. She sighed, a photo would have to do for now.

'They're lovely,' she said finally to the receptionist as she completed her viewing. 'I'll maybe come back later.' She didn't think she had fooled the girl who smiled neutrally at her.

'May I take one of these?' The girl nodded and returned to gazing at her computer as Isabel picked up one of Matthew's cards from a pile on the desk and slipped it into her bag. She had just turned out of the door on to the street when she saw Matthew walking towards her. She felt a twinge of embarrassment at being caught out like this but he seemed genuinely pleased to see her.

'Oh, you came! What did you think?'

'Very good. Well done. It must be great to be able to paint like that.'

There was a pause as they looked at each other.

'Have you got time for a quick coffee?' Matthew asked.

Isabel felt torn. She would love to go for a coffee with him but she had promised her mother she would be back by four. Normally, it wouldn't be a problem but now…

'I'm sorry,' Isabel looked glumly at him. 'That would be really nice but I need to get back to see my mum. She's ….'

'No, of course, I understand. Maybe next time?'

Then with a deft movement Matthew seized her hand and scribbled down his number with a biro he had pulled out of his pocket.

'Your call!' He laughed.

# CHAPTER 5

# HOME-COMING

ISABEL PICKED UP HER PHONE AND DIALLED HER MOTHER'S number. She tried to call her every few days since the funeral, just to hear how she was. She felt guilty that she was so far away. Not her fault of course but she wished she were nearer. On the face of it her mother seemed to be bearing up but then she wasn't a person given to great displays of emotion. But that didn't mean she wasn't finding it hard. They all were. There was a click as the ringing tone started. After a few seconds her mother's voice greeted her.

'Hello darling – lovely to hear from you.'

Her mother sounded tired.

'How are you?' The question was always the same. As was the answer.

'Pretty exhausted still. I miss him so much. But I've started with my walking group again which is nice. They're a great bunch and it's good to get out of the house. What about you?'

'Oh well, you know, one thing to be said for teaching there isn't much time to think of anything else and I'm so tired by the end of the day I just crash out. Better than sleeping tablets anyway.'

'Oh, Izzy!'

'How are you sleeping?'

'Not so well, very broken nights and the strangest dreams. And, no, I'm not on Diazepam in case you're wondering.'

'Mum, I wanted to ask you something.'

'Yes, of course, darling.'

Isabel paused before continuing.

'How would you feel if I moved back to Edinburgh permanently?'

'Permanently?' Her mother sounded surprised. 'But what about your job? Have you thought about this? Please don't do it on my account.'

Isabel felt a great wave of fatigue roll over her.

'I think I've fallen out of love with London, Mum. I need to be closer to my family and my home right now. Hopefully I'll find something in Edinburgh.'

'Yes, I understand. It would be wonderful to have you here if that is what you want. I'm sure there will be plenty teaching jobs up here. I'm always reading about the shortages.'

'Yeah, I hope so. If I'm leaving I have to hand my notice in by half term. So you might have an un-employed daughter hanging around for a while.'

'Well, I'll be very happy to have you hanging around.'

'You sure?'

'Of course I'm sure.'

The airport was full of Festival crowds as Isabel made her way to the taxi rank and joined the queue. Normally she would have hopped on the city shuttle bus but with so much luggage she decided to invest in a cab. Her mother had offered to come and meet her but Isabel had gently turned down the offer.

'Thanks, Mum, that's really kind but honestly I'll be fine in a cab. The traffic will be horrendous and parking is really expensive. You can do without that at the moment.'

Now the taxi drew up in front of the house and the driver checked his meter for the fare.

'Fifteen pound, that'll be. Card's fine.'

Isabel fumbled with the clasp of her bag, extracted her credit card and stroked it over the device being held out to her.

'You're staying for a bit then?' The cabbie queried of Isabel as he helped heave her two large suitcases on to the pavement.

'Yeah, new job,' Isabel responded non-committally.

'Oh well, good luck with that!' And with a friendly smile, he turned away.

Trying to prevent her bags from falling over on the short concrete path, Isabel approached the dark green front door and stretched out a finger to ring the bell. Her mother opened the door almost immediately, a broad smile of welcome on her face. It was so nice to see her mother look happy for once, thought Isabel, as they embraced.

'Those look heavy,' her mother remarked, nodding at the two suitcases which now stood impassively like standing stones in the hallway.

'Yep, they are. They did me for excess weight at the airport. Believe it or not I've given a lot of stuff away. I'll take it up in stages.'

Her mother started to walk upstairs. Following her, Isabel was about to turn left into her old room but her mother pushed open the door to the big double guest bedroom.

'I meant to mention that I've being doing some clearing and your old room's a bit of a storeroom at the moment. And I thought you would be better in here now that you are going to stay. It will give you more space for your things,' she explained.

Isabel suddenly felt emotional. She realised the last time she had slept in this room had been when she had still shared with David when they were little. She must have been about five or six. Before her pink and fluffy phase called for her own space and she had moved into the small back bedroom overlooking the garden. Dad had decorated it for her. It was one of her earliest memories, seeing him in his paint spattered artist's smock, roller in hand, during the summer holiday, before school started.

'I hope that's OK, Isabel? I rather assumed…' Her mother looked anxious.

'Yes, of course, that's fine. It's not a big deal one way or another. I was just surprised to be shown into the spare room. Nicely so.' Isabel smiled and gave her mother's shoulder a reassuring squeeze.

'Oh good, I hope you'll be comfortable. Get yourself freshened up, then come downstairs for a drink.'

Walking into the kitchen, Isabel sniffed appreciatively.

'Something smells good, Mum.'

'Pollo Cacciatore. One of your favourites I seem to remember?'

'Yes it is, thank you. I feel I should be cooking for you.'

'Nonsense!' replied her mother briskly. 'There'll be plenty of opportunities once you're settled in. Anyway, I enjoy cooking when I have someone to cook for. When you live on your own it's not quite the same. I seem to live off soup and cheese nowadays – and the odd glass of wine. It was nice to make an effort for you.'

'You are a bit thin, Mum.' Isabel appraised her mother with a concerned expression. 'I'll have to make sure you eat properly from now on.'

Isabel had picked up a bottle of Barolo, her mother's favourite, at the duty free. Now it sat in pride of place on the dining table in a slightly tarnished silver wine coaster. Isabel suspected that her mother didn't have much use for coasters nowadays but appreciated the gesture. Her mother reached out for the wine bottle and poured some of the ruby coloured liquid into each of their glasses, smelling hers approvingly.

'This is very kind of you, darling. I don't get this every day. Salute!'

'And here's to absent friends,' murmured Isabel, lifting her glass to her lips.

After dinner they sat quietly, finishing the wine. Isabel's mother broke the silence.

'Actually, I've got some news. Now that you're here we can discuss it in person.'

Isabel looked at her mother in surprise.

'I'm thinking about selling the house.' Her mother continued.

'Sell the house?' Isabel echoed in dismay

'Well, yes, darling. I'm sorry if this is a shock. There's no easy way to say it. Since Dad died, I realise it's really too big for me. I don't need a five bedroomed house. I couldn't really get my head round such an idea until now, but I think I've got to do this.'

'Does David know?'

'Yes,' replied her mother. 'I told him when I saw him last week. He didn't seem too bothered really. More surprised. Probably hopes I may be able to help him get on the property ladder.'

'How long have you been here, Mum?'

'Nearly thirty years.'

'That's all my life. I've never known anywhere else.'

Isabel suddenly felt she was about to cry. This wouldn't help at all. She had to support her mother. It couldn't be easy for her either.

'I'm just going to get some water, Mum.'

She stood up and went into the kitchen and turned the tap on in the sink until the water rushed out in a cold stream. Then she splashed her face and took a few deep breaths. After drying her face on a tea towel she picked up the water jug and filled it nearly to the brim.

'Sorry, Mum. Better now. Tell me more. Have you found somewhere?'

'No, not yet. But I'll stay in the area. Not far. Just a bit smaller and more manageable. There'll always be room for you and David, never fear!'

'So is this why you've been having a bit of a clearance?'

'Something like that.' And her mother smiled ruefully.

It took Isabel a long time to fall asleep. Her mother's news and the strange bed in the unfamiliar room combined to keep her wide awake. A multitude of thoughts turned over and over in her head. When she finally dropped off, her dreams continued as a jumble of places and faces and voices, while she tossed and turned restlessly.

It was still dark when she woke again. Peering at her phone she realised it would be at least another hour before daylight would start to creep into the room. After lying in bed for a few minutes, waiting until her eyes had grown accustomed to the gloom, Isabel slipped out of bed to go to the bathroom. She stuck her feet in her sheepskin slippers and pulled on a jumper. The room was cool and she shivered slightly. It was never easy leaving a nice, cosy bed. On her return she passed her old bedroom, the door slightly ajar. On an impulse she went in.

It was as her mother had warned her. Books were piled up on the floor and half open cardboard boxes had been placed on her old bed. Her father's colourful, lively paintings hung on the walls and old family photographs were lined up on the mantelpiece. Amid the shadowy jumble, Isabel's eye was caught by the outline of a small wooden box on her old chest of drawers. Fumbling for the switch on the bedside lamp she turned it on. A soft yellow light filled the room and reflected off the polished surface of the lid.

It was a rectangular mahogany box the colour of dark honey. The edges were embellished with a delicate strip of marquetry running in vertical stripes. A tiny piece had come off at the base but this was the only imperfection as far as Isabel could see. It was locked with a small silver key set in an ivory keyhole and on the top was a brass plaque, darkened over the years, with the name 'Miss Burnett' inscribed on it in old fashioned script where one of the 's' looked like an 'f'.

*This is beautiful. I haven't seen this before. I wonder where it came from?* Isabel asked herself, stroking the satin-smooth wood with her forefinger.

Clearing a space on the bed, she picked up the box and set it down on the bedspread. The little key was irresistible. Feeling like Alice in Wonderland, Isabel held it between her thumb and forefinger. She could almost imagine a label saying *Turn*

*Me.* Twisting the key gently clockwise, the lock released with a tiny click. Immediately, the lid was pushed up by the mass of papers and correspondence inside. There must have been dozens of letters, neatly tied together in bundles, little square white envelopes secured by pink tape. Very carefully, Isabel opened the lid fully to observe the contents properly. The box was lined with faded red paper and smelt slightly smoky. She leant forward, inhaled and closed her eyes for a moment. Then, before her curiosity got the better of her, Isabel sat up and gently closed the lid again. She would ask her mother about this in the morning.

# CHAPTER 6

# MISS BURNETT'S BOX

'Who was Miss Burnett, Mum?'

Isabel sat opposite her mother at the kitchen table. There was a smell of toast and the hiss of the kettle as it boiled for their mugs of tea.

'Miss Burnett? Well, she became Jane Black when she married Reverend Black. Burnett was her maiden name.'

'Ah, so that would make her my…' Isabel screwed up her face for a moment as she tried to work out the generations. 'Great-great-great- grandmother?'

'Yes, that's right,' her mother confirmed. 'Why do you ask?'

'Well, I hope I wasn't being nosey but I found a beautiful antique box in my old bedroom and it had Miss Burnett's name on the top. So I wondered who she was. Where did it come from?'

'Oh, I've had it since clearing out Granny's house after she died. I've been meaning to go through it. I did take a look inside at the time. I recall there was a lot of correspondence, family stuff that kind of thing, but there was so much there, it was rather overwhelming. You need time to do it justice. Granny never threw anything away, so here we are…'

'Could I look through it?' Isabel offered. 'Unless there's something top secret in there?'

Her mother laughed.

'Oh, I very much doubt that. Jane had a big family so I expect they will be letters from her children. They wrote a lot in those days – no phones or computers. I'm sure it will be very interesting if you have the patience and can make out the old fashioned hand-writing. Go ahead, Isabel. You have my blessing.'

They agreed she could use the dining room table. It would give her more space and just being the two of them, they could easily eat in the kitchen for now. Isabel laid the box down in front of her and turned the key. Once again the papers inside pushed up as though eager to see the light of day after so many years locked away. Then she started to lift out the contents and spread them in front of her. Judging by the stamps, Isabel reckoned most of the letters were over a hundred years old. Despite this they seemed in remarkably good condition. Many were addressed to 17 Melville Street in Edinburgh, then to an address in Buckinghamshire in decorative looped handwriting. Isabel was fascinated by the stamps. Maybe there was a Penny Black in there? Over the years they changed from a serene Queen Victoria to a stern Edward VII then an earnest George V. There were no more monarchs after that. Jane had died in 1930 her mother had told her.

Isabel was just about to close the lid when she noticed one more letter at the bottom of the box. It was not in a bundle with the others and it seemed to have been forwarded several times. Then she saw that it was not actually addressed to Jane Black as all the others had been, but to her husband, Reverend Black. So what was it doing in here? She picked it up to look at it more closely and it was then that she spotted the Canadian stamp in the top right hand corner – a little brown stamp with the King's head on it.

The envelope had been opened, very cleanly, presumably with a letter knife. Isabel turned it over. There was nothing written on the back. Very carefully, Isabel pulled out two sheets of smooth ivory paper and laid them on the table in front of her. There were no marks or blemishes and the letter looked as if it had been written just the other week. But it was dated 2nd January 1919. Nearly a century ago. To Isabel's modern eyes, the writing was, at first, frustratingly hard to decipher. The author had clearly taken time over the letter, forming each word carefully with the loops and joins of the period, the black ink still unfaded. The writer had lived in Halifax, Nova Scotia. Unaware of any Canadian relatives, Isabel quickly turned to the end of the letter, curious to discover their identity. Jessie Richardson. An old friend apparently. No, she hadn't heard this name mentioned at all during long family conversations over the years. And why had a long letter addressed to Frederick Black ended up at the bottom of his wife's sewing box?

Isabel wrestled with the Anglepoise lamp, pulling it down to illuminate the letter in front of her. The rest of the room was shadowy by comparison but that suited her. She wanted to be able to concentrate. To try and make out this hundred year old letter to her great-great-great grandfather. The strong light focused on it helped and after a few minutes, as her eyes grew more accustomed to the handwriting, she started to read.

*Halifax, Nova Scotia*

*2nd January 1919*

*My dear Fred*

*You will no doubt be very surprised to hear from me after all this time but I have often thought of you and wondered how you are and how your life has been? I do not know if this letter will ever reach you or indeed if you are still alive but I hope you are and that you will be able to read this. I have hesitated many times about writing to you but now that I have not long left to live, it is important to me that I write to you while I still can. We are both very advanced in years, so whether or not you receive my letter is in God's hands.*

*Things in the world are so different now especially after this dreadful war which has brought so much misery and destruction to so many people. Although it was a long ago I often think about our old life and the short time we had together. I can truthfully say I have never forgotten you. Although it was so hard to leave you, without meeting you and getting to know you I would never had the life I have had.*

*I recall I wrote to you before I left for Canada. I hope you got that letter at least? I was fortunate to obtain an assisted passage after a year staying in Glasgow. I was able to work to save up some more money and just managed to get enough for my ticket. It took five weeks and what a journey that was! There had been a tragedy the year before I left so I was mindful of the risks. Sometimes the ocean was flat as glass and other times the waves came nearly up to the height of the ship. It was terrifying. I have never prayed so much in all my life. But praise God, my prayers were answered.*

*I have lived in Nova Scotia since 1863 so I suppose that makes me more Canadian than Scottish now. I got work as a domestic almost immediately and then after a couple of years I went to work as a cook and housekeeper for a widowed farmer called Kenneth Richardson. His first wife had died in childbirth, poor soul, leaving him with five children under ten. Well, to cut a long story short, in 1870 Kenneth and I got married. We did not have any children of our own. He was so fearful of losing me and I loved his family as my own so they more than made up for it. And somehow I also did not want to overshadow the memory of my baby boy Jamie, who would be a middle-aged man now.*

*This brings me to my only real regret in life and I haven't spoken about it to a soul. But now before I die I need to share what happened to me all those years ago before I left Aberdeen. You may have wondered why I did not insist you marry me after the baby was born. Believe me it was very tempting but I could only be completely honest with you and I was not entirely sure you were the father. Let me explain.*

*After that Christmas when we were together, I returned to St Nicholas' Manse where I was living and working. I had believed Reverend MacDonald was interested in my welfare. He had always seemed a friendly sort. Well, I was mistaken. We were on our own in the house - his wife had taken her bairns to see the grandparents – and he came to my room one morning early and forced himself upon me. Even after all these years to see the words written fills me with shame and fear and sadness. And anger that I should have been so abused and betrayed by someone I trusted.*

*Then to find I was pregnant without knowing for sure whether you or MacDonald was the father was unbearable. I do not want to go through those terrible memories again but as I told you all those years ago, I called the baby Jamie, and then he was adopted. It is heart-breaking to think that he may be living somewhere in Scotland and does not know that I was his mother and that I loved him so.*

*So you can see why I wanted to confide in someone finally. I am sorry if this has been a huge shock or if I have offended you but it is the truth and as a man of God, I know you will understand. But I have had much to be thankful for. My husband was a good and kind man who loved me and we had a happy life together. He died in 1900 and left me the farm. The children are all grown but we stay in touch. One now lives in New York, one is in Montreal and the other three are still in Nova Scotia. My eldest stepson and his family live here with me on the farm. I have twelve grandchildren who come every summer to spend time with me which is wonderful. Despite everything I have been very blessed.*

*I hope and pray, my dear Fred, that your life has treated you well and that you have achieved great things in the ministry. I hope that you found love again and have had a loving family to support you in your old age.*

*I pray that we shall meet again in Heaven which may not be far off. Until then I send you my abiding love.*

*Your very old friend*

*Jessie Richardson*

By the time Isabel had come to the end of the letter, she was holding her breath.

'Oh my God!' she exclaimed out loud. 'She was raped!'

And Isabel realised she was shaking as she stared at the words in front of her. Poor woman - that's terrible! All those years and no-one knew. She had had a baby? Had Frederick Black known about this? He would have been an old man in 1919. More than eighty years old. The letter had clearly been read by someone but why would it have ended up in Jane Black's sewing box? It was so personal that most likely Frederick Black would have kept it to himself. How awful for Jessie not to know who her baby's father was and then to have the baby adopted. That's so sad. Izzy looked up, blinked and took a deep breath. Then suddenly she felt pure rage on behalf of Jessie Richardson. How dare she be treated like that! Taken advantage of and left with nothing. She must have been a very strong woman to overcome an experience like that and move on with her life. Isabel couldn't begin to imagine how difficult it would have been.

'How are you getting on?' Isabel's mother's voice broke into her thoughts. Reluctantly, Isabel turned round, and felt herself put on a smile.

'It's as you thought, Mum. A lot of family news, travels, school, visits – that kind of thing. A great archive. There's a lot more to see.' And Isabel swept her hand over the letters and papers spread across the table. Her left arm kept Jessie's letter covered, however.

'I wondered if you wanted a coffee.'

'Thanks, that would be great. I'll finish off for now and come into the kitchen. A bit more sociable.'

Isabel remained smiling at her mother until she left the room, then she looked down again at the pages in front of her. Why had she lied? Well, perhaps not lied exactly, but somehow she didn't want to share this heart-rending information. It was too personal. She was so glad it had been her who had discovered it. She could see that Frederick Black was just a normal man for all his public virtue and fame. Somehow she felt closer to him as a result. She wondered if he had ever seen this letter or had he died without knowing the truth?

'Isabel – it's getting cold.'

Her mother's voice called out from the kitchen.

Calmly, Isabel folded the letter once more and replaced it in its envelope, before returning it to the box. The safest place for it.

'Coming,' she replied.

# CHAPTER 7

# THE PORTRAIT

ISABEL EMPTIED THE CONTENTS OF HER BAG ON TO THE BED in exasperation. She couldn't find anything at the moment. No wonder, with so much junk accumulated in it. Receipts and coupons, old tickets and cards, tissues and hand-gel all fighting for space alongside her credit card, keys and phone. Time for a clear-out. As she scooped up the debris and walked towards the bin, a small business card fell to the floor. Isabel was just about to add it to the rest when the name caught her eye. Matthew Duncan. Artist. The Lawn Gallery. Ah, Matthew.

She remembered the electric moment outside the gallery when he had taken hold of her hand so unexpectedly. Until then he had been a passing figure, their first encounter completely overshadowed by the occasion of her father's funeral. She certainly wasn't looking for a new relationship at this stage. She just wanted to let the dust settle and restart her new life in Edinburgh unencumbered. That's what her head told her but looking at Matthew's card brought back her feelings when they had last met. The thought of contacting him gave her butterflies. He had made it very clear it was up to her. Perhaps he did this all the time and she would just make a fool of herself? But somehow she didn't feel this was the case. She wondered if her reactions would be the same if they met again.

She was in the corner shop near her mother's house, picking up some groceries for their lunch, when her phone buzzed. Settling up with Mr Patel, Isabel left the shop and put her carrier bag down on the pavement. Pulling her phone out of her trouser pocket she glanced at the screen. A text from an unknown number. But not unknown for much longer. It was Matthew.

*Hi Izzy, Glad you got in touch : ) Yeah, let's meet up. Lunch? I'll call you. M*

Isabel's mouth felt dry and she was aware her heart was beating faster than usual. So this meant she would now have to wait to hear from him again. *Hanging on the telephone…* Was this a big mistake? Possibly, but it was worth a try.

'Hi Izzy, how are you?' Matthew's voice sounded echoey at the other end of the phone. 'Glad you got in touch. Wasn't sure if I'd hear from you again to be honest.'

'Yeah, well things have changed a bit for me now. I'm back in Edinburgh to stay. Start a new job in a couple of weeks.'

'Oh well, yes, quite a change. Nice for your mum to have you back?'

'Yes, it is. That was one of the reasons.'

'How's she doing?'

'Not too bad, thanks. She's amazingly strong considering…'

'And you?' Matthew's voice had softened and Isabel strained to hear it properly.

'Up and down. I try to keep busy. It'll take some time I think.'

There was a silence.

'So, where shall we meet?' Matthew resumed the conversation. 'Do you know Cramond?'

'Yes, of course. Do you have a car?'

'I do. Tomorrow too soon?'

Isabel realised she was really looking forward to seeing him again but tried not to sound too eager.

'That should be fine.'

'OK, cool, I'll pick you up at midday.'

'Oh Matthew, you've forgotten something.'

'What's that then?'

'My address!'

Feeling like a school-girl, Isabel looked out of her bedroom window to survey the street outside. She had showered, dressed carefully and applied just the right amount of make-up. She had told her mother she was meeting a friend for lunch. Fortunately her mother did not ask any further questions. Isabel was cross with herself that she felt the need for subterfuge but this encounter might not work out and least said and all that. Once she had got started in her new job she would need to find somewhere of her own.

She jumped when her phone pinged suddenly. Matthew was outside in an old blue Golf. His description. Isabel left the house and approached the car. Matthew smiled in greeting and leaned over to open the passenger door. He was as Isabel remembered him, perhaps even better. Like her, he seemed to have made an effort with his appearance. Dark T-shirt with Japanese characters on the front, grey jeans, black and white Converse trainers and wet slicked-down shower hair. On his left hand he wore a chunky silver ring and round his wrist was a tangle of woven bracelets.

'Hi there!'

'Hi!'

In the confined space of the car Isabel was very conscious of Matthew's proximity. His hands rested on the steering wheel - long, slim fingers and arms lightly freckled with a dusting of sandy hair. He smelt of fresh-washing and nice cologne. They looked at each other without speaking and briefly Isabel wondered if he were going to kiss her. But then the moment passed and he turned his head and kissed her chastely on the cheek. Isabel realised she felt a little disappointed. Then Matthew started the ignition and put the car into gear.

The weather, which had been beautiful first thing, now looked as though it were going to change with stormy clouds starting to roll in from the east. By the time they got to Cramond and parked up, it had started to rain and the sea had turned a dark grey flecked with white foam. Matthew cut the engine and they sat looking doubtfully at the sky.

'Hmm,' grunted Matthew. 'Doesn't look very promising. We can wait a bit and see if it clears?'

'It must be nice to have a car,' Isabel ventured conversationally. 'In London hardly anyone does – most folk can't even drive.'

'It was my sister Sara's. She got a new one so I bought this off her. I can drive to work and it's useful for carting my art stuff about.'

'Is she older or younger than you?'

'Older.'

There was a silence and Matthew looked out of his window. Isabel wondered if she had said something wrong.

'I had a brother too …' he continued, still looking out of the window.

'Had?' Isabel queried, with a growing sense of unease.

'Yeah, three years younger than me. My wee brother Al, Alastair. He got knocked off his bike four years ago and went under a lorry.'

Isabel couldn't speak for a moment.

'Oh my God, I'm so sorry! That's awful!'

'Yeah, it was horrible. Still is to be honest. Very difficult for the family. I think it really tested my father's faith. Quite hard to be preaching about the love of God when your kid's in the morgue!'

Isabel felt cold. What could she say? She put a hand gently on Matthew's arm.

'I'm so very, very sorry, Matthew. Perhaps I shouldn't have brought it up?'

'No, it wasn't you, Izzy. I told you. I wanted to tell you. It's a big thing in my family so….'

Matthew turned towards her, his face just inches from hers. Isabel could hear him breathing, his nostrils pinched, and watched as his hazel eyes clouded over with the memory. She was so close that she could see specks of orange in the irises. Beneath his left eye was a small mole that looked like a dark tear-drop. Without thinking she reached out to touch it. Matthew leant in towards her and then suddenly their mouths met in great gulps of passion and all Isabel was aware of was Matthew's tongue, his hands and her heart going pitter-patter.

Beside them a car door slammed and they pulled apart, laughing self-consciously.

'I don't think we'll be doing much walking somehow,' said Matthew peering through the windscreen as rain coursed down the glass. 'I've got a better idea. Why don't you come back to my place? I could do with some company at the moment.'

Isabel stared at Matthew.

'I think that's a great idea!' she said softly, kissing him on the neck.

Isabel had expected to be more self-conscious but when she awoke she felt calm and relaxed. Beside her Matthew was asleep, lying on his back with one arm thrown above his head, his long pale legs tangled up in the duvet His lips were slightly parted and his breathing soft and steady. I wonder if I look that peaceful when I sleep, wondered Isabel enviously. Raising herself on one elbow, she resisted the urge to kiss him on the mouth. Instead, she ran her hand gently down his chest and kissed his shoulder. Matthew stirred and smiled dozily without opening his eyes.

'Hi, you,' he muttered.

'Hi, you too.' Isabel pulled herself on top of him and kissed him again.

Matthew opened his eyes and put his arms around her.

'That was nice. You OK?'

'Mmm, yes, very OK.' Isabel buried her head on Matthew's shoulder, taking in the warmth of him.

'You hungry? We never did get our lunch.'

'Well, now you mention it…'

'Look, I'll pop out for something. Bread and cheese, humus, that kind of thing sound alright?'

'Yeah, that'd be great!'

Matthew stood up and walked over to where his clothes were scattered over an armchair. Isabel watched as he bent down to pick them up – a long slim back, broad shoulders and a nice bum. She felt a renewed flicker of desire. What are you like, she told herself. Newly dressed, Matthew turned to her.

OK, I won't be long. Make yourself at home.'

Dressing quickly, Isabel took him at his word. The flat was on the top floor of a tall, sandstone tenement block in Comely Bank. From the living room window she could just see the Firth of Forth in the distance. Isabel loved being high up like this. As though you could just fly out of the window and away over the rooftops. Off the living room was a little box-room with a skylight. This looked like Matthew's studio. Isabel hoped he wouldn't mind her taking a look.

A big work table, covered in sketch books, took up most of the space. There was a small easel, holding a half completed canvas, in one corner. Underneath the table were several more small canvases while the walls were lined with shelves on which were stacked dozens of art and design books. On the top shelf, just at eye level, were displayed a random selection of objects – shells, ceramic figures, an old copper shaving mug, some quirky souvenirs and at the far end, propped up against the wall, a small portrait in an antique gilt frame.

Probably Victorian, thought Isabel as she picked it up to look at it more closely. It showed a good-looking young man of about thirty in a high-necked white shirt and a dark jacket, staring solemnly into the distance. He was clean-shaven with thick sandy hair brushed back from his face. Something about him looked familiar. Then it came to her. He looked just like Matthew. Obviously not the clothing or the hair style, but the mouth and eyes and the same colour of hair, the same thoughtful expression. And a mole under the left eye. He must be a relative.

Then she heard the sound of the front door opening.

'OK... mission accomplished. Sorry to take so long. There was quite a long queue for some reason. Hope you've been alright?'

Matthew walked into the living room and spread his purchases out on the dining table.

'Who's this?' asked Isabel approaching him and holding the picture up in front her. 'A relative?'

Matthew looked momentarily taken aback.

'No idea! I don't think so. Why do you ask?'

'Well, he looks just like you, don't you think?'

Isabel pushed Matthew gently in front of the heavy square mirror which hung in the hallway and held up the portrait beside him.

'See what I mean?' She persisted.

'Well, if you say so. I can't say I see it myself. It was at my parents' house. Actually, it was the frame I liked and Dad said I could have it. I'll ask them next time I see them. Now what about some lunch? I've got us a bottle of something as well.'

Isabel decided to walk home from Comely Bank. The earlier rain showers had passed and now the city was bathed in bright sunshine. The pavements had dried out and summer flowers in window-boxes looked clean and refreshed. She breathed deeply and a broad smile spread across her face. She had made the right decision to come back to this special place. She was just approaching her mother's house when she felt her phone buzz. Pulling it out of her pocket, she looked at the screen.

*Great day, Izzy. Miss you already. Btw my dad says the portrait is of Reverend Black – the old minister at St Ninians. M xx*

# CHAPTER 8

# RESOLUTION

17 Melville Street, Edinburgh - April 2019

The christening robe was laid out on the bed. Isabel's mother had given it to her a week earlier when she had wheeled the baby over to say hello to her grandmother. The tissue paper package had weighed hardly anything at all as Isabel sat down at the kitchen table and carefully started to unwrap the precious contents. Inside was an old-fashioned infant's dress, made from the finest, almost translucent, cotton lawn. Once white, the delicate fabric had yellowed with age and now looked the colour of thick cream. At the neck there was a miniscule label which read *Harrods London Ltd – Made in France.* The workmanship was flawless, from the precise pin tucks around the neck, to the cascade of embroidered daisies flowing down the front of the dress. The tiny puffed sleeves were edged with the narrowest band of handmade lace while at the hem was attached another wider band into which had been worked tiny rosebuds. Isabel had held the dress up to her face for a moment and breathed in the faint scent of laundry soap and mothballs.

It was so perfect and delicate her eyes had filled with tears.

'It's beautiful, Mum,' she had whispered. 'Thank you.'

'It is, isn't it? It was my grandmother Anne's. That makes it over a hundred years old. I'm so glad it's going to be used once again. Though strictly for special occasions I would say!'

And her mother had laughed as she stroked the fragile fabric.

There was a snuffling in the cot which told Isabel the baby was about to wake up. Then an indignant wail filled the air. The baby was awake and needed attention – now. Isabel went over to the cot. Leaning over she scooped up the child and nuzzled her soft silky head.

'Okay, okay, baby girl. It's your special day, dinnae fret'!'

On hearing Isabel's voice, the baby stopped crying and stared solemnly at her mother.

*She looks like one of those pre-Raphaelite cherubs*, thought Isabel, observing her daughter's unblemished pink skin and the dusting of reddish gold hair, smooth as velvet.

Then, responding to Isabel's smile, the little girl broke into a radiant grin and bumped her head against her mother's chest.

'You have no idea what I'm talking about, do you, my wee poppet?'

There was an excited intake of breathe from the family as Isabel walked into the living room holding her daughter. The baby was now wearing the christening robe but was also wrapped in a large crocheted shawl to protect her against the spring chill.

'I made that shawl for your christening, Isabel,' her mother informed her. 'Another heirloom!'

'She looks adorable,' Matthew's mother stroked the baby's cheek. The child opened a sleepy eye and then returned to her slumbers in her mother's arms.

'Yes, well let's hope she stays this way for the service. She's been getting a bit stroppy of late!' Isabel replied affectionately, as she laid a light kiss on her daughter's head.

'Well, it's half past. I think we need to get going if we're going to walk to the church.'

Matthew's father had taken a couple of steps towards the door. Following his lead, the others went in search of their coats and one by one walked outside.

What a beautiful day, Isabel remarked to herself as they approached St Ninian's. Although it was cold, a lemon yellow sun shone brightly and the threatened snow had held off for now at least. The church stood solid and grey, impervious to the changing seasons, but large pots of purple and white pansies had been placed at the entrance to welcome the congregation. Standing in front of the church, awaiting their arrival, were the godparents, David and Matthew's sister, Sara.

'Let's get a photograph of everyone in front of the memorial.' Isabel's mother suggested, pointing to the grey stone plaque set into the wall outside the church entrance. Frederick Black's profile stared out impassively.

Parking the buggy inside the church porch, Isabel picked the baby up and cradled her in her arms. Mathew stood beside her, his arm around her shoulders. Then the rest of the family crowded in around them.

'Let me take it,' volunteered Matthew's mother, holding her 'phone in the air. 'Say, fromage!'

The group laughed and tilted their heads at the camera. Then it was time to go in. Led by Reverend Duncan, the group filed into the church. The organ played softly and Isabel was aware of smiling faces turned towards her as they processed to the front where she could see a silver font set in a wooden stand, decorated with dusty pink and white hellebores. Matthew's father stopped and indicated the front row to Isabel and the family. On each seat was a printed order of service. Glancing through it Isabel was relieved to see that the baptism would take place early in the service. She doubted if the baby would hold out for the sermon as well.

'I bid you all a very warm welcome to this morning's service.' Reverend Duncan addressed the congregation. 'And I extend particular thanks to my son, Matthew, for asking me to carry out a very special and personal ceremony – the baptism of my grand-daughter.'

There was a murmuring of approval before Reverend Duncan continued.

'And this little girl also has a unique role in joining our two families. She is the great-great-great-great grand-daughter of one of the first ministers of this church, Dr Frederick Black. I am sure his soul is smiling upon us today. New life is something to be greatly cherished and I am very happy to share this significant occasion with you all. Let us open with a lovely hymn which always reminds me of my childhood, All Things Bright and Beautiful.'

There was a rustle as the parishioners got to their feet and listened to the organist play the first few bars.

*'All things bright and beautiful, all creatures great and small, all things wise and wonderful, the Lord God made them all.'*

Around her everyone was singing the familiar hymn enthusiastically. But Isabel's throat seemed to have constricted and she was finding it hard to join in. She was immediately transported back to her primary school at the age of five or six, with her teacher, Miss MacKintosh, accompanying them in the school hall on a slightly out-of-tune upright piano.

*'Each little flower that opens, each little bird that sings, He made their glowing colours, He made their tiny wings.'*

It was funny how all the words came back even though she hadn't sung this particular hymn for years. Then it was over and the congregation took their seats again. Her father-in-law beckoned to her and Matthew, Sara and David to join him by the font. In her arms, Isabel could feel her daughter start to fidget. At that moment, a shaft of spring sunlight shone through one of the stained glass windows and illuminated the little group. The baby waved one hand around as though conducting an invisible choir. For a moment there was complete silence, then Reverend Duncan smiled and turned towards Isabel.

'And the baby's name?'

Looking briefly at Matthew and then down at their daughter, Isabel replied with a strong clear voice.

'Jessica Jane. Her name is Jessica Jane.'

# ACKNOWLEDGEMENTS

ALTHOUGH MY NAME IS ON THE COVER, WRITING REALLY IS a team effort. I certainly would not be where I am today without the help, encouragement, support and guidance of the following people.

Firstly, my family, past and present, who were the inspiration for the novel and who have been my first readers and critics.

Thank you to City Lit in Covent Garden, London, who provided me with the first opportunity to develop my writing. Then to Neil Arksey and my writing group who provided me with a winning combination of encouragement, plain speaking, tough-love and cake to get me over the finishing line.

I am incredibly grateful to Keirsten Clark and Mark Leggatt of the Writing Consultancy for taking a fine-tooth comb to my manuscript to make it the best it could be and to Helen Cox for giving me the courage to launch my book.

They say you shouldn't judge a book by its cover, but actually you do. I am thrilled with the creative work done by Ken Dawson of Creative Covers to help bring my book to physical life and to the brilliant type-setting skills of Kate Coe of Book Polishers for doing just that.

Finally, I would like to thank my many friends who have followed my writing journey with interest and encouragement. It means a lot.

Printed in Great Britain
by Amazon

86770334R00176